Valentine's
FANTASY

Valentine's
FANTASY

ADRIANNE BYRD
and JANICE SIMS

HARLEQUIN® KIMANI ARABESQUE®

VALENTINE'S FANTASY
ISBN-13: 978-0-373-09150-8

Copyright © 2014 by Harlequin Books S.A.

The publisher acknowledges the copyright holders of the individual works as follows:

WHEN VALENTINES COLLIDE
Copyright © 2007 by Adrianne Byrd

TO LOVE AGAIN
Copyright © 1997 by Janice Sims

First published by Kensington Publishing Corp. in 1997

Recycling programs
for this product may
not exist in your area.

For questions and comments about the quality of this book, please contact us at CustomerService@Harlequin.com.

Printed in U.S.A.

CONTENTS

WHEN VALENTINES COLLIDE

This book is dedicated to the new angel on my shoulder—
Alice Coleman Finnley. I can still hear your laughter.

Chapter 1

"He's an egotistical, self-righteous son of a bitch," Chanté Valentine spat, storming through her best friend and publishing editor, Edie Hathaway's front door. "The man thinks he's God's gift to psychology."

"Please, come in," Edie mumbled in the wake of her trail, sighed, and then closed the door. Shaking her head and tightening her belt around her curvy, plus-size figure, she followed her friend back into the dining room.

"I can't do this any longer," Chanté announced as she marched straight toward the bar.

"It's eight in the morning."

"What can I say? I like vodka with my eggs."

Edie patiently watched her bestselling author splash out a glass of her expensive liquor. "You could add a dash of orange juice so I'd feel better about you getting something nutritional out of that drink."

Chanté smirked, but complied. "I want a divorce."

"Absolutely not." Edie crossed her arms. "It would ruin both of your careers."

Chanté downed a deep gulp and then came up for air. "I don't care."

"Sure you do." Edie shuffled over to the table where her breakfast grew cold. "Besides, you still love him... or you would've left him a long time ago."

"Ha! I've been trying to leave Matthew for the last two years, but it's always 'wait until after contract negotiations, wait until after you write your book, wait until after the book is published.' Now the blasted thing has been number one on the *New York Times* bestseller list for ten weeks running and you're still telling me to wait."

"You *should* wait." Edie shook her head as she slathered butter onto a biscuit. "How would it look if America's two top relationship gurus divorced each other? Don't you think we would have a credibility issue here?"

"Oh, give me a break." Chanté downed a second gulp. "If I didn't know any better, I'd think you, Seth and Matthew have all teamed up to drive me nuts."

"All right." Edie lowered her biscuit without taking a bite. "I know I'm going to regret asking, but what did Matthew do this time?"

One of Chanté's brows rose quizzically. "I take it you didn't watch Letterman last night?"

"Tivo. I'd planned to watch it this morning," Edie said, sounding concerned. "Why? What happened?"

Chanté's eyes narrowed as she simmered. "Letterman snidely pointed out the differences in our approaches in relationship counseling and then asked how people should choose whose advice to follow."

Edie leaned back in her chair and brushed back her thick straw curls from her face. "And...what did he say?"

"That people should follow the advice from the one who graduated from a *real* school."

Edie's mouth rounded silently.

"You should have seen him sitting there as proud as a peacock, cramming his overpriced education down everyone's throat." Chanté sloshed her drink down onto the breakfast bar and flailed her hands in the air. "Oh, look at me. I'm a Princeton graduate while my wife—"

"Graduated from Kissessme College in Karankawa, Texas," Edie finished.

"Which is a damn good school," Chanté snapped. "I busted my butt with two waitressing jobs to get my degree. I didn't have a rich daddy to write me a blank check."

Edie frowned. "I know you two are going through a rough patch—"

"This is more than a rough patch."

"But sometimes I wonder how the hell you two got together in the first place."

"Oh, that's easy." Chanté strode to the table and pulled out a chair. "Ten years ago, Matthew Valentine was handsome—"

"He still is."

"Charming—"

"Check."

"Successful."

"Double-check."

Chanté's lips curled wickedly. "And *great* in bed."

Edie's eyebrows rose with surprise and interest. "Oh?"

"Now he seems to think all he has to do is get his groove on and wait for a baby. A baby. That's all he ever talks about. After nine miscarriages you'd think he would give it a rest." Chanté drew a deep breath.

"So I take it you haven't told him you're—?"

"How can I?" She sloshed down another gulp, exhaled, and then finally slumped her shoulders in defeat. "Nine miscarriages. Five years. I should have started trying to have a family earlier."

"Come on. You wanted a career first. That's understandable."

"Yeah, but now I'm pushing forty and my body attacks every fertilized egg like I've caught a disease or something." She shook her head. "I can't help but wonder if I'd tried sooner I'd already have our baby as opposed to being on this wild race against my biological clock—a race Matthew is determined to win." Chanté shook her head during another sigh. "I just need a break—physically and emotionally."

"Is that why you kicked him out of your bedroom?"

"How did you—?"

"Seth." Edie filled in the blanks. "He'll never admit it, but those two gossip more than we do. If I remember correctly it's been…what—five months?"

Chanté took another gulp. "Something like that."

Her friend shook her head as she folded her arms and leaned back in her chair. "You know you're playing with fire when you let too much testosterone pile up. Not to mention, you seem a little wound tight yourself."

"If I'm wound too tight it's because I'm frustrated that Matthew and I can fix everyone's marriage problems but our own."

"That's because it always boils down to the battle of the wills with you guys." Edie shrugged and then returned her attention to her breakfast. "Both of you always have to be right."

Chanté grew indignant. "That's not true...entirely."

Edie continued eating.

"The problem is that two perfectionists should never marry each other."

"Or two stubborn people."

"Edie! You're supposed to be on my side."

"I'm on reality's side." Her friend finally cast her a long look. "It's not going to kill you to bend a little."

"If I bend any further you may as well remove my spine," Chanté snipped.

"Better flexibility can only improve one's sex life." Edie winked. "I can testify to that."

"I just bet you can."

Once a month, Dr. Matthew Valentine and his agent, Seth Hathaway, met at the International House of Pancakes for their favorite selection of Rooty Tuitty Fresh and Fruity pancakes.

"It was a joke," Matthew laughed, and then leaned toward Seth. "It was Letterman, for Pete's sake."

Seth leaned his six-foot-five frame over the table and settled his serene ocean-blue eyes on him. "Let me guess, Chanté didn't think it was funny?"

"Blew a damn gasket is more like it." Matthew rolled his eyes. "For punishment, I endured a four-hour rant about how I was undermining her authority and poking holes in her credibility—*not* the first time I heard that crap by the way." He stabbed his pancakes and twirled it absently in its strawberry syrup. "There's no pleasing her anymore."

Seth kept his face blank as he bridged his hands above his plate. "Far be it for me to give America's top relationship guru advice."

Matthew glanced up wearily. "But something tells me I'm not going to be able to stop you."

"Hey, I don't have a fancy degree, but twenty-five years of marriage—an interracial marriage at that—says I'm qualified."

Matthew flashed his million-dollar smile and forced a casual shrug. "All right. Shoot."

Seth waited until he'd captured Matthew's full attention. "Apologize."

Matthew waited for more, but concluded none was forthcoming when his agent returned his attention to his breakfast.

"That's it?"

"Yep." Seth shoveled food into his mouth.

Matthew rolled his eyes. "Good thing I didn't call you for help during the writing of my last book."

Seth smiled and dabbed the corners of his mouth. "C'mon. It's not rocket science. A man is just fooling himself if he thinks he could ever win an argument with a woman. Everything is always our fault. I don't care what it is. So apologize and move on."

"I didn't do anything wrong."

"You're joking, right?" Seth rocked back in his chair as his laughter rumbled. "Look, I don't mean to offend you or anything. I mean, you're my best client and all, but, when a woman gets mad it's usually for three reasons: something we did, something we didn't do or something we're going to do."

"Sounds scientific."

"Thanks. It is." He took another bite and quickly swallowed. "In *this* case, you went on a nationally televised show and made a lousy sucker punch to her reputation. Every man watching knew you'd get the couch last night."

"You don't understand." Matthew slumped back in his chair and refused to give credence to Seth's advice. "Once upon a time Chanté didn't take everything so seriously. She knew how to laugh at herself. C'mon. She graduated from Kissessme College. That's funny."

"She also has a syndicated talk radio show and is a bestselling author."

"I know about her accomplishments. I'm proud of what she's done—"

"So it's not so hard to understand she just wants to be taken seriously in her profession."

Matthew shook his head. "I'm telling you, I know my wife. She's not mad about something I said on Letterman. There's something else that's bothering her and she just won't spit it out."

"She keeps asking for a divorce," Seth reminded him.

Matthew shook his head again. "She doesn't want a divorce or she would have been gone by now. It's something else—I'm sure of it. She just won't talk to me."

"Two psychologists who can't talk. I think that falls under irony."

"Very funny."

Seth chuckled. "How long now since the Love Doctor has been locked out of his own bedroom?"

Matt grunted and lowered his gaze.

"Five months, right?" the agent continued, during Matt's silence. "Look, you're a big shot in your field—four number one *New York Times* bestsellers and a syndicated television talk show, but maybe it's time you listen to advice other than your own. *Apologize* and move back into your old bedroom. If you don't, things between you and Chanté are only going to get worse."

Chapter 2

Chanté breezed into WLUV's studio with her head held high but with her lips showcasing a nervous smile. The station's small crew greeted her with wide toothy grins, however, no one's eyes managed to meet hers. To top it off, on more than one occasion, she heard snickering whenever she turned her back.

"Oh, don't pay it any mind," Thad Brown, Chanté's extremely young, talented and laid-back producer advised as he settled behind the glass partition separating them and reversed his New York Yankees baseball cap.

"Easy for you to say," Chanté mumbled, and then placed on her headset.

"To be honest, I thought it was pretty funny," Thad said into his microphone. "Of course, I'm a little hurt

I didn't know this embarrassing tidbit about you. I thought we were best friends."

"Thad—"

"Yeah, yeah. I forgot. You have a *new* best friend— a hotshot publishing editor."

"Thad," she warned.

"Okay. Okay." He shrugged with a lopsided smile. "But when you start hobnobbing with Oprah...call me."

"First, I'll have to call my mother."

"You're on a hot streak. Hell, I bought your book yesterday and I'm halfway through it. Real good stuff. A lot better than—well, it could have been professional jealousy that sparked Dr. Matt's comment on Letterman the other night. Did you ever think of that?"

The On Air sign lit up.

"A little competition will do Matthew Valentine a world of good. Maybe his loyal readers will actually demand he write new material instead of rehashing the same trivial tripe of his last three books." She laughed and rolled her eyes. "And don't get me started on those Jerry Springer rejects he says he counsels on his show."

Still laughing, Chanté lifted her eyes to Thad and was stunned to see him frantically pointing upward. When her gaze landed on the sign, her voice failed her.

Static filled the airwaves.

Thad cringed and rolled his hands, urging her to speak.

"Good evening...and welcome to *The Open Heart Forum*. I'm thrilled you could join us. I am your host and friend, Dr. Chanté Valentine. If you're trying to salvage a relationship or if you're experiencing trouble moving on, I urge you to pick up the phone and talk to a friend."

Thad slumped back into his chair and sighed in relief.

With her nerves still tied in knots, Chanté settled into a groove.

From the computer screen on her desk, she read Thad's notes regarding her first caller and launched into her introduction. "Hello, Maria. Welcome to *The Open Heart Forum*."

"Hello, Dr. Valentine." A young, giddy voice filtered on to the line. "I can't believe I actually got through. I have to tell you, I read your book, *I Do,* and I'm a big fan."

"Why, thank you." Chanté smiled. "What's on your heart tonight?"

"Uhm…actually, I was wondering if everything was all right with you and *your* husband—The Love Doctor?"

Chanté blinked and glanced up.

Thad grimaced, shrugged, and then mouthed an apology.

Chanté forced a chuckle. "Yes. Yes. Everything is wonderful between Matthew and I."

"Oh. Well, I didn't think much about it when I saw Dr. Matthew on Letterman, but then I heard you a few minutes ago…?"

"No. No. I was just joking with Thad, my producer. Everything is fine," Chanté lied.

"Well, it just sounded like—"

"Maria, I'm reading here you called in about a friend of yours?" She kept her voice sugary sweet.

"Well, yes. You."

Chanté frowned. "I don't understand."

Maria laughed. "Don't you always encourage your listeners to view you as our friend?"

"Yes. Yes. Of course." Chanté covered quickly. "And thank you, Maria, for your concern. But I assure you, Matthew and I are fine. Thank you for your call." She disconnected the line and then returned her attention to the computer screen.

"Okay. Our next caller is Sienna. She's calling in from Decatur, Georgia. Hello, Sienna, what's on your heart tonight?"

"Hello, Dr. Valentine. I'm a first-time caller and longtime fan."

"Welcome to the show."

"Thank you. I just have one question."

Chanté relaxed. "Sure. What can I help you with?"

"I was looking on the Internet and I couldn't find anything about Kissessme College. Is that a real school?"

Chanté glared at her producer and slid her finger across her neck to let him know exactly what she was going to do when she got her hands on him.

"I'm going to kill her!" Matthew swore as he toted his autographed Reggie Jackson baseball bat and paced the spacious foyer of their multimillion-dollar home.

Their *dream* home. Ha! It was more like a palatial prison—one of their making.

"Maybe I imagined it," he reasoned, but then shook his head. His wife had turned on him on national airwaves. He couldn't believe it. "I should just give her that damn divorce."

Anything would be better than a public castration.

"Jerry Springer rejects," he mumbled under his breath. "I ought to—"

The front door rattled. Matthew stopped in front of the foyer's threshold leading toward the living room and turned to watch the door. As it crept open, he adjusted and readjusted his grip on the bat.

"Matthew?" Chanté's voice floated through the cracked door.

Waves of anger rushed up the column of his neck.

"Matthew?" she tried again, but didn't dare step into the house. "I know you're in the foyer. I can see you through the side paneling."

His shoulders deflated now, the element of surprise had been taken from him.

"What are you going to do with that bat?"

He'd almost asked "what bat?" when he became cognizant of what he must look like. "I think better with it." He placed the bat next to a crystal vase on the foyer table. "As much as I want to kill you, I'm not interested in doing the time."

As soon as he spoke those magic words, Chanté pushed the door open farther and entered the house.

Despite his anger, Matthew's gaze traveled up his wife's long, toned legs and black, mid-thigh skirt. Boy, she always did know how to wear the hell out of a skirt—or anything else for that matter. Just months away from the big 4-0, Chanté labored to maintain her Tyra Banks-like figure and there wasn't a man who'd crossed her path that didn't take a moment to appreciate all her hard work—including him.

His eyes continued their journey over her every luscious curve until they reached her thin, delicate neck. He sighed as he envisioned wrapping his hands around it.

"You're still up," she stated the obvious as she closed the door.

"Was there any doubt?" He drew another deep breath in hopes to cool his temper. "How was work tonight?"

Chanté set her briefcase down next to his baseball bat. "It was all right." She shrugged as she pulled the pins from her hair.

Matthew's heart squeezed at the sight of her long, thick, currently dyed auburn hair spilling down her back. Sidetracked, he struggled to remember the last time he ran his fingers through the soft strands—or tugged it during the throes of passion.

Five months.

She headed toward him and had almost passed by when Matthew broke through his reverie and jutted his arm across the threshold to block her escape.

"Surely it was more than just 'all right'?"

Chanté swept her dark, angry glare over him.

Heat flared anew within Matthew, but it had nothing to do with anger. Standing this close, staring into her fiery eyes, and smelling the soft fragrance in her hair, he was delirious with lust.

This made no sense. He couldn't stand her.

Five months.

"Move out of my way," she hissed.

"I want to talk more about your evening," he hissed back, and then added a smile. "Isn't that what all *loving* couples do—communicate?"

"We're not a loving couple so let's just skip the bull." She ducked under his arm and stormed to the bar. "And if you want to talk about that little comment I made about you on the air tonight…" She stopped and flashed him a smile. "It was a joke."

His anger returned. "A joke my ass. You did that to get back at me. Admit it."

Chanté folded her arms across her chest. "And what if I did? What are you going to do about it—divorce me?"

"Don't tempt me!"

Frustrated, Chanté stomped her foot and glanced around the room to throw something—anything. She grabbed a nearby statue, but was stunned when the damn thing wouldn't move.

"What the—?"

"Superglue," Matthew replied with a smug smile. "Your screaming tirades have gotten a little on the expensive side."

Big, bright patches of red flashed before her eyes and she reached for something else, only to discover it, too, had been glued down.

Her husband laughed, plunging deeper under her skin. In a last desperate act, she pulled off a shoe and hurled it at him.

Matthew ducked. "Hey!"

She launched the second shoe and it nailed the side of his head.

"Ouch!" He rubbed his bruise and then took off running toward her. "You've lost your mind."

Chanté squealed as she lunged from him. "Get away. Leave me alone." She bounded up on the sofa and rushed across its cushions.

"I'm going to make you pay for that."

"Don't you dare touch me!" She jumped down, slid on her stocking feet, then raced in the opposite direction.

Matthew crashed into a bookcase and yelped in pain when a few hardcovers landed on his head. "Damn it!"

Chanté glanced over her shoulder as she exited the living room. To her surprise, her husband was right on her tail. She'd crossed the foyer and was just inches away from the staircase, when his strong fingers bit into her shoulders.

"Gotcha!"

Chanté swung as she pivoted.

Matthew ducked, lost his balance, and fell backward—taking her down with him. He landed with a hard thump and had no time to register the pain before his wife knocked what little air he had left out of his lungs.

In no time, her hands and legs flailed out in attack.

"Will you stop it?" He wrestled with her, trying to catch hold of her.

"I hate you. I hate you. I hate you."

He latched on to one arm, but failed to catch the other one before it landed a hard blow against the same spot her flying shoe had hit. "Ouch!"

Matthew captured the other hand. He rolled on top and pinned her beneath him.

Even then Chanté kicked and squirmed.

"Be still," Matthew demanded.

"Go to hell," she spat.

"What? This isn't 666 Hell's Drive?"

"Very funny." She gave a last futile tug, and then went limp beneath him.

"Give up?"

"Never."

Her chest heaved while she dragged in deep breaths. It, consequently, drew her husband's lustful gaze. It was crazy, but she felt good lying beneath him—her curvy body soft but pulsing with raw energy. He was turned on—and she knew it.

Five months.

"What are you doing?" she asked in alarm.

He leaned down close until their faces were just inches apart. He filled his senses with her floral-scented hair and the faint hint of Chanel No. 5.

"What will you do if I kiss you right now?"

"What?"

"I want to kiss you."

Chanté renewed her escape efforts, but the wild bucking and squirming only succeeded in turning them both on more.

When his lips landed on hers with surprising gentleness, Chanté's mutinous body melted as though cold water had been splashed onto a fire.

Their tongues danced, caressed, and sent small shock waves of pleasure clear down to her toes. She wanted him, and judging by the hard bulge in his pants, he wanted her, too.

She could give in just this once. After all, it had been five long months. What was the harm? God knew she still loved him—probably always will.

"Tell me you want me," he commanded softly. "We don't even have to go upstairs. We can do it right here. Right now, but I want to hear you say it."

I want you. Chanté panted and tried to gain control of herself.

"Tell me."

She met her husband's fevered gaze while the war continued to rage inside of her. Bend—be flexible. But giving in to him wouldn't magically erase their problems.

"Who knows, tonight might be the night…"

A baby. She closed her eyes. *Always a baby.* Forcing ice into her veins, Chanté lifted her chin, and with her next words extinguished the small fire crackling between them. "I want you to get the hell off of me."

Chapter 3

Matthew didn't sleep a wink.

How could he when all he could think about was marching down the hall to the master bedroom—his old bedroom—and demand his wife perform her wifely duties?

Fat chance.

He chuckled under his breath and watched as the sunlight beamed through the thin slits in the venetian blinds. The rays warmed his face but he wondered when it would touch his heart.

This was not supposed to be his life.

He was never the type of man who trembled at the idea of settling down, having the white picket fence or having the customary two point five children...

Children.

Coming from a large family of four brothers, four sisters and a host of cousins, nieces and nephews, Matthew had always assumed that one day he, too, would raise a small army of children. He'd originally delayed those plans to support his wife in her career. But when they actually started planning five years ago, there was a snag. Chanté could get pregnant, but ten weeks into the pregnancies, like clockwork, her body would reject the fetus.

Five years. Nine miscarriages. Nine heartbreaks.

Matthew swung his legs over the side of the bed and sat up. Children were what was missing from their home—from their lives. He knew it, she knew it and all their friends knew it, too.

And yet, it wasn't in the cards for them.

He sighed; mourned for the children he didn't have, and then reached for his copy of Chanté's latest book, *I Do.* "Following an argument, we need time to cool off. When one person hisses a sarcastic comment and the other, hurt and angry, feels justified in topping the insult. The volleys begin. By the time we realize the mistake we're making, it's too late to 'take it back.'"

He slapped the book closed and hung his head in shame. Seth was right. "I should have apologized."

A loud rip caught his attention and he jerked his head toward the door. When he heard it again, he frowned and went to investigate. Upon opening the bedroom door, he couldn't wrap his brain around what he was seeing.

"What in the hell are you doing?"

Dressed in sexy, silk pink boxers and a matching lace

chemise, Chanté stood with a large roll of duct tape and a pair of scissors. "What does it look like I'm doing?"

"It *looks* like you've lost your mind." He took another glance at the silver duct tape running down the center of the floor, the wall, and even the ceiling. "Do you know what's going to happen when you peel that off?"

"I'm not going to peel it off." She huffed. "Since a *real* divorce doesn't suit either of our interests—at the moment—it doesn't mean that we can't go ahead and divvy things up."

He heard her and his brain replayed what she'd said, but it still wasn't making a lick of sense.

"Split everything in half," she clarified at his look of confusion. "Fifty-fifty."

Matthew crossed his arms over his bare chest and leaned against his bedroom's doorframe. "You don't think people might notice? I mean, the tape clashes with the furniture."

"Then we won't invite anyone over," she settled, turning on her heels and marching away.

"You're joking, right?" He started after her.

"No."

He reached the top of the staircase just as she bolted from the bottom of it. "Can we please talk about this like two rational adults?" he shouted.

"I'm through with being rational."

"Obviously."

Chanté stopped and glared up at him. "I'm tired of this lie—this life. I'm tired of…"

He sucked in a deep breath as his eyes narrowed on her. "Go ahead. Say it."

Chanté clamped her mouth shut and stormed away.

Matthew descended the stairs two at a time, ignoring the ugly silver tape down the center. "Say it, Chanté."

She ignored him and continued toward the kitchen. It, too, had been duct taped in half. The sight of it ignited his anger.

"You have something to say, Chanté. I want to hear it."

"Since when?" She rounded on him.

He stopped within inches of her. "I'm standing right here."

Their glares fused as they stood in a stalemate.

"What else are you tired of, Chanté?" he asked.

"You." She lifted her chin, now that she'd said the word. "I'm tired of having to deal with you. Satisfied?"

"Quite." Matthew turned and stomped out of the kitchen.

Chanté watched him leave with a wave of regret and relief. She had no explanation as to why she baited him. She also didn't understand why she was so angry all the time. She could psychoanalyze herself. After all, she was a professional; but the truth is: doctors made terrible patients.

Why couldn't she just say what was really on her mind? Because it would destroy him. She shook her head and turned toward the sink and filled a glass with water, where she proceeded to take her morning vitamins and pills.

The phone rang and Chanté snatched the cordless from the kitchen's wall unit. "Hello."

"What on earth did you do?" Edie asked in a high, strained voice. "No, scratch that. I know what you did. I need to know why you did it."

Chanté sighed as she pinched the bridge of her nose. "You're talking about last night's program?"

"Are you kidding?" Edie's voice rose another octave. "That's all everyone is talking about. My boss has left six messages on my voice mail. She's worried how all this is going to affect your book sales."

"Edie—"

"Not to mention, my assistant has fielded calls from the big three networks. Even *The Enquirer* called and stated they're going to run a story about you two not sleeping in the same bedroom."

"How did they—?"

Something loud roared from outside. Chanté lowered the phone. Was Matt doing something in the yard? She placed the phone back against her ear.

"—we're going to have to do some damage control on this thing."

"Edie, let me call you back."

"No. We need to talk about this now."

Chanté peeked out of the kitchen window and didn't see her husband.

"Seth and I have a few ideas. What do you think about going on *Larry King Live?*"

"What? Are you sure all of this is necessary?" Chanté headed toward the front door.

"Vital. If this doesn't work, we'll have to sell our souls to get you on Oprah."

Chanté opened the door, screamed and dropped the phone. "Stop! Stop!"

Now dressed in protective clothing, Matthew headed toward his wife's brand-new Mercedes with a chainsaw.

"What are you doing?" she yelled.

"Divvying our assets, hon." He smiled as he lowered his goggles and proceeded to cut the car in half.

"Stop, stop!" she screeched, but the loud buzz of the chainsaw drowned her out. Chanté raced toward the car, but jumped back before sparks showered onto her flammable outfit. "You're crazy," she shouted and stomped her fluffy pink house slippers.

Matthew didn't spare a glance in her direction, but he smiled like a kid in a candy shop as the saw cut through the car like warm butter.

Chanté charged toward the garage, looking for something—anything. From the corner of her eye she spotted a pile of steel pipes on Matthew's workbench and quickly grabbed one before returning to the yard.

The chainsaw jammed halfway through the Mercedes' roof and Matthew climbed down, wondering if he had something stronger to finish the job when he saw an angry pink blur rushing toward him and he removed his goggles.

With a firm grip on the steel pipe, Chanté swung at her husband's head like Barry Bonds going for another home run record.

Matthew ducked and felt the air swoosh past his head as he dropped the chainsaw.

The force of the swing twisted Chanté around in a

complete circle and before she could adjust, her husband charged and tackled her to the ground.

This time the air was knocked out of Chanté's lungs as the steel pipe bounced out of her hands.

"What the hell were you trying to do—kill me?" Matthew barked.

"Damn right," she growled and tried to twist away and reclaim the pipe.

"Oh, no you don't." Matthew scrambled above her and pushed the pipe further out of reach. "You're absolutely certifiable. You know that?"

"Me?" she shrieked. "Look what you did to my car!" Chanté squirmed and then started pelting him with her hands—a constant occurrence, especially in the last six months.

While the wrestling match grew fast and furious in the grass, the sprinklers came on and immediately drenched the couple from head to toe.

"My hair," Chanté sputtered. "I just had it done. Let me up!"

Matthew tried, but the grass was slippery now and he had a hard time getting his footing.

"Get up!" she insisted, smacking him again.

After one too many pops against the head, Matthew waved a finger at her. "Has anyone ever told you that it's never okay to hit?"

Her answer was to smack him again.

"Uh, excuse me."

Chanté and Matthew froze, and then slowly turned their heads to see old man Roger, the lawn guy, peering curiously over at them.

"Uh, is everything all right, Mr. and Mrs. Valentine?"

Their smiles were instant and their expressions as innocent as they could manage.

"Everything is f-fine," Matthew said, finally climbing off his wife and pulling her up with him. For a few strained and awkward seconds they stood before the elderly gentleman in the sodden grass while the sprinklers continued to drench and plaster their clothes against their bodies.

"Uh-huh." Roger eyeballed them as if they were Martians.

Chanté snuggled against her husband and slid her arms lovingly around his neck. "We were just trying something new. You know…to keep things…fresh." She planted a kiss on Matthew's cheek. "Isn't that right, hon?"

Matthew's smile tightened. "Right…hon."

Roger's dusty brown face wrinkled as he scratched his short-cropped, cotton-white hair. "Uh-huh."

"Well, hon," Matt said. "I think we better move this lovefest back into the house." Before Chanté had a chance to respond, Matthew swept up his wife, tossed her over his shoulder, and smacked her hard on the butt.

"Matthew!" Her fist pounded his back.

"Patience, baby." Matthew winked at Roger. "She gets a little impatient from time to time."

"Right." Roger nodded as he watched Matthew march toward the house. From behind, Chanté lifted her head and waved.

At last, Roger turned toward the Mercedes. "Hey,

what happened to the car?" He glanced back to his employers, but they were already entering the house.

Mrs. Valentine screeched. "Now put me down!"

The door slammed closed, leaving Roger to scratch his head and glance from the car to the front door. "I swear those two are as loony as they come."

Chapter 4

Master interviewer, Larry King, dressed in a starched periwinkle shirt, black suspenders and matching striped tie performed his trademark haunch over the desk and welcomed the audience to the night's show.

"It's always a pleasure to welcome Dr. Matthew and Chanté Valentine to the show. Dr. Matt is the host of the highly-rated TV talk show, *The Love Doctor*. He is the author of four *New York Times* bestsellers…"

Matt smiled and scratched at his collar.

Chanté drew a deep breath and forced steel into her spine while keeping her smile on full wattage. This interview called for her finest performance.

Matt shifted in his chair, scratched his arm and then jerked the arm to scratch at his back.

Mr. King flashed Matt an inquisitive glance but kept on with his spiel.

"And this little lady, Dr. Chanté Valentine, has quite a résumé as well," Mr. King praised. "She is the host of her own syndicated radio talk show *The Open Heart Forum*. Her first book, *I Do*—I have the book right here—has been on the bestseller list for ten weeks running. Welcome to the show."

"Thank you." She smiled and leaned closer toward her husband.

Matt jerked his head back and tried to scratch at his neck, his chest, his back and his crotch.

"Is everything all right, Dr. Valentine?"

"Oh, uh. Yeah, just fine," he panted, jerking this way and that. "I just seem to have a little itch."

Chanté smiled serenely, thinking about the itching powder she'd sprinkled in his clothes. *That'll teach him to destroy my car.*

Off set, Edie and Seth Hathaway took turns experiencing chest pains as they watched the Valentines attempt to charm their host, but watching them was like watching and expecting a train wreck.

"This was a mistake," Edie whispered and glanced nervously around.

"This is damage control. We needed to do something other than let them continue taking public potshots."

"Look at her. She looks like a plastic Stepford wife and he…what the hell is he doing?"

"Calm down." Seth looped an arm around her shoulder. "They're doing fine. Look, Larry is eating it up."

"Larry is the least of our worries. It's the court of

public opinion that matters here." She hid her face in the palms of her hands. "Why did she have to call his TV guests Jerry Springer rejects?"

Seth chuckled. "Because some of them are."

"What?"

"You didn't know?" He shook his head. "You're probably the only one who didn't."

"Well, we wouldn't have to do any damage control if your client reined in his jealousy on Letterman."

"C'mon. If you graduated from a place called Kissessme, you should grow a thick skin."

Edie stepped away from her husband. "Are you saying all of this is Chanté's fault?"

Stagehands, cameramen and the director glanced toward them and Edie realized she'd forgotten to use her "inside" voice. "Sorry," she whispered to the set.

On camera, the Valentines smiled lovingly at each other and their host. But then Matt started raking at his skin like a madman again.

"I'm not saying that it's anyone's fault," Seth resumed the conversation. "But I do think we're sitting on top of a time bomb. We may be able to fool the public right now, but how long do you think they'll be able to keep it up?"

Edie thought of Chanté's constant demand for a divorce. "Not much longer."

"Right." Seth's voice lowered. "Which is why I think it's up to us to do something about it."

"Us?" She laughed. "How are we going to help professional psychologists—the top in their field, by the way—mend their own relationship?"

Seth's lips slid into a wide grin. "An intervention."

"An intervention?" Edie repeated and turned her gaze back to Chanté and Matt, just as Matt twisted one too many times and fell out his chair, then proceeded to writhe on the floor. "Forget the intervention, I think we need an exorcist."

"Oh, *hell* no," Chanté snapped at Edie above the den of diners at the prestigious Gramercy Tavern. When all eyes shot to their table, Chanté quickly covered with a bland smile, and then added under her breath, "I'm not going to marriage counseling."

Unfazed by her friend's outburst, Edie calmly peered over the rim of her glasses. "If you look me in the eye and tell me that you honestly want a divorce, I'll back off."

Chanté opened her mouth to make her daily proclamation, but when the words failed her, she closed it and shifted in her chair.

A triumphant smile bloomed across Edie's lips. "I didn't think so."

"Explain to me how it would look for two relationship experts to seek relationship counseling. Wouldn't that also put a dent in our precious credibility?"

"The public will never know," she assured.

"Come on. We live in the information age." Chanté stabbed at her spinach salad. "Secrets always come out—usually on the Internet."

Edie slumped back in her chair, thoughtful. "Then we could release the information ourselves." She bobbed her head, warming to the idea. "Hear me out on this."

She sat up again. "You and Matthew promote counseling. What better way to show that all relationships hit rough patches? Right now, you guys appear to have the perfect marriage. There are a good percentage of people who think you guys can never understand their problems because you have it so good. But if they see perfect marriages being not-so-perfect then we can tap into a few more readers."

"What are you talking about? People see those marriages all the time. They're called celebrity marriages."

"Be serious. No one takes celebrity marriages seriously. We're talking about two famous love doctors, and when you fix their marriage, it will renew hope."

"*If* we can fix our marriage." Chanté bit into her salad and rolled her eyes. "And that's a very big if."

"Okay. We'll keep it out of the papers for now, but if a leak happens we'll be prepared."

Chanté lowered her gaze and stared at her half-eaten salad, remembering the first time she'd laid eyes on Matthew. He'd blown a tire out on the main highway and walked ten miles to Sam's Café on the edge of Karankawa, Texas, where she waitressed. It didn't take a rocket scientist to figure out with his perfect speech, soft manicured hands and expensive shoes that he wasn't from around those parts.

Chanté chuckled aloud from the memory, but snapped to attention when Edie's sharp gaze zeroed in on her.

The last thing she expected today was to be ambushed with an intervention for her own marriage. However, her own solution to surviving the rest of her life with her self-absorbed, self-righteous and pretentious husband had already cost her a new Mercedes.

However, the question was whether she wanted to fix her marriage. As she struggled for an answer, her vision blurred, but she blinked away the tears and forced down another bite of food.

Edie watched Chanté from over the rim of her glasses for a long time before she prompted, "Well? You have to do something before you kill each other or kill yourselves. You know psychologists have the highest suicide rate."

"Where did you hear that?"

"I read it somewhere."

"Huh. I always thought it was dentists who had the highest rate."

"C'mon. What do you say? Will you go to marriage counseling?"

Matthew Valentine, handsome in a royal-blue suit, stared over the heads of his studio audience and into the camera. "Today we will be talking about how to take the bitterness out of your marriage." He smiled, but remained serious. "Oftentimes, it's not the big things that break a marriage. It's the small things." His voice quivered and for a brief moment, Matt appeared to have lost his concentration.

Seth shifted his gaze from one of the monitors to glance at his client on the stage.

The ultimate professional, Matthew recovered and continued with his spiel. The irony of today's subject matter didn't escape Seth so he found himself paying close attention to how Matthew interacted with his guests and the advice Matthew gave them.

"Couples tend to argue over something safe or superficial during battle, but they avoid talking about the serious problems."

Seth nodded as he listened. Everything Matthew said was sound advice. Everything made sense to him—so what were the serious problems between Matthew and Chanté? Where had they gone wrong?

While Matthew continued to mingle with his audience and offer handkerchiefs to sobbing guests, Seth thought back to when he first sensed trouble between Matthew and Chanté. Actually, he didn't sense, more like he dodged a glass vase when he'd entered the Valentines' home during a heated argument. Chanté was a small woman but she had one hell of an arm.

Two hours later, with the day's show finally completed taping and the last of the audience filtered out of the studio, Seth made it to Matt's dressing room and lingered just outside the door while a young, petite, yet curvaceous intern fawned over her employer.

"Great show today, Dr. Valentine," she said breathily. "I swear it's like you really know how a woman thinks and feels."

Seth lifted an inquisitive brow.

"Thank you, Cookie." Matt didn't spare the young girl a glance as he stripped the light coat of makeup from his face.

However, Cookie ignored his indifference and stepped forward until her perky bosom brushed against Matt's arm. "I know I've only been here six weeks, but

I have to tell you—working with you has been like a dream come true." She reached out a hand and gently stroked the side of his face.

Belatedly, Matt flinched from her touch.

"You're using the cologne I bought you for your birthday."

"Yeah, I decided what the hell. I've been using the same cologne for ten years."

Smiling like a seasoned temptress, she winked. "If there's ever anything you need—I'll be more than happy to help."

Matt finally met her gaze, but didn't respond.

Enough was enough. Seth cleared his throat.

Matt jumped again and then his face flushed a deep burgundy. "Seth," he boomed too loudly. "C'mon in. Cookie, that will be all for today."

The vixen's lips managed to spread wider as she demurely cast her gaze down. "If you say so, Dr. Valentine." She turned and walked saucily toward the door.

"Remember, if you need anything—anything at all— call me." Cookie winked and disappeared from the door.

"Can you spell *trouble?*" Seth asked, blinking from the trance her swaying hips induced.

"Who—Cookie?" Matt asked. "She's harmless."

"So is a starved lion—as long as you're not locked inside its cage." Seth folded his arms and leaned against the doorframe. "Look, Matt. I don't know how to say this other than to just come out and say it."

Matt cast a curious glance at the mirror and met Seth's reflected stare. "All right. Let me have it."

"I think you and Chanté should see a marriage counselor."

A silence roared on the heels of his words and judging by the intense glare from Matthew, he expected the vanity mirror to crack at any second.

"Have you lost your mind?" Matthew asked, standing from his chair and storming toward the door.

Seth managed to jump out of the way before Matt slammed it on his arm.

"Chanté and I are fine. The last thing we need is a marriage counselor," he said and barked a humorless laugh.

Seth glanced around the room and feigned surprise to find there were no other parties surrounding him. "I'm sorry. Are you talking to me—or someone else who hasn't refereed a few screaming matches at your home?"

"All couples have disagreements," Matt answered flatly and then exchanged his starched white shirt for something more appropriate for the tennis court. "Of course, they usually refrain from putting itching powder in each other's clothes."

"Or cutting each other's cars in half."

A wide smile monopolized Matt's face. "That was pretty good." He jutted a finger. "Extreme—but pretty good."

"Come on. What's the big deal?" Seth shrugged. "You encourage and educate people everyday about the importance of counseling. What's the big deal in practicing what you preach?"

Matthew unzipped his pants and jerked them down his legs. "The big deal is there isn't a damn thing that a psychologist can tell us that we don't already know. We're both controlling perfectionists with hot tempers. Theories and overblown rhetoric are not what we need. Especially when you're dealing with someone who is stubborn as an ox."

Seth frowned. "Help me out. Who's the ox in this scenario?"

"Not funny." Matthew tried to pull his left leg out from the bunched pants leg, but instead lost his footing and fell face forward. "Goddamn it."

Seth covered his mouth in time to cork his laughter.

By the time Matthew recovered and climbed back to his feet there was no trace of amusement on Seth's face—despite Matt's sock suspenders and Daffy Duck boxer shorts.

Matthew cleared his throat and then launched into an explanation for the boxers. "Chanté burned just about everything in my underwear drawer after the car incident."

"I think you got off lucky."

At last, Matthew smiled as he reached for his pristine-white tennis shorts. "I do, too."

A knock rapped on the door.

"Come in," Matt shouted.

Cookie peeked inside with a sheepish grin. "Your package arrived, Dr. Valentine."

Matthew's eyes lit up as he clapped his hands together. "Oh. Bring him in."

Seth's brows furrowed in curiosity but the feeling was quickly sated when Cookie entered the dressing room with the most adorable brown-and-white puppy.

"There's my little man," Matt exclaimed, finally stepping free from his trousers to reach for the dog. "Thank you, Cookie."

"My pleasure. Do you know what you're going to name him?"

"I'm not sure yet." Matt scratched behind the puppy's ear. "I have to spend some time with him and get a sense of his personality."

Cookie leaned over and kissed the dog on top of the head. "Well, keep me posted. I love dogs!"

"Will do."

The intern gave either Matt or the dog a wink, Seth couldn't tell which.

"Call if you need anything," she reminded him again and then disappeared with another wink.

"Excuse me, uhm," Seth said once the door closed. "But isn't Chanté allergic to dogs?"

"She's not allergic," Matt said unconcerned. "She just hates them."

"I stand corrected."

Matt sat in his makeup chair and began to coo and imitate baby talk to the bundle of fur.

"What kind of dog is he?"

"Bulldog. Isn't he handsome? Maybe I should name him Buddy? As in *my* Buddy."

"You know your wife is going to hit the roof when she sees him."

"Probably." Matt smiled. "But I'll just keep him on my side of the house. Besides, everyone needs companionship. A fact my wife seems to have forgotten."

Seth stared at his friend. Finally, he decided to stop

pussyfooting around. "Let me ask you something. And be honest if you can. If you and Chanté continue on the way you have been, how long do you think it will be before you finally accept Cookie's invitation?"

A flash of anger returned to Matthew's eyes. "You're out of line."

"And you're in denial."

That loud silence returned to the room, but this time it was layered with a tension usually reserved for heavy-weight boxers on fight night.

"Look, I'm your friend."

"You're my agent."

Seth thrust up his chin at the verbal blow. "All right. I'm your agent. As your agent I think I should warn you that a marriage counselor is better for your reputation than getting caught with your hands in the *Cookie jar*."

Matthew's heated black gaze snapped up to Seth as he opened the door.

"Think about it, Matt." His gaze shifted to the puppy. "Good luck, Buddy. Something tells me that you're going to need it."

Chapter 5

"Hello, Shawanda. Welcome to *The Open Heart Forum*."

"Dr. Valentine? Oh, Lawd, girl. I didn't think I would ever get through."

Chanté chuckled as she glanced up at Thad through the glass partition. "Well, I'm glad you did, Shawanda. What's on your heart tonight?"

"Yeah, well, I need to get some advice on what I should do about this (beep!) that's been creeping around with my man."

"Whoa, whoa, Shawanda." Chanté laughed. "I got to tell you this isn't one of those trashy talk shows, so I'm going to have to ask you to watch the language. You think that you can do that?"

"Yeah, girl. Just tell me what I should do about this…

heifa stalking my man 'cause I'm seriously about to catch a case if she calls my house one more damn time."

"Well." Chanté shook her head and braided her fingers. "Have you confronted your husband about this woman?"

"Oh, we ain't married or nothing. We've just been living together the last fifteen years."

Thad slapped a hand around his mouth while Chanté remained composed.

"I see. Before I address your question, Shawanda— do you mind if I ask you a question?"

"Uh, well, I guess not."

"Why have you wasted fifteen years of your life on a man who clearly doesn't respect you enough to marry you?"

"Hey, that's my baby's daddy. The ring will come. I mean, you know, he first has to get his wife to sign the divorce papers."

"His wife?"

"Yeah, she's been trippin' ever since he chose me over her trifling behind."

"So let me get this straight—" Chanté straightened in her chair. "You're calling because your man is exhibiting the same behavior you benefited from fifteen years ago when he left his wife for you. Do I understand that right?"

"Look, Rufus left my sister because she didn't know how to treat him right. She never could keep a man, if you know what I mean."

"Unfortunately, I think I do." Chanté sighed. "All right, Shawanda and the rest of you ladies out there who think that hanging on to a man, any man, by any means necessary is the road to eternal bliss. Snap out of it!"

Chanté drew a deep breath and shook her finger at her desk microphone like it was an errant child. "This sort of behavior is unacceptable, despicable and downright counterproductive. It's bad enough that you destroyed one family, but you're calling me to help you stop someone from paying you back for what you put out in the universe. The way I see it, Shawanda, you have two choices, get out or suck it up.

"If you have any sense left you'll do the right thing and crawl to your sister on your hands and knees and beg for forgiveness. Got it?"

A loud click followed by a dial tone filled the airwaves.

"Humph. Another woman who can't take the truth." She shook her head. "Look, ladies. One of the hardest things you'll ever have to learn is to know when to let go. It's not always healthy to only listen to your heart. Your heart can convince you to give up things you have no business giving up. Trust me, I know."

Chanté stayed her tongue, realizing that she'd nearly said too much. To her surprise, Thad had already removed his headphones and was stretched out in his chair, shaking his head.

"We cut to Dr. Laura Schlessinger's repeat show about a minute ago."

"Oh, thank God." Chanté sighed and dropped her head on her desk. "I was about to experience a serious case of verbal diarrhea."

Thad stood from his chair and strode out of the control room and into the studio booth. "Hey, what do you say we grab some coffee at our favorite diner? We could talk and...talk."

Chanté rolled her head to the side and peeked up at him. "Talk?"

Somehow, she managed to lift her head and smile. "Thanks, Thad...but I think I'm going to have to take a rain check." She removed her headset.

He nodded with obvious disappointment. "All right. But I got to tell you—the rain checks are stacking pretty high. I'm going to start cashing them in soon—real soon."

"Tomorrow?"

"Tomorrow night it is." Thad slid the bill of his Yankees cap to the front and winked. "Get some rest. You look like you need it."

Chanté watched the young producer as he shuffled out of the studio and then felt herself tumble back into a void so complete, she barely had any energy to pack up her belongings. "Sleep," she mumbled under her breath. "What a novel idea."

Like a zombie, she headed out to the employee parking lot. Despite exhaustion, Chanté knew when she climbed into bed, sleep would be rationed out in fitful doses. Such had been the case for the past five months. Ever since she'd kicked Matthew out of their bedroom.

She was angry. He was angry. She threw things. He shouted hurtful things at the top of his lungs. Neither apologized. To do so would mean that one of them was wrong. After eleven years of marriage, Chanté was tired of always being wrong.

Chanté's heels clicked louder against the asphalt, renewed anger brewed in her blood. Over the past five months, she'd lamented over every argument they had ever had and not once had Matthew apologized.

Not once.

As she approached her parking space, the sight of the rented Mercedes only fed her anger. Matthew deserved more than just some itching powder sprinkled in his clothes—maybe being thrown into a cage with a wild animal would elicit some sense of satisfaction.

"Okay, maybe that's a little too harsh," she admitted, but a smile curved her lips all the same.

As Chanté merged into traffic, she wished that she'd taken Thad up on his offer for coffee and a talk. She wanted to talk to someone, but hated feeling pressured to do so. The irony of that didn't escape her.

She drove for hours, most of the time going back and forth over the same stretch of highway—never really ready to make the right exit for her house. No matter the hour, she knew Matt would be waiting up for her in the living room, although he would never admit it. He'd always claimed to be working whether his laptop was on or not. That still meant something, didn't it? What about the other night when he'd nearly made love to her on the floor of the foyer?

Wasn't that a sign that he still wanted her?

At least her body…or what her body should be capable of giving him.

A child.

The white lines of the road blurred at the sudden sting of tears. Why couldn't Matt just let it go? Not every couple had children. Not everyone was meant to be parents.

But in the last six years her husband had grown obsessed. From endless tests to new and innovative positions, Matthew was determined to have a child. Making love had become sex and sex had become a dull, emotionless act that had left her feeling more empty and dissatisfied than when they started.

Matt never noticed. After all, to a man, an orgasm was an orgasm.

Chanté reached the point that she didn't even bother faking it anymore. And if she wasn't enjoying it, then why do it?

Still, the other night, an old familiar spark had flared between them. Or had she imagined it? She mulled the question over a moment, but in the end was no closer to an answer than she was that night.

But I wanted to make love to him.

That was an inescapable fact.

After a marathon of hot and sweaty sex, Edie and Seth curled into a nice spoon while they waited to catch their next wind.

"God, you're beautiful," Seth panted, peppering his wife's back with butterfly kisses.

"You just make sure you don't forget it," Edie purred and wiggled her rump against his growing erection.

Seth laughed but reached over and snatched a white Kleenex, a surrender flag, from the nightstand and waved it in front of his wife. "I give up. I can't go on without the aid of a medic."

Edie groaned and then inched out of their beloved spoon to roll over and face him. "You know if you keep conking out on me, I just might have to get myself a younger man."

"Then I'll just have to get myself an older woman. Someone who knows how to roll over and go to sleep after four rounds."

"Better not." Edie giggled before she laid another long, hot kiss on him. When she pulled away, she gazed deep into his eyes. "Promise me that we'll always be like this."

"I promise that we'll always be like this."

"Even when I grow old and my skin gets all wrinkly?"

"Even then."

"Even when my hair turns all gray and I'll have to put my teeth in a glass next to the bed?"

"Ooh, no teeth, huh? That could come in handy."

Edie popped him on the arm. "Promise."

Seth chuckled and drew her soft body close. "I promise to love you until my dying breath." He kissed her upturned nose.

Edie released a long sigh and tried to relax against him.

"Something else is on your mind. Out with it."

"Oh," she said disconsolately. "It's nothing."

"It sure doesn't sound like nothing."

She hesitated a moment, kissed his firm chest, and then tilted her head back so that she met his gaze in the dimly lit room. "Did you talk to Matthew today?"

It was Seth's turn to sigh wearily. "Yeah, I guess you can say that."

"I take it you ran into the same brick wall I did with Chanté?"

"Unfortunately." He rolled onto his back, but kept Edie locked in his arm. "I think they're worse off than I originally thought."

"What do you mean?"

Seth relayed his suspicions about Matt's potentially straying eye and waited for the eruptions he knew that would follow. Edie and Chanté were best friends, after all. Jumping to her girl's defense was only natural.

But she said nothing.

In a way, the quiet was more unsettling than any explosion.

"Baby?"

"Do you think he'll have an affair?"

Seth drew in a deep breath while he replayed what he'd seen in Matt's dressing room and what he knew of his friend's character. He wanted to say "no, absolutely not," but something kept the words from falling from his lips.

Edie sat up. When their eyes met again, Seth read the sadness she felt for her friend. It had nothing to do with book sales or public image.

"We have to try harder," she whispered. "Everyone knows they're soul mates."

"That doesn't mean anything, if they don't know they're soul mates," he reasoned, caressing her arm. "We can lead deer to water, but we can't make them drink."

With a slow nod, she turned toward the window. As she gazed out at the full moon, Seth watched as a smile crept across her face.

"We're going to have to do more than just lead them to the water," she said.

Seth frowned, lost on her meaning.

Edie faced him again. "We're going to have to throw them in."

Chapter 6

Somewhere around two a.m., Matthew began to worry. Would this be the night Chanté decided not to come home? He held his breath as his eyes scanned the dimly lit property. For the last five months he tried to prepare himself for such an occasion, but at this moment he realized he could never truly be prepared for that.

Day after day, he taught and counseled couples on how to rebuild a broken marriage, but he was absolutely clueless on how to fix his own. The sudden beam of a car's headlights piercing the night made Matthew's shoulders deflate with relief.

His marriage would see another day. Break out the champagne.

Matthew moved away from the window and returned to the sofa. He opened his laptop and spread out a folder of paperwork around him. When the door opened, his heartbeat sped up while he questioned if his wife would buy his "working late" act.

The door closed and he heard the locks engage. Soon their nightly script of light bantering would ensue.

Juvenile—yes. Necessary—absolutely.

However, at the sound of Chanté's heels clicking up the stairs, Matthew realized there was an unexpected change in the script. He removed the computer from his lap and rushed to the living room's archway.

"I'm glad to see that you remembered our address," he quipped, crossing his arms. He mentally berated himself for saying the words with blatant concern. He was supposed to sound aloof and nonchalant.

Chanté stopped halfway up the stairs and turned to face him. "Can we not do this tonight? I'm really tired."

Matthew moved from the archway, instantly concerned about the overwhelming sadness in her eyes and her slumped posture.

"Is there…?" He stopped himself at her sudden flash of anger.

"I think you've done enough, don't you?"

He had no response for the soft reprimand. All he could do was watch her turn and climb the rest of her stairs. Exactly one minute later, her high scream filled the entire house.

Matt's heart leaped into the center of his chest as he flew up the stairs. When he rounded the corner to Chanté's room, he quickly skidded to a stop while his eyes grew wide as silver dollars.

The entire room looked as if a tornado had hit. Curtains were pulled from their rods, paper, cotton and goose feathers were spawned across the floor—along with most of the bedding.

"What the hell happened in here?" Matthew asked, though the moment the question was out of his mouth, he suspected the answer.

Chanté rounded on him with fire in her eyes. "You know damn well what happened. You did this!" She stalked toward him.

Raising his hands in surrender, he took a retreating step. "Wait, it's not what you think."

A low growl caught their attention and Chanté slowly turned toward her walk-in closet.

Buddy trotted out, growling and shaking his head with a leather pump clenched between his teeth.

"What in the hell?" Chanté screeched.

"Buddy, no." Matthew raced into the room and knelt to rescue the prized possession. "Give me that. How did you get out of my room?"

"Buddy?" his wife snapped. "This mongrel belongs to you?"

Matthew pried the shoe out of the dog's mouth, but then groaned at the numerous teeth marks around the heel.

Chanté approached with her fist jabbed into her hips.

He glanced up. "Uh, looks like we were a little too late."

"Uh, you think?" She snatched the shoe from his hand. "These are Weitzman pumps. Do you know what I had to do to track these down?"

He quickly scooped the dog into his arms before his

wife did something rash. As a matter of fact, he realized that he better stand up if he wanted to keep his own teeth. "Chanté, calm down. This was an accident."

"An accident? You expect me to believe that? What the hell is a dog doing in this house in the first place? You know I don't like dogs."

"Well, I do. And I think it's high time I had one. I need something around here to be happy when I come home."

She sucked in an indignant breath. "And who is going to take care of him?"

"I'll take care of him!"

Chanté swept out an arm to indicate her bedroom. "Does this look like you're taking care of him?"

"He must have gotten out of his crate."

"Did you come to that conclusion all by yourself, Dr. Valentine?"

"It was an accident. It won't happen again."

Rage trembled through Chanté's body like a bolt of lightning. "Get out!" she seethed through her clenched teeth.

"Chanté…"

Pivoting on her heel, she marched toward the door and held it open. "I said, get out."

Realizing that she wasn't going to listen to reason, Matthew waltzed out. He'd barely crossed the threshold when the door slammed behind him.

Matthew stood still for a long moment, reviewing what had just happened.

Just apologize. Seth's advice rang in Matt's ear and reverberated through every cell of his body.

But apologize for what? Okay, maybe he could start with the car and the damage the dog did to her room— or even his callous remarks on national television. But all of that transpired in the last week. It would hardly cover the past five months.

It's a start.

Matthew turned around and knocked on the door.

Chanté didn't answer.

He drew a deep breath and tried again—this time a little louder. When she didn't answer the second time, he knew he was officially being given the silent treatment.

"I just wanted to say I'm sorry," he murmured to the door.

Buddy lifted his head and delivered a sloppy lick against Matthew's cheek.

"At least you still like me." Turning, Matthew followed the gray duct tape back to his room.

Thinking she heard something, Chanté shut off the shower and waited to see if she'd hear it again. After a minute, she shivered from the cool chill of the bathroom and turned the hot water back on. The steady, warm pulse of the water did a considerable job of easing the tension from her body.

However, she fully intended to make herself a hard drink once she climbed out of the shower—maybe even two.

As she lathered and rinsed, lathered and rinsed, she churned an inventory of Matthew's prized possessions over in her mind. Which item would pack the most wallop and which one would hit below the belt?

How long are you going to keep this up?

The question threw her, mainly because she didn't have an answer. This tit-for-tat game they played was taking on a life of its own, and in a weird way, it fed something in her—in Matthew, too, if she wasn't mistaken.

She shut off the water again and stepped out of the shower. Wrapping the towel around her body, she traipsed back into the adjoining bedroom. She stripped everything off the bed, and then put on fresh linens before she crawled on top.

Sighing, she stared up at the ceiling and laughed. She laughed so hard and so long, the voice inside her head questioned her sanity.

Sitting up, she took a long look around her gilded cage—albeit a trashed cage—and felt an incredible loneliness. It hadn't always felt this way—not when Matthew used to lie beside her. Chanté groaned. Why did her heart constantly flip-flop where Matthew was concerned?

She loved him. She hated him. She loved him. She loved him.

"Aw, hell. Maybe Edie was right. Maybe we do need help." After all, it had been easy to fall in love with Matthew, though many of her friends thought they were oil and water from the start.

Growing up, she hadn't known any affluent black families—not in a small Texan town like Karankawa. She was charmed by everything from the way he talked to the way he walked. She was in awe of his intelligence, captivated by his sophistication and seduced by his good looks.

While wallowing in a moment of honesty, she realized he still had those qualities. Maybe she was the one who'd changed. Maybe if her body had given them a child, she wouldn't be so bitter.

She stretched out across the bed, hoping to fill the empty spaces—but it didn't work. Chanté closed her eyes and struggled to remember all of their firsts. The first time he took her into his arms. Their first kiss. The first time they made love. After a while, the memories flooded her senses.

The first time they were together they'd lain on a bed of rose petals. Roses were her favorite flowers. That night, she thought she'd die from the sheer joy of their consummation. The tenderness of his probing and inquisitive hands. He was masterful in figuring out all her hot spots.

She remembered his mouth tasting like a fusion of heaven and sin. One minute, she was his precious angel and in the next, his little devil. Back then, Matthew kept a beautifully groomed goatee and her sensitive skin always quivered beneath its light tickle.

Lost in the memories, Chanté unwrapped the towel from her baby-oiled body and fanned her fingers across her chest. Oh, what she wouldn't give to travel back in time and experience that night again. Love seemed so effortless and happiness was always just a kiss away.

Nothing is stopping you from going to him now.

Her eyes snapped open. For a second her eyes darted around to see if someone else had actually made the comment. When she realized she was still alone, she sighed in relief.

But the bud of her femininity began to ache for fulfillment.

"I could go," she whispered, warming to the idea. Heck, who said that she had to apologize in order to get laid? Hell, she didn't even have to talk.

Chanté sucked in her bottom lip and nibbled for a little while. *There's the danger of Matthew thinking that sex would be some sort of peace offering.*

The ache between her legs intensified.

Then again, I could correct him in the morning. Chanté liked that idea and bounded off the bed, in search of the perfect negligee to seduce her husband.

Chapter 7

After a half bottle of Jack Daniels, Matthew dreamed of his wife's creamy thighs, firm breasts and perfect apple bottom. He tossed and turned and even smacked his lips while remembering her distinctive taste. The wanting, aching and longing had stripped him of his sanity.

No matter how many times he tried to think or concentrate on something else, Chanté's teasing body would crystallize in his mind. If he thought about work, Chanté would materialize as a naked cue-card girl. When writing material for his next book, Chanté would be the naked girl on his Internet pop-up, asking him if he wanted to see her in action.

It was maddening…and a complete turn-on.

In need of relief, Matthew grabbed hold of his erection and tried to assuage the ache. Even at this desperate hour, his hand was a lousy substitute.

You could always go back and knock on the door again.

Matthew's hand stilled. The thought had possibilities. But then he remembered how Chanté had turned him down the other night and how she closed the door in his face tonight. How many times could he face her rejection?

Knock. Knock.

Matthew remained frozen in the bed with his erection still throbbing in his hand.

Knock. Knock.

Buddy barked from his crate.

"Yes?" he asked sluggishly.

Instead of an answer, he listened as the doorknob turned and the heavy door creaked open. Pushing himself up, he wasn't quite sure what to expect—an intruder, his wife, or an intruder impersonating his wife.

He waited until the curvaceous figure illuminated under the silvery moonlight. Even then he wasn't sure he believed what he was seeing or if his old buddy Jack now had him hallucinating.

"Chanté?"

She glided toward the bed and pressed a slender finger against his lips. It didn't take a rocket scientist to catch her meaning—and he was only too willing to oblige.

Damn it, it's been five months.

Wait, his brain screamed. *Something wasn't right.* Matt eyed her suspiciously. "Is this a trick?"

Again, she didn't answer. Just gave him a slight shake of her head.

Matthew weighed whether to believe her. Then again, if this was a hallucination, what harm was there in having a little fun?

A bright smile bloomed across Matthew's face and glowed in the moonlight. "Hey, baby. You finally decided to come pay Big Daddy a visit?"

Chanté frowned. "Have you been drinking?"

"Maybe. Maybe not. There's no law against a man drinking in the privacy of his own home, is there?"

"Never mind. This was a mistake." She turned.

Matthew hopped out of bed and clutched her arm. "Don't go, baby. You know we've both been waiting for this for a long time," he slurred.

She hesitated, giving Matthew all the confirmation he needed.

"Why don't you give me a big, fat juicy kiss to seal the deal?"

Eager, both Chanté and Matthew leaned forward, only to bang their foreheads together.

"Ouch."

"Oh. Sorry about that." Matt fluttered a nervous smile before trying again. This time, their lips connected and their bodies sagged with relief.

However, when Matt leaned her back onto the bed, he'd forgotten about his laptop and piles of paper occupying the other side.

"Ow, ouch." Chanté shoved him off.

"Oh, just a minute." Matt pitched everything, including the laptop, over the side of the bed. "See? All gone." He flashed another toothy smile and clumsily reached for her again.

Buddy barked.

"Shh. Buddy, be quiet," Matthew warned. "You'll scare my dream girl away."

Chanté hesitated.

"Don't worry, no more surprises," he assured, patting the empty bed for emphasis.

After another beat of hesitation, Chanté decided to give it another try. She glided effortlessly into his arms and imagined herself cast into her own romance novel. But everything didn't play out quite the way she'd hope.

Matthew grabbed for her like a starved man before an all-you-can-eat buffet. He fumbled and cursed while he tried to pry her out of her lingerie.

"Here, let me do it," she offered before he had a chance to destroy one more thing of hers. Three snaps later, she chiseled on another smile and then lay back on the bed in all her naked glory.

That was when the real pawing began.

Matt's once tender and caressing hands were now rough and forceful. Lips that once gave loving worship to her sensitive nipples now seemed determined to chew the damn things off.

"Easy. Easy," she coached, wanting him to slow down and enjoy the ride. Instead, her husband skipped foreplay and went straight for the main attraction.

He entered with one mighty thrust and nearly split her in two.

What the hell?

Chanté gripped his bulging biceps and tried to hold

on during the ride. However, she was nearly rendered senseless several times as her head was rammed into the headboard. Meanwhile, Buddy continued to bark his head off. This was like nothing she'd ever experienced before.

"Shh, Buddy. Shh, Buddy," Matthew hissed in between his "Oh, Gods." His hips hammered away while his eyes damn near rolled to the back of his head.

Chanté watched in resolute boredom until Matthew stiffened with one last thrust, and then collapsed in a sweaty heap.

Is that it?

"Oh, baby. I missed you so much." Matthew panted and peppered sloppy kisses across her face and eyes.

"Uhm." She searched for the right words. "Matt?"

"Hmm?"

"I, uh, didn't...well, you know."

Matt lifted his head and stared down at her. "You didn't?"

Chanté shook her head. *Not even close.*

"I, uh, I'm so—well, I guess, I did get a little carried away. It being a while and all." He absently wiped the sweat from his brow.

She nodded in feigned understanding. "That's all right. You can try again."

"Yeah, yeah." He smiled and wiggled his hips.

To Chanté's dismay, she noted Matt Jr. wasn't exactly standing at full salute.

"Just give me a minute to...catch my breath," Matthew panted.

Chanté's brows furrowed, but she had no choice but

to bob her head in agreement and wait for her husband to catch his second wind.

Two minutes later, Matthew was fast asleep.

At breakfast the next morning, Seth decided it was time he dusted off his culinary skills to make his wife breakfast in bed. Unfortunately, his specialty was cold cereal.

"Oh, honey." Edie smiled brightly when he appeared at their bedroom doorway with her breakfast tray in hand. "You shouldn't have."

Seth beamed proudly as if he'd prepared a five-course meal. "My baby deserves the best."

"Special K, huh?"

"Special K with strawberries."

"Then bring it on!" Edie set aside the pamphlets in her lap and punched up her pillows before her husband delivered her meal.

"What are these?" he asked, picking up one of the pamphlets.

"Some brochures I picked up yesterday before my talk with Chanté."

Seth frowned as he opened one and then another. "Sex therapy? I thought the idea was to get them to see a real counselor?"

"They're real." Edie snatched one of the brochures back. "I've heard some great things about these places."

"Where? On one of those women's talk shows?"

Edie poked out her bottom lip as she shrugged her shoulders. "What if I did? A reference is a reference."

"Okay, this job just went from difficult to impossible." Seth laughed. "Sex isn't the problem. Their ability to stay away from sharp objects is."

"Are you sure about that?" she asked, scooping out her first spoonful of cereal.

"No," he acquiesced. "It's not the sort of thing we talk about."

"Well, what do you talk about?"

"His lack of sex. Five months and counting." Seth shook his head with great sympathy. "I don't care what anyone says, that's cruel and unusual punishment. No wonder he's demolishing cars."

"I hear you." She chomped away for a moment while her gaze returned to the pamphlets.

"Actually, I really think I'm on to something here. Last week when Chanté stormed over here about the Letterman incident, she said that Matthew *used* to be great in bed."

"What the hell? Do you two give each other blow-by-blow recaps?"

"Don't worry, sweetie. You're still a ten in my book."

Seth straightened his shoulders as his chest swelled from the compliment. "Ten is easy when I have an eleven in my arms."

For that, he was rewarded with a kiss.

"So you think this sex therapy will work?"

"It certainly can't hurt."

"Not unless there's a chainsaw on the premises."

Edie chuckled.

"Any idea how we're going to get them to one of these places?" Seth asked.

"Yes. We lie."

Chapter 8

Chanté was beyond pissed.

No car. No foreplay. No orgasm. Enough was enough.

She slammed the kitchen cabinets as she made coffee, took her morning pills, and slaved over the hot stove. Every time she thought about last night's lousy performance, she broke a glass, a cup or a dish. How and when did Matt become so selfish and so clueless in bed?

Not only had he fallen asleep, he snored loud enough to wake the dead.

Crash!

Another plate bit the dust.

"Good morning."

Chanté's gaze snapped to her husband as he entered the kitchen, and for a brief moment she weighed the consequences of smashing his head in with a frying pan.

The temptation nearly won out—especially since the bastard had the audacity to be in a cheerful mood.

"What smells so good?" he asked, with a beaming smile.

"Breakfast," she answered with an overdose of saccharine. "Hungry?"

Suspicion glimmered in Matt's eyes. "You're cooking me breakfast?"

"It's not unusual for a wife to cook for her husband."

Matthew's brows shot up.

"Why don't you just take a seat at the table? The food will be right out."

Matt didn't move. Instead, he studied the angles of her plastic smile. "Uh…about last night," he began. "Did we…you didn't come to my room last night, did you?"

The jerk doesn't even remember! Chanté crossed her arms and weighed her options. "Only in your dreams," she lied bitterly.

"Oh, I didn't think so." He shook his head and gave an awkward laugh. "I knew I had a few too many."

Chanté glared and contemplated the frying pan again. "Breakfast will be out in a minute."

He hesitated again.

"Go on now. I'll be out there in a second."

Finally, he gave her a slight nod and then turned in the direction of the dining room.

I'll fix you breakfast all right. One you'll never forget.

Matt knew he was in trouble. Why on earth would Chanté fix him breakfast after what Buddy did to her room? The way he saw it, he still had options. He could either run from the house screaming like a banshee, put in a precall to 9-1-1, or drop to his knees and beg for mercy.

The first option had potential.

"Breakfast is ready," Chanté sang, carrying plates to the table.

Too late. Matthew swallowed a lump in his throat while his brain threatened to short-circuit with trying to come up with an excuse to miss breakfast.

"Uh, Chanté." He followed his wife to the table.

"Yes, dear?"

Dear? "You know, I'm not all that hungry," he said with a nervous smile. However, the sight of fluffy scrambled eggs, crisp bacon and golden-brown biscuits made his stomach roar at the lie.

Chanté lifted an inquisitive brow.

"Maybe I am a little hungry."

Chanté smiled and pulled out a chair. "Sit."

Matt hesitated. His fear accelerated at the sight of her lips sliding wider.

"Come on." She patted the back of the chair. "You're not afraid of me, are you?"

How could he back down from a challenge like that? "Of course not." He walked over to her, searched her eyes for any telltale signs and then slowly eased into the offered chair.

"There. See?" She patted his shoulders. "That wasn't so bad, was it?"

The corner of Matthew's lips quivered and then

he glanced down at the meal before him. Everything looked good—perhaps too good.

Chanté hummed a merry tune like a Disney princess as she walked to the other side of the table to take her seat. "Dig in," she said.

Matt glanced around. "You know, I think I'd like some orange juice," he announced, scooting back his chair. "Can I get you any?"

"I'll get it." She jumped up from her chair and nearly raced out of the room. "You sit there and eat."

When she disappeared around the corner, he reached across the table and switched the plates. A second later his wife rushed back into the room carrying two glasses of orange juice. "Here you go."

"Thank you, honey."

Her smile thinned at the endearment and Matthew grew suspicious of the drink she handed him as well. Mercifully, Buddy chose that moment to waddle into the room.

"What in the hell is he doing in here?" Chanté snapped and jumped up from the table.

"Hey, little Buddy." Matt scooped up the dog. "How do you keep getting out of your crate?"

"Get him out of here!" Chanté screeched.

Matthew cradled the dog against his body. "All right. Calm down. Don't have a conniption fit. I'll go put him back in his crate."

"Apparently he needs a stronger crate. Tie him up somewhere outside."

Buddy barked.

Chanté stuck her tongue out at the dog.

"Now is that mature?" Matthew asked.

"After what he did to my bedroom, he's lucky we're not having him for breakfast."

Buddy whimpered and snuggled against his owner.

Unmoved, Chanté stomped her foot. "Outside."

"Come on, Buddy. Let's see if Roger can get you situated somewhere." Matthew rose from his chair and marched out, all the while cooing and apologizing to the dog for his wife's behavior.

Chanté leaned across the table and craned her neck to see if the coast was clear and then quickly switched the breakfast plates back.

Minutes later, her husband returned with a pinch of annoyance in his expression. The emotion vanished when he discovered his wife had already started eating her meal. He eased into his chair and watched her expression.

Chanté stopped chewing and frowned.

"Is something wrong, honey?" Matthew picked up his fork.

"No." She smiled but it faltered. "Everything is… fine."

He returned the smile when she placed a hand over her stomach. "Good." He dove into his food triumphantly and moaned aloud to emphasize how wonderful everything tasted. "You know, honey. I think this is the best breakfast I've had in a long time."

"Glad you enjoy it." Grimacing, she cupped a hand over her mouth. "Excuse me." She bounded out her chair and raced out of the room.

Matt shoved another forkful of food into his mouth

while chuckling to himself. *You have to get up pretty early in the morning to pull one over on me.*

In the half bathroom on the bottom floor, Chanté was doubled over with laughter.

The studio audience for *The Love Doctor* show grew restless waiting for their host to take the stage. The warm-up team had long run out of jokes and prizes to hand out and the camera crew and stagehands were growing bored.

"Where is he?" Trish from the sound department inquired. "Production is going to run over."

"Love Doctor! Love Doctor!" the crowd chanted.

"We'd better do something or we're going to have a studio of emotionally imbalanced women storm the stage," Trish warned.

"Love Doctor! Love Doctor!"

"I'll go check his dressing room," Cookie volunteered cheerfully and sashayed off.

Matthew wasn't feeling too good. In fact, he was feeling downright miserable—and he knew why.

"I'm never going to forgive her for this," he vowed, exiting his private bathroom. Despite his black mood, he finally managed to pull himself together and leave his dressing room.

"There you are!" Cookie approached, wearing a wide smile. "Everyone is waiting for you." Studying his face, the intern frowned. "Are you all right? You don't look so well."

"Fine." Matthew flashed a smile but proceeded to

take tiny steps toward the stage. "Never better." He stopped and closed his eyes as another wave of nausea threatened to send him back to the toilet.

Cookie stopped, fearful that whatever he had was contagious.

After a few seconds, Matthew sighed in relief when his stomach settled and he continued his slow journey to the stage.

"Love Doctor! Love Doctor!" the crowd chanted.

"There he is!" a spectator shouted from the crowd, and the studio thundered with applause.

Matthew smiled, waved and hit his mark in front of the cameras. However, the moment he opened his mouth his stomach dropped to his knees and his nausea was no longer ripples but huge tidal waves.

"Hello, everyone," he greeted, struggling to remain professional. Yet, the moment the stage lights turned up, he literally felt beads of sweat pop up along his forehead. "Thanks for coming…and good night." Matthew turned and bolted off the stage, praying that he would make it back to his private bathroom.

"What type of conference is this again?" Chanté asked Edie for the third time as they perused the shoe aisles. "And why do both Matt and I have to attend?"

"It's a relationship conference and you're going because it's an excellent promotional opportunity. A lot of press is covering this thing so you and Matt need to be on your best behavior."

Chanté sighed and rolled her eyes. "I don't know, Edie. I sort of need a break from Matthew—especially

after last night's fiasco. I wanted to kill that damn dog…
and him." She hesitated and then cast a sidelong glance
over at her friend.

"What?"

Chanté debated on whether she should tell everything that had happened. "I went to Matthew's bedroom last night."

Edie's eyes lit up. "You did? Well, good for you!"
She gave her a strong hug and noticed Chanté's lack of
response. "Not good?"

"I'd rather have played Scrabble."

Edie grimaced.

"No kissing. No foreplay. No nothing," Chanté whispered angrily. "He just tossed me back onto the bed,
pumped like an Olympic record was on the line…and
then rolled over and went to sleep."

"Ouch."

"Damn right. I wanted to kill him." She stopped
there, not confessing to tampering with Matthew's
breakfast. No need to paint herself in a bad light. "I
just don't get it," Chanté complained. "He wasn't always like this. I remember a time— Ooh, girl. The earth
moved, angels flew down from heaven and I thought I'd
need physical therapy in order to walk again. Now? It's
wham-bam-thank-you-ma'am and, by the way, where
is the baby?"

Edie fell silent as she cocked her head in sympathy.

"I used to think we were just in some kind of rut. You
know, stress from the jobs, the pressure to try and beat
my biological clock. Before I knew it, long lovemaking

sessions were downgraded to quickies and we've been stuck in that same gear ever since."

"I'm sorry." Edie draped an arm around her friend's shoulders. Now she was convinced more than ever that she was doing the right thing in tricking Chanté and Matthew into sex therapy. "Look, go to this conference. When you get back, I'll make sure you get a break. I'll talk to Julia in the publicity department and arrange a book tour for you. That'll keep you out of the house for a little while."

"True." Chanté sighed, but then perked up. "Ooh. These are nice." She picked up a pair of leather pumps.

"Don't you already have a pair like that?"

"No. It doesn't have this cute little buckle on the side. I'm going to try them on."

Edie just shook her head as she followed her friend to a nearby chair where she asked a saleswoman for the correct size. "No offense, but how many shoes can one woman own?"

"Hey, when I was growing up, I never owned more than two pairs of shoes at a time."

"And now you have a whole department store in your closet."

"All right, I admit it. I love shoes. Sue me."

Edie continued to shake her head. "So what do you say? Will you do the conference?"

"Separate hotel rooms?"

"C'mon. How will that look at a relationship conference?"

"Like we're trying to preserve our sanity."

"Chanté."

"All right. All right." She held up her hands.

"You'll do it?" Her editor perked up.

Chanté drew a deep breath and tried to figure out just how long she and Matthew could share a hotel room without a homicide detective showing up.

"Please?" Edie folded her hands in mock prayer.

"All right. I'll do it," she huffed. "Just make sure the room is stocked with enough alcohol to dull my pain."

Edie smiled smugly behind Chanté's back. *One down, one to go.*

Chapter 9

"I'm not going anywhere with that psycho!" Matthew spat to Seth and then ducked his head back over the toilet bowl. "If you haven't noticed, she damn near tried to kill me this morning."

"Am I to believe that you did nothing to provoke her attempted murder this time?"

"No," he lied, coming up for air again. "Well...not exactly."

"Uh-huh." Seth finished wringing cold water from a face towel and then tossed it to his client. "What exactly did you do? It wouldn't happen to have involved a four-legged friend I told you not to take home?"

Matthew placed the towel over his face, in part to cool his forehead and in part to hide his guilt while he reviewed last night's major disasters…and one mind-blowing sex dream.

"If it's taking you that long to answer the question, I don't think I want to know what happened."

"That's probably best." He paused and then added, "I think my, uh, streak ended last night."

Seth's eyebrows rose in surprise, but then quickly crash-landed. "You think? I take it since the porcelain god is your best friend today that it didn't go too well?"

"Horrible," Matthew groaned. "I was drunk and it had been so long…I grew too excited…and was a little quick on the trigger." He glanced up at Seth. "And that's not the worst part."

"You didn't."

He nodded. "I did. I fell asleep…and then this morning I wasn't sure if I'd dreamed the whole thing. When I asked Chanté about it, she said that it never happened, but I don't know."

It was Seth's turn to groan.

"I didn't mean for it to happen," Matthew said defensively. "It just did. And then this morning when she was cooking breakfast I started to apologize…and I couldn't quite get the words out. Me! King of the talk shows couldn't find the words to apologize to my wife. How pathetic is that?"

"No wonder she tried to kill you."

"Nothing excuses that."

"And what excuse is there for taking a chainsaw to someone's car?"

"Hey! Just whose side are you on?"

"No one's side since you're both crazy as hell." Seth

folded his arms as he leaned back against the sink. "C'mon, Matt. About this conference—it's going to be great for you publicly. A few of the other top relationship gurus are going to be there."

"Dr. Phil?"

"If I'm not mistaken," Seth lied smoothly. "It's just for a couple of days. Surely you and Chanté can put your differences aside for a couple of days to pose as the perfect couple?"

Matthew groaned his doubt, especially since his mind was already churning for his next payback for being damn near poisoned. "I don't know, Seth. I think what we need is a vacation from one another. Maybe you can set me up with a book tour or something. Get me out of the house before I make America's Most Wanted list."

"All right. You do this conference and when you get back, I'll get you your tour."

After hosting another long night of *The Open Heart Forum,* Chanté broke her promise and issued Thad yet another rain check. Mostly, she didn't feel like hosting another pity party. What good would it do?

"Piss or get off the pot." How many women had she told that to over the years? If you're not happy, why stick around?

"And the hypocrisy award goes to…me."

At two a.m., she turned the rental car into the driveway, but sat behind the wheel long after she shut off the engine. To be honest, she was afraid to go inside. Matthew was not likely to let a little thing like spiking his food go unavenged. Of course it was harmless—at most he was nauseous for a couple of hours—at worst he spent the day hugging the toilet.

Like always—she had options. Grab a hotel room for the night, sleep in the car or brave out Matthew's next chess move. In the end, her curiosity was too strong to back down.

Opening the front door, Chanté peered cautiously inside. The first clue that something was up was that all the lights in the house were turned off. Matthew was giving the appearance that he hadn't waited up for her.

She didn't buy it for a minute.

Chanté inched across the threshold with bated breath and her ears strained to catch the slightest sound. Closing the door, she effectively stamped out the only light resource she had. She knew the layout of the house by heart and rushed across the foyer to take the stairs two at a time. If she could just make it to her bedroom, she'd be safe.

But once in her bedroom, she discovered Matthew's revenge.

The scream she released was more bloodcurdling than all the horror movie scream queens put together. There, strung from the ceiling like party favors, were hundreds of her precious shoes: Prada, Gucci, Ferragamos and even her $14,000 Manolo Blahnik alligator boots, with all their heels severed.

Her shoes. Her babies.

She screamed until she realized this was not a dream or, better yet, a nightmare. "I'm going to kill him," she seethed. Glancing around, Chanté looked for a weapon—any weapon.

"Payback is a bitch," Matthew drawled from behind.

She spun around and launched at him.

Matthew never imagined his wife could move so quickly. Before he could think to block the attack she was already on him like white on rice. After she landed a few blows upside his head, he lost his balance and toppled onto the floor where they rolled around like seasoned wrestlers.

"I hate you! I hate you!" Chanté shouted at the top of her lungs. "How could you do such a thing?"

Because you tried to kill me, he tried to say, but the moment he opened his mouth, she socked him in it.

"Chanté, it's never okay to hit," he managed to scowl.

"Screw you!"

They continued to grapple. She took the top position, then it was his turn, and then her turn again.

"Goddamn it, Matthew. You've gone too far this time."

"Me?" he thundered incredulously. "I could have ended up in the hospital over that stunt you pulled this morning."

"If only I could be so lucky," she snapped.

The rush of small padded paws rushed across the hardwood floor and Chanté glanced up in time to see the short squat bulldog barreling and barking toward her. She jumped just as Matthew shoved and flew back, and smacked her head with a loud thump on the corner of the bedroom's doorframe.

"Chanté!" Matthew sat up. "Are you all right?"

"Oww." She sucked in a deep breath and rubbed at the instant knot on the back of her head. "That hurt." As Buddy continued to bark at full volume, Chanté had an evil image of skewering the dog and roasting him over an open pit.

"Shut him up!"

Matthew scooped Buddy up and jogged him back to his room. By the time he returned, Chanté managed to pull herself up off the floor and limp to the bed.

"Are you all right?" he asked again.

"Of course." She didn't attempt to look in his direction. "Don't I look all right?"

Matthew crossed the room to her bed. "Mind if I take a look?"

His gruff baritone held a warmth she recognized from years long past and she was surprised by a sudden flutter in the pit of her stomach. She jumped when his hand gently touched the back of her head.

"Be still. I promise I won't hurt you…this time."

Why in the hell did she smile? Had he finally knocked the rest of her marbles loose?

Tilting her head, Chanté's sanity was again called into question when her husband's fingers combed through her hair and her heartbeat quickened.

It had to be a trick of the mind when time crawled at a snail's pace during her examination. Sitting still and trying not to make any additional contact, she noticed for the first time his change in cologne. For years his signature scent was the sandalwood-based Hugo by Hugo Boss. She had been the one to introduce the fragrance to him as a Christmas gift back in '96. He loved it because she loved it and he'd worn it ever since.

Now this tangy scent reeked as being a gift from another woman. Chanté sucked in a breath from the sudden conclusion and she pulled away.

Misinterpreting her reaction, Matthew held up his hands and backed away. "Looks like you'll live."

Chanté eyed him suspiciously, looking to see if there were any other clues that hinted that there was another woman in the picture. She found none, but once the thought escaped Pandora's box, she couldn't force it back inside.

"I want a divorce," she said in a croaked whisper.

Matthew sighed.

"I mean it this time," she added as tears gathered in her eyes. "We can't keep living this way." Standing from the bed, her head bumped against a pair of Jimmy Choos. "It's time we let go."

Her words skillfully carved Matthew's heart out of his chest. It was probably the millionth time she'd asked for a divorce and probably the first time he knew that she meant it.

And it was the first time he was truly scared.

"We'll talk about it in the morning," he said, almost failing to get the words out of his constricting throat.

"I'm not going to change my mind," she informed him softly. Her eyes swam in a pool of tears. "The only reason we're still together is because of our careers. How pathetic is that?"

Chanté reached up and began pulling the shoes down

from the ceiling. Fat tears rolled like boulders down her face.

"I went too far—"

"We both did," she said sadly. "I, uh, did promise Edie we would attend some big conference coming up."

"Yeah. Seth asked me about it today."

"I think I can manage one last happy face for the public. How about you?"

"Piece of cake."

She nodded and wiped her face dry. "When we return, I'm seeing my lawyer."

Matthew clenched his jaw at the sound of the final nail being hammered into their marriage's coffin and turned to leave before his tears fell.

Chapter 10

For three days, the Valentines' household had transformed into a multimillion-dollar tomb. Even Buddy
seemed to take on his owner's melancholy and gave
up barking.

At seeing the short, stout mongrel following her to
the kitchen, Chanté couldn't bring herself to get angry
with him for having escaped his crate again. Especially
not with him looking up at her the way he did. His wide-
eyed stare seemed to urge her to tell him her problems.

More than once, she found herself doing just that—
usually when she found herself filling his dog bowl
with kibble.

"I just don't know if I can handle four days pretending to be happy when I'm not," she told Buddy. "And

I don't know what I'm going to say when the divorce becomes public."

Buddy whined as he put his head down on the cold kitchen floor.

"I know," she whispered, retrieving a box of cereal. "I still can't believe it's over." She filled a glass with water, took her morning pills and then finished fixing her breakfast. She settled on a stool at the breakfast bar. In her head, she scrolled through a list of questions she usually asked her callers who were at the end of a relationship.

Have you exhausted all avenues for reconciliation?

Before she lied to herself, Edie's voice floated around her head. *Maybe you and Matt should seek counseling.*

Like before, she scoffed at the idea, but then looking around her kitchen and imagining what it would truly be like when Matthew moved out, she reconsidered.

The moment her morning meeting with the marketing department was over, Edie raced back to her cluttered office ready to dive into a stack of unread manuscripts, but instead was surprised to see her handsome husband waiting for her.

"Baby, what are you doing here?" She eased into his arms and delivered a quick smooch against his smooth-shaved skin.

"Came to see if I could take my favorite girl to lunch…and to see if you have those fake itineraries printed up. I'm running by the studio this afternoon and I promised Matthew I'd bring them to him."

"Got them right here on my desk." She moved to her in-box and then handed him a glossy folder.

"The Marriage Quest conference," he read aloud. "Catchy."

"Why, thank you." Edie's smile beamed as she rocked on her heels. "I can't take all the credit. Julia in Publicity helped."

"The Tree of Life Spa and Resort," he continued reading. "Sounds interesting."

"Oh, it is. The tree of life is a part of the map of the seven chakras."

"The what?"

"Chakras. They are energy centers that represent the dynamic flow of cosmic energy within the human body."

"Uh-huh." He snapped the folder closed. "Fascinating."

"It is," Edie went on. "You know, I was thinking— maybe we should go with Chanté and Matthew."

"Why? There's nothing wrong with our sex life." Seth stepped back and folded his arms. "Is there?"

"No. No. Of course not." She slyly opened his arms and eased back into his embrace. "But I thought it would be fun for us to try out new things. Plus, we'll probably need to keep an eye out on Matthew and Chanté. We have to stop them from bolting when they discover they've been tricked."

"What are we supposed to do—tackle them?"

"Love is a contact sport." She laughed at her own joke.

Seth failed to see the humor.

"C'mon. We should really be there for them."

Never being able to resist his wife's pleading brown eyes, Seth gave in with a sigh. "All right. All right. I'll clear my schedule."

"Good. I already bought our tickets."

"Of course you did."

Matthew spent another day cruising on autopilot. He listened with great apathy to his guests' problems, doled out his earnest opinions and advice, and then smiled and laughed with his staff once they wrapped taping.

In the coming week, the network would broadcast repeat programming while he attended his last conference with his wife. A part of him knew that he should at least give his producers a heads-up about the pending divorce, but the other part of him still hadn't come to terms with it.

That was silly, considering their wild fights and inexcusable behavior. Deep down, he never thought she would go through with it. She was his yin to his yang. If she got crazy, he went crazy, too.

But leave?

"I should have followed Seth's advice and just apologized," he mumbled to the vanity mirror inside his dressing room.

"I'm sorry. Did you say something?" Cookie asked, handing him his coffee.

"No. No. I was just…talking to myself." He smiled blandly and dropped his gaze to the steaming black liquid in his favorite *Open Heart Forum* coffee mug.

"Oh." Cookie clasped her hands behind her back and

thrust her surgically-enhanced bosom high into the air. "Well, is there anything else I can do for you?"

"No. I think that's all. Thank you." He sipped from his cup and prepared to dive back into his desolate thoughts.

"Are you sure?" The young girl stepped forward and purposely rubbed her breasts against his arm. "Can't you think of anything else you might need?"

Surprised, Matthew instinctively pulled his arm away and repositioned himself in his chair to avoid physical contact. Yes, she was a beauty by any man's standards and there was no misinterpreting the open invitation written in her eyes, but he was a married man and...

His thoughts froze. He wasn't going to be a married man much longer. His war against his advancing depression ended in a crushing defeat.

His marriage was over.

Old man Roger agreed to keep an eye on Buddy for the Valentines. When he showed up to pick the puppy up, he innocently asked, "You guys going to a funeral?"

Matthew handed their luggage to the chauffer and shot a look over at his wife.

As if a director had shouted action, she gave an Oscar-worthy performance by laughing off the question and patting the groundskeeper's arm. "Nothing as serious as that. We're guest speakers for a marriage and relationship conference in New Mexico."

"Ah." He nodded his head, but his eyes darted between the couple.

Matthew thought the man didn't look convinced, but at least he had the decency not to probe further.

"Well, you two have a good time. Don't you worry none about Buddy. I'll take good care of him."

A few minutes later, they headed off to the airport. Within five minutes, the drive already seemed too long. Matthew sat ramrod straight while trying not to glance over at his wife. The few times he caught a glimpse of her, she stared resolutely out the window.

"You know, it's not too late to back out of this," he said, breaking the chilly silence.

Chanté glanced at him, seemingly annoyed that he was speaking to her.

"We could just give them some type of excuse...or tell them the truth."

The way she pressed back into her seat and carefully folded her arms, Matthew surmised she was tempted by the suggestion. In turn, it felt like another nail being driven into their coffin.

"I promised Edie I would go," she admitted softly. "Might as well go ahead and just get it over with."

"Yeah," he agreed, returning his attention to the scenery sliding past his own window. "Might as well."

Later, the husband and wife team arrived at the airport and stepped out of the limousine with wide toothy smiles. Matthew, being a sort of television celebrity, was more immediately recognized and was approached for autographs.

"Oh, my Lord. It really is you," one woman gushed, covering her heart with both hands. "Oh, I absolutely love your show." She turned her dancing eyes toward

Chanté and dug through her large purse. "And I just purchased your book this morning. Will you sign it for me?"

"I'd love to." Chanté returned the woman's infectious smile.

The woman handed over the book and prattled on. "I was telling my girlfriend the other day about what a beautiful couple you two make."

"Why, thank you," Matthew and Chanté responded like robots.

"Look, it's the Valentines," another woman gasped and then proceded to drag her unimpressed companion toward them. Within seconds it was apparent the woman had a major crush on Matthew.

"Honey, make sure you keep your claws in this one," gushing woman number two whispered loudly to Chanté. "Trust me. They don't make them like him anymore."

A few inches evaporated from Chanté's smile as she cast a sidelong glance at her husband. No question about it, Matthew was indeed a fine specimen. His aura of confidence and warm baritone practically had the women melting all over him.

Her, too, if she wasn't careful.

The Valentines worked their way toward their gate, smiling and giving one another adoring glances.

Sometimes it was forced, sometimes it wasn't.

After settling into their first-class seats, Chanté and Matthew blinked in genuine surprise when Edie and Seth took the seats across the aisle from them.

"What are you two doing here?" Chanté asked with a rush of relief, easing into her bones.

"What do you think?" Edie chided, and then lowered her voice. "We're here to make sure you two don't kill each other."

"Personally, I welcome the protection," Matthew joked, and was rewarded with a sharp elbow jab. "See what I mean?" he added.

"All right, you two. Behave," Seth warned, shaking his head. "Don't make us put you in time-out."

"He/She started it," Chanté and Matthew complained in unison and then gave each other sharp looks.

Seth leaned into his wife's ear. "Still think this is going to work?"

Edie thrust up her chin and gave him a reassuring smile. "Trust me. Once we get to the resort they'll be thanking us."

Chapter 11

"What the hell do you mean there's no conference?" Chanté rounded on her best friend once the group arrived at the front desk of the Tree of Life Spa and Resort. "I have a full itinerary and workshop program—"

"I sort of made those up," Edie admitted and then used her husband as a human shield in case Chanté put her good pinching fingers to use.

"You made them up?" Matthew and Chanté barked.

"Why would you do something like that?" Chanté asked. "Do you know what I had to do to get this time off from the radio station on such short notice?"

"Mr. and Mrs. Valentine?" A calm, gentle female voice spoke from behind them.

Chanté and Matthew turned cautiously toward an elderly white-haired woman who was just shy of five feet tall.

"Hello, I'm Dr. Margaret Gardner. Welcome to the Tree of Life Resort. I can't tell you how excited I was that you two had registered for our Sexuality and Liberation program."

"Come again?" Matthew shot a glare at Seth.

"Don't worry," Dr. Gardner continued. "Nothing is more important to us than our guests' privacy. We're just thrilled for the opportunity to introduce an alternative method to relationship healing."

"Uh-huh." Matthew digested the kind woman's words and then reached over to close his wife's gaping mouth. "This Sexuality and Liberation program of yours…exactly how does that work?"

Before Dr. Gardner could respond, Chanté finally found her voice. "Excuse us for a minute, won't you?" She grabbed Matthew by the arm and tugged him aside. "I don't care how it works. We're not staying!"

"Oh, c'mon, Chanté." Edie jumped uninvited into the conversation. "Give it a try. What do you have to lose?"

"You, stay out of this!" Chanté jabbed her finger in the center of Edie's breastbone. "What were you thinking tricking us to come to a place like this?"

"We," Edie said as she dragged her groaning husband into the argument, "are trying to help you, since both of you are too proud and stubborn to do the right thing. I mean, really! Duct taping the house, cutting up expensive cars and tampering with food. Does any of that sound like what two rational, mature adults do to resolve conflict?"

"Don't forget what he did to my shoes," Chanté added, crossing her arms with a great huff.

Edie gave her friend an annoyed look as she slid her hands onto her hips. "Look, Seth and I know you two are a little on the neurotic side. We're your friends. We accept that. We also know you two still love each other."

Chanté lowered her eyes and then stole a side-glance at Matthew. His deep onyx gaze softened as it roamed her face. "A marriage needs more than love."

"Yes, it needs communication and hard work," Edie answered. "Somehow in your crazy quest to always be right, you've forgotten how to connect. You've forgotten how to touch each other."

"Hey, I've tried to connect with her."

"When? In between getting drunk and passing out?"

"I knew that wasn't a dream!"

"No, it was a nightmare."

"Okay. Okay," Edie snapped. "The bottom line is that you guys need help."

The group fell silent.

Finally, Matthew cleared his throat. "I'm willing to give it a try, if you are."

Chanté looked up again, this time her eyes were glossed with unshed tears. "I…guess…we could give it a try."

"Yes!" Edie jerked her arm back as if her favorite football team had scored a touchdown.

Dr. Gardner cleared her throat and everyone turned toward her with guilty smiles for having forgotten she stood behind them.

"Uh, yes. About that program?" Matthew asked again with a widening smile.

Dr. Gardner clasped her hands together and rocked

excitedly on the balls of her small feet. "Our Sexuality and Liberation program gives our couples the framework and tools for lovemaking."

"Tools?" Seth asked, and then grinned at his wife. "I'm already liking the sound of this."

Edie smacked him on the arm. "Behave."

"I believe that great sex is a rarity even for couples who are in love. I'm interested in making it a repeatable reality."

"Now I like the sound of that," Chanté said.

Edie turned around and gave her girl a high-five.

Seth frowned and curled his bottom lip. "How come she didn't get smacked?"

His wife playfully smacked his arm again. "Don't worry about it."

"Since you'll be staying," Dr. Gardner chuckled, "how about I show you to your private lodges?" She winked.

Seth and Edie took the lead, linking their arms together.

Chanté and Matthew followed, moving like shy teenagers out on their first date.

The Tree of Life Resort was nestled comfortably in the Sandia Mountains, halfway between Santa Fe and Albuquerque. Walking down the long, curvy multicolored stone walkway, everyone had a breathtaking view of the dusty rose and lavender skyline.

The stunning desert landscape easily transported Chanté back to her Texas days. She nearly laughed at the thought. When had she started thinking of those days as simple?

She looked over at Matthew. At least when they had first gotten together, it had been simple. Hadn't it? Shaking her head, she concluded that she didn't know anymore.

"Here we are, Mr. and Mrs. Valentine." Gardner slid a card key into a door lock. "I trust you'll find everything to your satisfaction."

Chanté drew a deep breath and fluttered a smile as she crossed the threshold. The southwestern decor continued in their grand lodge. Handsome leather chairs, handwoven coil baskets and even Native American patchwork quilts gave the room an authenticity, but it was the giant stone fireplace that quickened her heart and tickled her imagination.

"Very nice," she said, setting her purse on what appeared to be a hand-carved wooden table.

Matthew nodded his agreement and slid his hands into his pants' pockets.

Dr. Gardner beamed and clasped her hands to her chest. "Great! You'll find everything you need in the folders laid out on your bed. It has your workshop overviews, schedules and instructions. You'll have one class tonight before dinner and then there's a small mixer."

"Great. We get to meet the other couples," Matthew said. "So much for privacy."

"Are you saying you want to leave?" Chanté asked, afraid he was having second thoughts.

"No. No. That's not what I meant…unless—you want to leave."

"No. I mean, we're already here."

Edie rolled her eyes. "Let's leave these two alone,

Dr. Gardner. They can go at it for hours. Trust me."
She addressed her friends. "See you guys at dinner?"

"Sure. Meet you there," Matthew answered with a
smile that didn't quite reach his eyes and then waited
patiently for the group to exit.

When the door finally clicked closed, he dropped his
artificial smile and deflated his shoulders.

"Quite an interesting turn of events," Chanté commented with forced amusement.

"I'd say." Matthew nodded and then failed to think
of anything else to add.

Chanté turned and exaggerated her interest in the
room's decor. However, her husband's gaze grew heavier
on her back while the silence became deafening. Was he
expecting her to say something—do something?

"Do you think this will work?" he finally asked when
she completed her circle around the living room.

She shrugged. "I don't see why not, it's a fairly large
place."

"No. You know that's not what I meant."

He stepped forward and crowded her personal space,
but she stepped back when that unfamiliar cologne tickled her nose. "I don't know. In the past six months we've
said a lot…we did a lot to hurt each other."

Matthew lowered his gaze and grudgingly nodded.
"But it doesn't mean that I stopped loving you," he
added tenderly. At her soft gasp, he chanced another
look up and watched her beautiful amber eyes fill with
tears.

"I still love you, too," she responded in a trembling

whisper and closed her eyes. "Do you know how long it's been since we've said those words to each other?"

While his mind tumbled over recent months, Matthew's face heated with shame and embarrassment for failing to do the number one thing he advised the world to do: always tell the people in your life how much you love and appreciate them.

"I'm sorry," he said, taking another step forward.

Chanté blinked. "What?"

"I said I'm sorry. I've been an incredible asshole and you deserve better."

Something certainly had to be wrong with her hearing. Dr. Matthew Valentine had never apologized for anything—not that she should be keeping some sort of scorecard, but it just never happened.

Her husband frowned at her. "Did I say something wrong?"

She shook her head as a few tears skipped down her cheeks. "No. In fact, you said everything just right."

Matthew smiled and erased the remaining distance between them. Their gazes remained locked as his hand cupped her chin and tilted up her lips.

Butterflies emerged from their cocoons and began batting their new wings in the pit of Chanté's stomach. She even held her breath in anticipation as Matthew's head slowly descended. When their lips finally touched, a dam of emotions broke within her soul and tears streamed down her face.

Matthew groaned and pulled her tighter. Despite a surge of urgency and testosterone, he took his time exploring her mouth and dancing with her tongue. What was undoubtedly his millionth kiss from her, this one had every bit of sweetness as their first.

Matthew allowed hope to bloom in his heart. He didn't know what to expect in the next four days, but he vowed to do whatever it took to win his wife's heart back.

Chanté didn't know whether this place could save their marriage but, at least, they were off to one hell of a start.

Outside the Valentines' lodge, Edie and Seth stood with their ears pressed against the door.

"I can't hear anything," Seth complained.

"I think they're kissing," Edie whispered with a widening smile.

"You're kidding me." He pressed his ear to another spot on the door. "I can't believe it," Seth whispered back in genuine amazement. "They're not trying to kill each other."

"Oh, ye of little faith." Edie moved away from the door and pulled her husband along. "You know if this all works out according to plan, we should write a book."

"Yeah. We can name it: *Lie, Sneak and Trick Your Friends to a Happier Marriage*."

"Catchy. I like it."

Seth rolled his eyes.

Chapter 12

Chanté held Matthew's hand firmly as they entered the first workshop of their Sexuality and Liberation program. Edie and Seth were already there, mixing and mingling with the group as if they did this sort of thing every day.

Given the Valentines' celebrity status, most of the participating couples made the assumption that Chanté and Matthew were teaching the course. When they learned the celebrity duo were actually participants, everyone's excitement level increased.

"This experience is going to change your life," Wilfred, a seventy-something gentleman with a George Hamilton tan and a whistling ear aide confided. "This is me and Mable's ninth time here at the Tree of Life Resort," he said, nodding his head vigorously. "Each time we come, we learn something new. Ain't that right, Mable bear?"

Mable, a very tall, Bea Arthur look-alike nodded and expanded her crimson-red lipstick smile. "That's right, Willicums."

"The last time we came, we learned the principles of the Kama Sutra. Now that was fun!"

Matthew and Chanté shared an amused glance before another couple introduced themselves.

"Hello, Dr. Valentine." Jeff, according to his name tag, looking considerably younger than eighteen, pumped his hand. "My wife and I love your show." His wife, though attractive, was three times the boy's age. However, they were clearly crazy about each other.

"I keep tellin' her that age ain't nothin' but a number. Ain't that right, Dr. V?" Jeff went on about his and his wife's winter/spring relationship.

"As long as everyone's legal," Matthew agreed good-naturedly.

Chanté muffled a laugh behind her hand as she turned away and then introduced herself to another couple. In total, there were fifteen couples. Some were newbies and some were veterans. Chanté found that the other couples attended the workshops as a way to either spice up their love life or because they were just plain curious.

"Good evening, everyone," a bald Asian man said upon entering the room. "Please take your seats, so we can get started."

The seats were actually large, multicolored velvet pillows spread in a big circle. Matthew followed everyone's lead by sitting more toward the back of the pillow and then spreading his legs so that Chanté could sit in the vee he formed.

The only couple that alternated from this pose was Wilfred and Mable—mainly because Mable was a whole foot taller than her husband.

Their instructor smiled as he took his place in the center of the circle. "Good evening," he said again. "My name is Dr. Dae Kim. I'm happy to meet each of you as you prepare to embark on a wonderful journey. With our simple techniques you will be transformed. In the next four days, you will learn the ancient art of love-making. You will learn how to generate powerful surges of sexual energy."

Mable let out a loud "whoop" and the group crackled in amusement.

Dr. Kim smiled at the elderly couple. "Ah, Mable and Wilfred. Welcome back."

A beaming Wilfred gave the instructor a high thumbs-up. "Wouldn't have missed it for the world!"

Chanté was enchanted by the loving couple. Despite the height difference, they appeared comfortable in their skins and with each other.

"The most important thing I want you to go away with tonight," Dr. Kim continued, "is how through some simple exercises and rituals, sex can be used to heal and free the mind, body and soul. Each one of you can achieve a state of bliss. But first, you must identify past hurts whether they are real or imagined."

Chanté and Matthew shifted in their seats.

"The reason it's important to identify these various

hurts, rejections or abuses is because it's the only way to release the emotions attached to them. Once you do that, you then replace those hurts with positive experiences and emotions."

Dr. Kim's words floated inside Chanté's head long after class and dinner. Could she and Matthew truly get past all the temper tantrums and arguments in the past year? Four days hardly seemed like enough time.

The men were excused from the evening mixer so they could get started on their homework. Before Matthew left, Chanté did her best to wheedle clues as to what their mysterious homework entailed.

"If I tell you, then it would ruin the surprise," Matthew chuckled and then kissed the tip of her nose before he left the dining room.

"Stop obsessing," Edie said after reading her friend's pensive expression.

"I wasn't," Chanté lied with a forced shrug of indifference. However, she took one look at her friend's dubious expression and broke out into a wide grin. "This is sort of exciting," she confessed.

"So you forgive me for tricking you?"

Chanté tilted her head high and pretended to mull the question over.

Edie popped her lightly on the shoulder. "C'mon. You two were being stubborn and you know it."

"All right. All right." Chanté swung her arm around her friend's shoulder. "Thank you for caring so much."

"Don't mention it," Edie said, waving off the praise. "I'm sure you would have done the same thing for me."

"If you say so."

The women continued to mill excitedly around the plush room. The Tree of Life staffers didn't miss a trick with surrounding them with various exotic flowers, filling the trays with sinfully rich chocolates and playing soft classical music.

Being that it was ladies' night, waiters who looked like models roamed about the room in scantily-clad genie outfits that boldly and proudly displayed their bulging muscles. Once, Chanté caught sight of seventy-something Mable slipping a twenty-dollar bill in the lining of a young man's waistband and then giggling like a young schoolgirl.

"You think we'll be like that when we get older?" Edie inquired.

"God, I hope so."

At precisely nine o'clock, Dr. Gardner entered the room, tinkling a small, gold bell. "It's time ladies," she sang merrily. "Each of your husbands or partners has prepared a special evening for you. Tonight, you will be the center of attention. As you learned in class, the pathway to the perfect state of bliss is finding the perfect balance. To give and receive. Traditionally women are givers—the nurturers. And men—well, you know where I'm going with this."

The women laughed.

"Tonight. Your only role is to be the receiver. Abandon your natural instincts. Let your partner pour everything they have into you. Take it all in. Give your body freedom to move in the way that it wants. Lose control. Do you think you can do that?"

"Yes," the women thundered.

"Good." Dr. Gardner glanced around at the smiling women. "Enjoy your evening." She jingled the bell again.

Before Chanté could set down her flute of champagne, she had to jump out of the way as the women took off like a pack of thoroughbreds at the Kentucky Derby—Edie included. Not that she wasn't equally excited as the others, she was. It was just that she was more nervous than anything.

Which was silly, wasn't it?

Shrugging the question off, she strolled back to her private lodge with an arrhythmic heartbeat and trembling legs. At the door, she fidgeted, drew several deep breaths and finally mustered up the courage to knock.

Immediately, the door flew open and Matthew stood, looking devilishly handsome in a loose, black silk robe. "I was afraid you got lost," he said.

Chanté's jaw slackened at the sight of her husband's broad, chocolate chest and a tease of his rippling six-pack.

He smiled at her reaction and stepped farther back. "Please, come in, my beloved." He gestured with a wide sweeping hand. "I've been expecting you."

Beloved. Chanté tingled from the word as she crossed the threshold. Immediately, a wondrous blend of jasmine and vanilla wafted under her nose and brought a smile to her lips.

Matthew closed the door and then quickly appeared at her side. "May I take your purse and shoes for you?"

Fighting not to laugh, she handed him her purse and started to kick off her shoes when he stopped her.

"No, no. Let me do that for you."

He knelt before her and Chanté's brows shot up in surprise, and then relaxed in delight when he gently lifted one leg at a time to slide off her pumps.

"You have very beautiful feet," he said, looking up at her. "Would you like for me to massage them for you?"

Chanté couldn't stop grinning. "I'd love a massage."

Matthew stood and put away her things. When he returned, Chanté gasped as he swept her up into his arms.

"You're taking your job a little seriously this evening."

"I hope that doesn't displease you. I am at your service, devoted to your pleasure, my beloved."

Chanté's toe tickled at that word again. "Why would I mind you being my love slave?"

"Ah, that's the spirit," Matthew chuckled as he carried her to the bedroom.

Chanté gasped again at the beautiful sight of low-lit candles, crushed roses on the bed, champagne on ice by a small alcove and a lamp that projected stars across the ceiling.

"You've been busy."

"I hope that means you like it."

"I more than like it," she said, catching his dark gaze. "I love it."

Neither spoke as Matthew carried her to the small alcove and lowered her onto a bed made of plush, black velvet pillows. Next, he brought over a large basin of warm water.

"Would you like some champagne while I bathe your feet?" he asked.

"I would love some."

As attentive as a maître d' at a posh restaurant, Matthew popped the cork to the champagne and then poured the overflowing bubbly into a thin flute. "For you, my beloved."

She tingled again and accepted the champagne.

Matthew returned his attention to bathing her delicate feet. The feel of his strong hands cupping and massaging the soles had Chanté squirming against the pillows. "If you like, I've also prepared a bath for you."

"This night keeps getting better and better."

"That's the whole idea."

Her smile widened. "In that case, I would love a bath."

Once again, Chanté found herself swept up into Matthew's arms and this time carried into the adjoining bathroom. There, another army of scented candles awaited her and on top of the foam of white bubbles were more crushed rose petals.

Suddenly overwhelmed, Chanté felt tears burn the back of her eyes. It wasn't that her husband had never staged a romantic evening, it had just been so long since he had done so. Between their hectic schedules—his working during the day at the studio, her working at night at the radio station and their writing—such grand romantic gestures were lost in the shuffle.

"None of those," Matthew said, catching her errant tear with the tips of his fingers. "I only want you to feel beautiful...and loved."

"Mission accomplished."

"But we've hardly gotten started. I have a whole evening plan dedicated to pleasuring you." He gave her a conspiratorial wink. "May I unzip your dress?"

Unable to help herself, she leaned up on her toes and pressed a kiss against his lips. "Yes, you may."

Chapter 13

Chanté was in heaven.

Sinking deeper into the tub, she was certain every muscle in her body had turned into mush at the feel of Matthew's hands roaming her body as he took his time bathing her.

"More champagne?" he asked.

His rich baritone seemed deeper than usual and when she opened her eyes, she noticed his onyx gaze was polished with passion. Was he getting as hot as she was?

"I would love another glass."

Like a skilled magician, Matthew produced the champagne bottle, without having left her side, and poured her another glass.

"There is one last place I have yet to clean, my beloved," he whispered. "May I have permission to enter your secret garden?"

Chanté choked on her champagne. "My what?"

Her husband looked as though he was having a hard time keeping a straight face as well. "According to the worksheet we are to use a different vocabulary for body parts."

"And you came up with 'secret garden'?"

"It's not without a certain charm," he said, stroking the small vee of curls between her legs. "Of course, if you don't want me to…" He slowly drifted his hand away.

"No." She grabbed his arm with her free hand. "I didn't say that."

"So that's a yes?"

Suddenly shy, she bit her lower lip and nodded.

Their gazes locked as his hands glided languidly up her inner thigh. Though she was expecting the probe of his fingers, she nevertheless sucked in a small gasp as he slid one inside of her.

Matthew set a slow, lazy rhythm that made it difficult for Chanté to hold on to her champagne glass. Without her having to ask, he removed it from her hand.

"How do you feel?" he asked.

"Wooonderful," she moaned, licking her lips and sliding her legs farther apart.

"You look so beautiful right now," he said. "What in the world did I ever do to deserve you?"

"You just got lucky," she joked, but then closed her eyes when he glided in another finger, instantly doubling her pleasure.

"I think you're just about clean," Matthew said.

"No, no. Don't stop," she panted.

"As you wish," he whispered.

Chanté shivered at the feel of his warm breath drifting across the shell of her ear. In the next second, an explosion of lights flashed behind her closed eyes and her body shook with incredible tremors.

"That's it, baby. Let it go."

Quaking in the aftershocks of her orgasm, Chanté stilled Matthew's hand in order for her to catch her breath.

"Do you require any more cleaning, my beloved?"

Still panting, she shook her head. "I think I better climb out of this tub before I drown."

"As you wish." Matthew stood and offered a hand to help her stand.

Chanté accepted his offer and loved how a few of the tub's soapy bubbles slid down her body and how the bathroom's cool air drifted across her skin and hardened her nipples.

This time, her husband magically produced a thick, terry cloth towel and wrapped it around her body as she exited the tub.

"After you," Matthew said, sweeping a hand toward the door.

Excited to see what awaited her, Chanté strolled back into the bedroom and glanced around. The romantic setup still caused her heart to beat in double time.

"If it pleases you, I would love to give you a full body massage."

For the first time, Chanté noticed a massage table at the opposite end of the bedroom. Next to it was a long line of body oils.

"If you keep this up, we may never leave this place," she threatened.

"You'll get no complaints from me," he said, leading her to and helping her up on the table.

At the first drop of warm oil against her back, Chanté teetered on the edge of her second orgasm. But then Matthew's large hands rubbed, caressed and teased her body and she quickly found herself back straddling that edge.

"Has anyone ever told you that you have wonderful hands?" she moaned.

"As a matter of fact, yes," Matthew chuckled. "I ran out and married her as fast as I could."

"Then she is a lucky woman," she joked back, but then her husband's hands stopped their massaging.

"No. I'm the lucky one."

Chanté carefully turned onto her side so she could look up at Matthew. It had been a long time since she could read his emotions so clearly and what she read took her breath away.

He still loved her.

"Kiss me," she whispered, feeling that she would wither away if he didn't.

A small smile tugged his thick lips. "As you wish."

As his head descended slowly, Chanté stretched forward to meet him more than halfway. The moment their lips touched her body continued to melt lazily on the table.

Matthew wavered on his feet and it had nothing to do with the heady taste of champagne on his wife's lips. In fact, he felt certain it had everything to do with the raw energy transmitting between them. He knew by the way her body trembled beneath him, that she felt it, too.

Determined and eager to give her the best night of her life, Matthew gently repositioned her to lie on her back and then broke the kiss. For long seconds afterward, he maintained eye contact. Her emotions were clearly reflected in her gaze.

She still loved him.

"Would you like for me to continue your massage, my beloved?"

"You're welcome to do whatever you want."

He pressed another kiss against her lips and with a great sigh, reached for another warm bottle of oil. He watched in delight when aromatic oil kissed her skin.

"That smells divine. What is it?"

"Chocolate massage oil."

Chanté slid her finger between her breasts and then tasted the oil. "Mmm. That's good."

"Does that mean it meets with your approval?" he asked with a wicked grin while he rubbed the oil over her breasts.

"I'm not sure. I'd like for you to taste it and give me your opinion."

"As you wish." He met and held her gaze again while he lowered his head.

She sucked in a small gasp as his warm tongue settled over her marbleized nipple, and with slow deliberative strokes, Matthew polished it clean of the oil.

"Mmm. I'm not sure. Let me taste the other one." Matthew stretched over and popped the second nipple into his mouth.

Chanté instinctively arched her back and lolled her head from side to side. While he continued to lick and suck her nipple dry, his hands massaged the oil down her flat belly and even between her legs.

Briefly, she wondered if anyone has ever died from such pleasure. If not, then surely she would be the first.

Matthew's tongue, at long last, trailed away from her glistening nipples, only to explore the valley between her breasts.

But he didn't stop there.

Lower and lower he went, setting off tiny tremors. He even smiled to himself when her breathing quickened to someone running a marathon. He squeezed more oil from the tube and ran his hands down her legs and in between her thighs.

When he finally reached the end of the table, he slid his hands beneath her buttocks and then grabbed hold of her waist so he could slide her down to the edge.

"You know, I think I can get a better taste of it this way," he said huskily and then lowered onto a small chair while settling her legs over his shoulders.

Chanté's eyes widened at the feel of her husband's tongue sliding into her. Then they drifted closed as it began moving inside of her. Every thought emptied out of her head and all that was left were these wonderful sensations heating up her body.

Matthew paid particular attention to the hard pearl in the heart of her "secret garden." The strokes were languid at first then accelerated to a pace with which she could hardly keep up.

Vaguely, she was aware of herself moaning, but she

lacked the ability to monitor or control how loud she cried. When the pressure started building, she tried to squirm and crawl back up the table.

It was too big and too intense, she realized, but Matthew would not let her get away. "Oh," she cried and then screamed as she tried to brace herself.

However, there was nothing she could've done to prepare herself for the earth-shattering explosion that detonated from one deft stroke of Matthew's tongue.

Chanté discovered a new octave as blinding lights flashed behind her closed eyelids. Shortly after, she struggled for breath and gripped the sides of the table. She arched her body as high she could, trying to break the intimate kiss, but Matthew stood with his tongue still delving deep inside of her, driving her insane.

The pressure began to build again and the squirming and twisting became mindless. She wanted to beg for time to catch her breath, but somehow she'd forgotten how to speak. All she could manage were senseless moans and orgasmic cries. In the next second, another orgasm slammed into her and sent her soaring through an endless sky.

"Baby?"

A lazy smile drifted across Chanté's lips. "Hmm?"

"How do you feel?"

"Like water," she murmured truthfully. Nothing in the world would convince her that he hadn't drained her of muscle and bone.

Her husband's soft laughter danced through the air like music.

She was unaware of being lifted from the massage

table, but she was aware of being placed onto the bed's silk sheets.

"I think I've come to a decision," Matthew said.

"Oh?"

"Yeah." He nibbled on her ear. "I love chocolate."

She giggled and lolled her head away.

"Of course," he said, reaching across her. "We could always try the strawberry."

Chapter 14

The next morning, Chanté woke with a smile as wide as a football field and a body completely rejuvenated. Memories from the previous night began to spin lazily inside her head and she released a moan of contentment as she leaned back against Matthew.

Glancing over her shoulder, she smiled when her eyes met her husband's. "Good morning," she whispered.

"That it certainly is." He kissed the tip of her nose and continued to hold her in their spoon position. "It's been a long time since I've seen that kind of smile on your face."

She twisted around so she could lie on her back and stare up at him. "You know, you're smiling, too, and you wouldn't let me—"

"You weren't supposed to." He kissed her. "Last

night was your night. Of course, it shames me to say that after years of training, I never thought to do that for you on my own, to just give a whole night dedicated to you. What does that say about me?"

"That you're not a mind reader," she offered. "You had no idea I was unhappy until I kicked you out of our bedroom. Then I was a crazy woman."

"Amen to that."

"Hey!" She gave his chest a playful shove. "I wasn't the only one who flew over the cuckoo's nest. You're buying me a new car and replacing every shoe you destroyed in my closet."

Matthew laughed and rolled over onto his back. "I really did lose it, didn't I?"

Chanté now moved onto her side and ran a finger down the length of his chest. "I don't ever want us to get like that again."

"You know, I always said that if we had a child—"

She groaned and also rolled onto her back.

"What?"

"Nothing," she mumbled, but it was clearly a lie.

Matthew launched back onto his side and took a cue from her by drifting his own finger up her chest and then around her breasts. "That was not a nothing. That was clearly something."

She shook her head, but a thin sheen of tears coated her eyes.

"C'mon, talk to me. We're supposed to be starting over, remember?"

Chanté didn't speak for a long moment, but her husband was determined to wait it out. "It's just that you're always talking about children and..." She shrugged. "Maybe it's not in the cards for us. Maybe we're just not meant to be parents."

He took her hand in his. "Look, I know that we had our difficulties conceiving, but there are a lot of options we haven't even tried yet. Now that your book is such a success, I was hoping that you would let the radio station go..."

She pulled her hand away and rolled out of bed.

"Where are you going?" he asked.

"It's nine o'clock. We have a ten o'clock class and we haven't taken a shower or had breakfast yet."

"We also weren't finished talking," he pointed out.

"No, no. You're right." She shrugged again. "We still have a lot of options." Chanté flashed him a smile and trotted off to the bathroom where she closed the door firmly behind her.

Matthew fell back against the pillows, wondering what in the hell had just happened. Whatever it was, he guessed that it was somehow his fault. Maybe it was one of those times he should follow Seth's advice and just apologize.

Groaning, he fell back against the pillows. Would he ever understand his own wife?

In the bathroom, Chanté turned on the shower, but she didn't immediately step inside the tub. Instead, she reached for her cache case and pulled out her morning pills. At the sink, she cupped a handful of water and used it to wash the pills down.

When she was done, she stared at her blurring reflection in the mirror. "Quit my job," she mumbled under her breath. "Why does his dream mean I have to give up what's important to me?"

And why can't I just tell him the truth?

She shook her head and turned away from the mirror. Standing beneath the steady stream from the showerhead, Chanté continued to grapple with the question until she heard the shower curtain slide on its rail.

Matthew stepped in behind her wearing a wide smile. "Care if I join you?"

It was just on the tip of her tongue to tell him that it was a free country when she realized that she needed to check herself. Her husband was doing his best to make this four-day excursion work. The least she could do was meet him halfway.

"Actually, it looks like you arrived just in time to help me with my back." She winked.

"As you wish." Matthew grinned and took the loofah from her hand.

She turned and waited while he squirted more liquid soap onto the loofah and then smiled when he began scrubbing her back.

"Uhm, about what happened in the bedroom," Matthew started awkwardly. "I'm sorry if I said something that upset you." He cleared his throat. "I was thinking and, you know, you really don't have to quit your job if you don't want to. I know how much you love it at the station. I was just making a suggestion."

This was the second time in two days that Matthew had apologized and it still had the effect of having the rug pulled out from beneath her. "Thank you," she whispered.

Matthew stepped forward so that her soapy back pressed against his chest. "I just want to do whatever it takes to make you happy."

Tears sprang to her eyes at the complete sincerity in his voice. *Tell him.*

Chanté turned around with the full intent to tell him the truth, but one look in his handsome face, and she simply couldn't do it.

"We'll get pregnant again," Matthew said. "And I'm willing to wait however long it takes."

She twitched her lips into a smile and nodded her head like a good little girl. As her reward, Matthew leaned forward and gave her a kiss that nearly took her breath away.

Matthew and Chanté weren't the only ones late for their morning workshop. Mable and Wilfred, as well as Seth and Edie tiptoed in more than thirty minutes late. Every woman had a certain glow about them that wasn't there the day before, while every man held their chest about three inches higher.

Dr. Gardner, dressed in a bright sun-yellow gown, moved about the room as she lectured about the importance of soul gazing.

"I want everyone to turn on their pillows and face their partners," Gardner instructed.

Matthew and Chanté complied, folding their legs into the Indian position.

"Now, for the next twenty minutes, all I want you to do is stare into each other's eyes. I know it will seem awkward maybe even silly at first, but this exercise is to get you into the practice of truly connecting with your partner. We've all heard the phrase 'The eyes are the windows to the soul.' You need to go beyond just eye color, you need to connect with the soul."

Dr. Gardner was right, Chanté felt silly just staring at her husband. And for the first five minutes, they did little more than give each other goofy smiles.

"Now concentrate on calm, even breathing as you continue soul gazing," the doctor said.

Again, Chanté did as she was told and after a few deep breaths something happened. Her husband's dark gaze somehow felt like an industrial magnet that pulled her into its depth. She grew lightheaded but comfortable at the same time.

Sighing in contentment, Chanté suddenly felt loved. But a renegade question as to whether she was worthy of his love and trust derailed her soul gazing and brought her out of her trance.

"Very good, class." Dr. Gardner clapped her hands together. "How do you feel?"

The crowd murmured different answers while Matthew leaned forward. "That was sort of weird how that worked."

Chanté agreed and returned her attention to the instructor. The class went on to learn the Yab Yum position—where the man sits cross-legged and the female sits on top of his legs and wraps her legs around his waist. Keeping the Yab Yum position, they learned how to transfer each other's sexual energy by leaning close to soul gaze and synchronize their breathing.

By the end of the class, Matthew and Chanté felt

less like educated doctors and more like flower children from the sixties.

"How are you liking it so far?" Edie asked Chanté as they sat down for lunch.

"I—it's definitely different," she answered, glancing over at her husband.

"Forget that," Matthew cut in. "I feel like a kid in a candy store."

"You and me both," Seth snickered. "Who knew a woman had so many sex buttons to push?"

"Or that you could push them all in one night," Matthew volleyed.

"Duh," Chanté and Edie intoned together and then slapped each other a high-five.

The men rolled their eyes but knew better than to continue with the touchy subject.

After lunch, the men and women were once again split up, this time to learn different techniques to awaken and honor the god and goddess within them. Overall, Chanté thought it was a fun class and made a mental note to do more research on the subject for possible future books.

"Now's the time for us to discuss this evening's homework." Dr. Gardner beamed at the crowd of excited women.

In response, everyone clapped, except for Mable who shouted, "Bring it on."

"Your assignment, ladies, is to give your partner the best night of his life. Last night, you were just the receiver. Tonight, you will cultivate your natural instincts and become the giver. It's important that you become subservient to his needs. Reassure him that you are there to please him and he does not have to do anything in return. Any questions?"

Everyone shook their heads, but Chanté was already experiencing a mild case of panic. Being an independent woman and always an equal partner in the bedroom, the word "subservient" made her nervous.

"You're obsessing again," Edie said, cutting into her thoughts.

"No, I'm not."

Edie lifted a dubious brow.

"All right, so I was. Sue me."

"What's the matter? I thought that you were having fun?"

"I was—I—I mean, I am." She shook her head. "Don't pay any attention to me. I'm just making things harder than they need to be—as usual." She sighed. "You know, it's not easy realizing that the biggest problem in my marriage is me."

Edie cocked her head to the side. "What do you mean?"

Chanté's talk with her husband that morning flashed through her mind. "Nothing. Forget it. I can do this."

"Well," Edie said, swinging her arm around her shoulders. "Speaking as your friend and not your editor, I'm really happy to see you and Matthew giving this an honest try. As crazy and neurotic as you both are I truly believe that you two are soul mates."

Chanté smiled and also swung her arm around Edie's shoulders. "Despite your lying and scheming, you're the best friend a girl could ever ask for."

"Well said," Edie boasted. "Now what do you say we go and give our husbands a night they'll never forget?"

"Separately, right?"

"Of course," Edie laughed.

"In that case, you're on."

Chapter 15

Matthew couldn't concentrate on the flow of conversation around him during the men's networking hour. Various scenarios of what awaited him had Matt Jr. throbbing painfully against his thigh.

"You're panting like a dog that hasn't had a bone in two years," Seth joked, handing his friend a Heineken. "Calm down, Cujo."

Matt frowned. "Didn't Cujo have rabies?"

"Well, I was going to say Lassie, but she was a girl. At least Cujo would explain your foaming at the mouth."

"I'm just a little anxious. What time is it?" He glanced at his watch.

"I'm guessing two minutes later than the last time you asked," Seth chuckled.

"Very funny." Matt rolled his eyes because it was

exactly two minutes later. He took a swig of his beer. "I have to tell you, man. This trip saved my marriage." He held his friend's gaze. "Thank you."

"Don't thank me. Thank my lovable scheming wife. Frankly, I thought this whole thing would blow up in our faces and I would have lost my best client. I still can't believe it worked."

"Well, so far so good." He looked around. "You know, I should do an exposé on this place and others like it. I'm loving what this whole place is about."

"I'll get on it."

As the hour ticked on at an excruciating pace, Matthew noted that he wasn't the only man glancing at his watch every minute on the minute. When Dr. Dae Kim jingled a gold bell to draw the men's attention, he made sure to stay away from the door in case of a stampede.

Turns out, there nearly was one and Matthew wasn't ashamed to be the leader of the pack. By the time he reached his private lodge, he was a rocket ready for blastoff.

Calm down. Take a deep breath. He barely tapped the door. The door opened, but his wife wasn't in view. His heart thumped against his chest as he crossed the threshold.

When the door closed behind him, he turned around and then blinked in surprise to see his wife in a sheer white gown. He could see every curve of her body.

"Welcome, my love. I've been waiting for you."

"And I've been going crazy waiting for this moment."

Chanté smiled, but kept her head lowered. "Would you like for me to take off your shoes?"

Matthew pressed his big toe against the heel of his shoes and kicked them off one at a time. "What shoes?" He then pulled his shirt off over his head, unbuckled his pants and rushed toward her.

This time Chanté couldn't help but laugh and she had to press her hands against his chest to stop him from jumping her bones right then and there. "Slow down, baby," she cooed up at him.

His pants slid off his hips and hit the floor.

She stifled a laugh at his eagerness. "We have all night."

Was it going to take all night to get to the good part? "Yes. Yes. You're right." He smiled painfully.

"Good." Chanté beamed a smile at him. "I prepared something for you in the living room." She started to walk off and then stopped. "Uh, would you like to see it?"

Matthew understood the slip. His wife was not the submissive type, which made him appreciate the effort she was putting into this. "I would love to see it." He stepped out of the pants pooled at his feet and followed her, wearing only his boxers and socks.

She nodded slyly and then escorted him into the living room area. Just like the night before the place was littered with candles, but instead of the clean floral scents, these candles gave the room a more cinnamon and spice smell. On the room's portable radio was the unmistakable music of Miles Davis.

"Would you like to sit down?"

"Don't mind if I do." He settled onto the leather sofa

like a king on a throne. Only then did he notice the spread of food on the large, square coffee table.

"Uhm." She cleared her throat. "I was sort of hoping you'd like to sit on one of the velvet cushions." She gestured to the ones on the other end of the table.

"Oh, yes. Of course." He shot back on his feet and raced over to the cushions.

Chanté took a deep breath and tried to remain in character.

Matthew watched in a dreamlike trance as his wife's beautiful silhouetted figure glided toward him. He almost wanted to pinch himself to make sure he wasn't dreaming, but he decided against it in fear that he would wake up.

"Would it please my love if I took off my gown now?"

Hell yes! He nearly laughed aloud at his eagerness. "It would please me very much."

Like the great tease she was, Chanté's hand drifted to the small zipper in the center of the gown and then slid it down one inch at a time.

Matthew couldn't decide whether this was pleasure or torture. Every impulse in his body demanded that he jump up and rip the damn thing off of her. As much as he loved everything he did for her the previous night, it had been pure agony not to satisfy his own carnal desires—and there was no way he could do it two nights in a row.

At long last the zipper reached the end of its track and Chanté parted the sheer gown to proudly display her womanly curves to his greedy gaze. *Mine. She's all mine.*

"Do you like what you see, my love?"

"No." Matthew licked his dry lips. "I love what I see."

Chanté's lips bloomed wide as she allowed the gown to glide off her body. "May I join you on your pillow?"

"You most certainly may."

She stepped forward and placed each of her long cinnamon-brown legs on opposite sides of his hips, pausing just long enough for him to run his hands against them and enjoy their smoothness. She then lowered her naked body onto his lap and assumed the Yab Yum position.

"Comfortable?" Matthew asked, mainly because if he didn't have on his boxers, they would have been joined together.

"Yes," she answered, her minty breath blowing softly against his face. "Would my love like some fresh fruit to whet his appetite?"

"Don't mind if I do."

Chanté reached out to her side and selected a plump strawberry and carefully dipped it into a bowl of chocolate before she brought it to her husband's lips.

As he bit into the juicy fruit, their eyes locked together to do a bit of soul gazing. It was no surprise to Matthew to see so many different layers to his wife. The most dominant trait was her fierce independence, but just below that were layers of uncertainty and even a tinge of vulnerability.

"How is it?" she asked.

An instant smile slid into place. "You know how I

feel about chocolate. Both it and the strawberry remind me of you."

Chanté's cheeks darkened even beneath the low candlelight. "Does that mean that you'd like another bite?"

"Yes, to both." He took the rest of the strawberry into his mouth while their gazes remained locked. He allowed her to continue hand-feeding him an assortment of fruit and even a few oysters before she offered him a bath.

The routine was similar to the night before with the exception of him trusting her to give him an old-fashioned shave.

"Don't worry, I used to do this all the time with my father," she assured.

Still, he would have preferred something made in the twenty-first century, but this night was also about developing and deepening their bond of trust. So in the end, he sat still with his head tilted back while his wife shaved him.

"There. That wasn't so bad, was it?"

Matthew rubbed his hand against his face and was more than a little impressed. "Wow. I should have had you doing this all along." He waited until she put the blade down, and then pulled her into the tub.

Chanté yelped and caused a huge wave of soapy water to splash over the tub's rim and flood the floor. "What are you doing?" she giggled and floundered around until she lay flat against his chest and smiled into his handsome face. "You know, all you had to do was ask me to climb in."

"What—and miss that surprised look on your face?"

He blew a cluster of bubbles off the tip of her nose and then leaned in close for a kiss. "I love you."

Her eyes suddenly glossed with tears and she responded in a shaky whisper. "I love you, too."

Matthew looped his arm around her small waist and drew her back down for another kiss. He took his time exploring and savoring her hot mouth. Despite the tub's cooling water, he grew hard against her body.

Chanté moaned as she stretched her hand down in between their bodies and wrapped her fingers around his shaft. With light, feathery strokes, she moved just her fingers up and down and around the tip.

Matthew, lost in a rapture of soft, silky flesh, continued to arch his erection against the loving strokes of her hands. Meanwhile, he roamed his hands lazily down the blades of her shoulder, then kneaded the skin along the planes of her back, and then finally cupped her firm, yet curvy butt, giving it a gentle squeeze.

She sighed and opened her mouth wider and allowed him to deepen the kiss. His tongue skated over her slick teeth, danced with her tongue, and savored her unique flavor. Nothing on earth tasted this sweet.

He worked his hands in a circular motion—caressing, squeezing and parting her cheeks. In seconds, he set a slow, hypnotic rhythm that Chanté began, rotating her hips to join the fun.

A long groan rumbled in Matthew's chest as his wife's fingers accelerated their strokes and increased his need to be inside of her, but first, he had to make sure she was ready to receive him. Releasing one of her butt cheeks, he glided his soapy hand farther down and then dipped it between the tuft of curly hair between her thighs.

His wife moved as her body quivered against the intimate invasion. Delighted that the slick passageway was just as warm and inviting as her mouth, Matthew navigated another finger inside and began a languid pump.

Chanté stopped rotating her hips and instead rocked against his plunging hand. Almost immediately, her breath became erratic and the soft lapping of the tub's water became just as melodic as the jazz music playing throughout the lodge.

"I need you, baby," Matthew rasped. "I need you right now."

"Yes, love." She moved to climb out of the tub. "Let me get—"

"No. I don't want to get out of the tub." He took his erection out of her hands and held it up straight up so that the tip poked out of the water. "Slide it in for me, baby."

Chanté's lustful gaze met his own while a mischievous smile curled her lips. "As you wish." She reclaimed possession of his hard shaft and inched her body upward and slid her knees to opposite sides of his hips. The porcelain tub made for a tight fit, but she managed the task set before her.

As she eased down his long, throbbing shaft, they moaned together in mutual satisfaction.

Matthew lolled his head back against the tub as he reveled in the unbelievable sensations of her sweet, tight body.

His deep, guttural moans echoed and bounced off

the bathroom's tiles as Chanté continued to rise and
fall against his powerful thrusts while squeezing her
internal muscles. Heavy-lidded, he watched her lust-
fully through the mesh of his lowered eyelashes and felt
his mouth water for the taste of her bountiful breasts
bouncing above him.

Pulling up into a sitting position, he pressed her wet
body closer, and then drew a pearled nipple into his
mouth.

Gasping, she quivered again, but didn't stop rocking
her body. As he suckled and polished the black pearl, his
wife's hand clawed at his wet back, running her nails
over his shoulders and driving him crazy.

With a rarely displayed strength, Matthew planted
his feet firmly at the bottom of the bathtub, wrapped
an arm around her waist, and propelled their bodies upward with one mighty push from the tub's rim.

Water splashed and ran down from their soapy bodies. Matthew remained careful as he carried his wife
out and sloshed through the bathroom. They fell onto
the bed not giving a damn about ruining the silk sheets.
The only thing that mattered was finishing what they
started.

He reentered her body with a long, easy thrust.
Her body's warm honey was so unbelievably slick he
clamped his teeth together as if it would help him maintain some type of control. Slowly, he moved within her,
trying his best to practice restraint but that was shot to
hell when Chanté matched his rhythm, thrust for thrust,
and then urged him to a faster tempo with her hips.

He was more than accommodating.

Soon, they were rocking at an exhilarating pace and Chanté's cries of pleasure drowned out his own. When she reached the brink of her climax, she tried to inch higher along the bed, but Matthew's hips dogged her trail and he could feel her body explode and tremble around him.

One of her body's tremors detonated his gargantuan climax as he tensed and drove deep, burying his head against her neck and releasing a throaty growl.

Holding him with both her arms and legs, Chanté rocked with him until he quieted and his shaft stopped pulsing. At this moment their bodies and their hearts beat as one. This was how they were meant to be— none of the craziness that had filled their lives in the past few months.

Matthew finally rolled onto his side, but remained welded inside of her. After their hearts returned to a normal pace, he brushed a lock of hair from her eyes. "Whatcha thinking about?"

"You. Us." She fluttered a shy smile. "The last two nights."

His arms tightened around her as he drew in a deep breath. "What about us?"

"I was just thinking about how nice it is to fall in love again."

Matthew met her steady gaze unblinkingly. "Yes, it is."

Chapter 16

Matthew and Chanté made love throughout the night. Each time, the pleasure intensified and strengthened the newly formed bond between them. By the time morning spilled sunlight through the windows, they were no more than two heaps of flesh piled onto each other.

"What time do we have class?" Chanté asked, lacking the strength to even lift her head.

"Who cares?" he groaned. "I may never leave this bed for as long as I live."

She chuckled and then yawned lazily. When she realized that she was still lying on top of him, she asked, "Am I too heavy?"

"Don't even think about moving," he warned and yawned himself. "As soon as I get my energy back, I'm going to make love to you again." Another yawn. "Any minute now."

"No worries, baby. I'm staying right here." She planted a kiss against his chest and drifted off to sleep again.

The next time she opened her eyes, the daylight had softened and there was the unmistakable sound of rain drumming against the windows. Still straddling her husband's hips, she sat up and glanced groggily about the room.

Matthew groaned as his eyes fluttered open. However, a smile quickly slid into place at the sight of his wife's breasts. "Now this is how a man should be greeted in the morning." He reached up and ran his hands over the soft mounds and loved the way her nipples hardened at his slightest touch.

Before he could get the party started, they jumped from the phone's sudden ring.

Matthew frowned. "Who in the hell would be calling us?"

"I'll give you one guess," Chanté said, reaching over and snatching the headpiece off the receiver. "Good morning, Edie."

"Morning? Try afternoon," Edie corrected. "Wait. How did you know it was me?"

"Simple deduction, my dear Watson," she said, laughing and dismounting her husband.

"Wait. Don't go." He reached for her, but she bounced off the bed, leaving him to grasp nothing but air.

"Was that Matthew?" Edie pried.

"No. Denzel Washington," Chanté shot back. "Who else would it be?"

"Then I take it that last night was another success?"

Chanté watched her husband as he stretched lazily among the sheets. "You can say that," she said, as another wave of desire spiraled through her.

"Good," Edie said triumphantly. "I told Seth you were okay, but he thought that I should double-check to make sure that neither of you reverted to your old ways and tried to kill each other."

"Well, he can relax. We're both alive and breathing."

"Just barely," Matthew shouted. "She wore me out!"

Edie "whooped" loud enough for Matthew to hear and the three of them laughed good-naturedly. "All right. Are we going to see you guys for dinner?"

"Dinner?" Chanté glanced around. "What time is it?"

"Two o'clock," Edie sang merrily. "But don't fret. I was told a lot of people missed the morning classes."

"Told?"

"What—you think you're the only ones who can work it all night long? I am the original Energizer Bunny, baby."

Chanté rolled her eyes and quickly disconnected the call.

"Well, what did our self-appointed babysitters want?" Matthew asked, sitting up. "Or should I even bother to ask?"

"Nothing too serious. She was just spying on us and reserving us for dinner." She waltzed over to him on the edge of the bed and popped a squat on his lap. "But I'm starving now." She leaned forward and nibbled on his ear.

Matthew opened his mouth but he was unable to

respond with her warm tongue getting him all excited again.

Chanté chuckled at seeing her husband rendered helpless and decided to cut it out—especially if she wanted to eat anytime soon. "You call room service while I go freshen up," she instructed with a departing kiss.

"Ah, we're not going to eat in the nude?"

"We can." She shrugged as she headed toward the bathroom. "But don't you think we should go to at least one class today?"

"The point is for us to have sex. I think we have the gist of it now," he joked. "We just needed a refresher course."

Laughing as she entered the bathroom, she gave him one final reminder to call room service, then closed the door.

Surprised to see just how much water they had splashed on the floor, Chanté retrieved a few towels from the rack and made floor mats out of them before she went about washing her face and brushing her teeth. When she reached inside of her cache case for her morning pills, she stopped.

"What are you doing?" she asked her reflection. She waited as if her mirror image would actually give an answer. If this was to be a new beginning then she needed to start with being honest—and doing the right thing.

Chanté left the pills in her bag, and then turned to the tub to let out the previous night's water and to take a quick shower. When she finally emerged from the bathroom, wrapped in one of the resort's robes, their late lunch was just being delivered to the room.

Matthew, who'd put on a pair of white boxers to answer the door, glanced up. "Hey, honey, we had a note on the door from Dr. Gardner. She wants to schedule a one-on-one consultation. Do you feel up to it?"

"Psychologists seeing psychologists. Maybe Tom Cruise was right and we're all just crazy."

"Or we all just need someone else to talk to."

Chanté lowered her gaze as she slid her hands into the pockets of her robe. "We should be able to talk to each other."

"True," he said thoughtfully. "But when you're dealing with a proud man who finds it difficult to apologize, then talking to him may not be the easiest thing in the world to do."

"Or when you're dealing with a woman who thinks it's easier to leave than deal with a problem." Sadly, she shook her head as she moved over to the sofa. "It's funny. I give millions of listeners and readers advice, but when it comes to me...?"

"Neither of us has claimed to be perfect. It's hard for teachers to be students and for doctors to be patients. We're learning and growing from our mistakes just like everyone else. Sure we have issues. You like to poison people and I like to cut things up. We're perfect for each other."

Chanté laughed and loved him for brightening her mood. "Hey, did you know that psychologists had the highest rate of suicide?"

"Huh, I thought it was dentists."

* * *

Chanté and Matthew emerged from their daylong hibernation to rejoin their group for a class in tantric dance. At first, Chanté thought she would never be able to master the belly rolls and simultaneous hand gestures, but soon, she found the sensual snakelike movements fun and exhilarating.

Plus, Matthew was completely turned on by her efforts.

After class and a pleasant dinner, Edie asked Chanté to join her for a trip to the ladies' room.

"I take it that you want to talk to me about something," Chanté said, checking her appearance in the mirror.

Edie nodded and turned toward her friend with her arms crossed. "Have you told him yet?"

Chanté's genial smile melted from her face. "Told him what?"

"Come on. This is me you're talking to."

Turning away from the mirror, Chanté met Edie's laserlike gaze dead-on. "Not yet."

Edie rolled her eyes with a loud sigh. "Mind if I ask what you're waiting for?"

"I don't know." Chanté's shoulders slumped as she exhaled. "Something called the right moment?"

"He talked nonstop throughout dinner about it."

"I know. I know." She shook her head. "It's just that it's so important to him and after so many…I can't…" She stopped herself and closed her eyes. "He may not forgive me."

"Aww." Edie moved in close and wrapped her arm

around her friend's shoulder. "Of course he'll forgive you. He's in the forgiving business."

Chanté had her doubts but didn't voice them. Instead, she lifted her head and wiped a few errant tears from her eyes. "Maybe you're right. Tomorrow we scheduled a one-on-one therapy session with Dr. Gardner. It's as good a time as any to talk about it. Who knows—maybe there's something to this therapist needing therapy thing."

"That's my girl." Edie squeezed her shoulders. "Let's take those men back to our rooms and work up a black sweat, separately, of course."

Laughing, Chanté quickly fixed her makeup and waltzed arm in arm back out to the resort's grand dining room. However, through the rest of their meal, Chanté's reservations and doubts began to pile on top of one another. Soon, she found it difficult to keep her smile angled at the appropriate levels while the beginnings of a migraine throbbed at her temples.

Matthew leaned to her side and whispered, "Honey, are you all right?"

"Huh? What?" She blinked out of her reverie and glanced around the table to see she'd become the center of attention. "I'm sorry, I didn't catch what was said."

"You were rubbing your head so I just asked if you're okay."

"She does look a little pale," Seth noted.

"Oh, it's nothing." Chanté waved off everyone's concern. "It's just a little headache."

"Well, it looks like the sex gravy train has come to a halt," Seth joked with a whack across Matthew's back.

"Looks like you may be the only man not getting good use of those belly dancing moves tonight."

"Seth!" Edie smacked her husband on the back of the head. "Don't be crude."

"What? He knows I'm just joking with him."

"Keep it up and you'll be on the couch." Edie's annoyance melted when she turned her attention to Chanté. "Do you have any Tylenol or anything? I have some in our room, if you'd like some?"

"Actually, I think I have some in my cache case," Chanté said, massaging her pressure points again.

"We should call it a night." Matthew stood and then offered to assist her from her chair.

"Well, maybe I should go take something." She accepted his offer and stood. "I guess we'll see you in class tomorrow."

The group of friends finished their goodbyes and Matthew and Chanté returned to their private lodge. During the entire walk, Chanté practiced the next day's confession in her head, and each time her vision of Matthew's reaction intensified her migraine.

"You really don't look well," Matthew commented as he led her to the bedroom. "Why don't you lie down and I'll go get your medicine and some water for you."

"Thanks," she murmured. "I'm sure I'll be all right in a little while." She eased back against the bed's pillows.

"Don't worry about it, my beloved." He leaned down and kissed the top of her forehead. "The most important thing is to get you feeling better."

Beloved. She really did love it when he called her that. "Thanks, my beloved."

Matthew's eyes lit up at the use of his endearment and he rewarded her with another kiss; this time a light, sensual one that was as effective in curling her toes as well as fluttering her heart.

"Be right back," he promised.

She smiled as she watched him move away from the bed. Lavishing in her love haze, she couldn't quite remember how she'd allowed things to get so bad between them. Now, she just hoped tomorrow's session with Dr. Gardner wouldn't change all of that.

She closed her eyes and tried to lie still until Matthew returned with her pills, but then her eyes flew wide open when she remembered what else was in her cache case.

Matthew stood above her. In one hand he held a glass of water and in the other, her circular compact of birth control pills.

"Why in the hell do you have these?"

Chapter 17

Chanté bolted out of bed like a light and snatched the pills out of her husband's hand, as if doing so would magically make him forget that he'd ever seen them. Once the damning evidence was in her hand, she felt an overwhelming sense of nausea.

"I believe I asked you a question," Matthew said, setting the glass of water down on the nightstand and settling his darkening gaze on her.

She opened her mouth to launch into the prepared speech for the following day's session, but what came out of her mouth instead was, "You weren't supposed to find those."

Silent, he glared as if he enjoyed watching the room's mounting tension choke the living daylight out of her.

Chanté wasn't used to that sort of combat. She much

preferred it when there was a lot of yelling and screaming involved. She was in her element in verbal combat
and petty revenge tactics.

How did anyone fight silence?

At long last, Matthew turned on his heel and headed
toward the closet. It wasn't until he pulled out his suitcase and propped it up on the bed that Chanté's panic
hit her at full throttle.

"What are you doing?" she asked.

"I'm packing," he growled.

She rushed toward the bed. "You're leaving?"

He didn't answer.

"You can't leave. W-we have class tomorrow and—
and what about our session with Dr. Gardner?"

He stopped and pierced her with another dark glare.
"Tell me about the pills."

Her mouth went dry and after a full minute of struggling for the right words, she gave a flat response. "It's
complicated."

Matthew clenched his jaw so tight, a singular vein
protruded from the center of his forehead. He turned
back toward the closet, grabbed the few clothes he had
hanging from the rack, and shoved them—hangers and
all—into his suitcase.

"Wait. You can't go." She threw the pills onto the
bed and started snatching his clothes back out of the
suitcase.

Matthew stepped back and slowly settled his hands
against his hips. "Tell me about the pills," he stressed
evenly.

"Matthew, it's just that… I tried to tell you but—"

"Tell me about the goddamn pills," he roared, reaching out and grasping her painfully around her arms.

Her vision blurred with a sudden rush of tears. "I've been taking them for a year."

The confession was like a hard slap and Matthew's grip tightened on her arm.

"Let go, Matt. You're hurting me."

He released her immediately, but it didn't stop his hands from trembling.

The silence returned and Chanté squirmed fitfully beneath his murderous glare. She made an attempt to reach him through the windows of his soul, but she couldn't journey past the blackness of his stare.

"A year," he finally growled. "All those times we were trying…or should I say *I* was trying to have a child, you were taking birth control pills?"

"Look, Matt, try to understand—"

"Understand?" he roared. "How can I understand anything if you don't say anything? How could you let me believe that we were in this together?"

"We were in it together. It just got to be too much— too many miscarriages and too much heartbreak. I couldn't…I couldn't keep putting myself through that."

"And what about me?" he shouted. "Don't I have a say about any of this? Why wasn't I a part of the decision-making? Or is this another grand standing position that since it's your body, you get to make all the decisions?"

"That's usually how it works," she snapped back, finally feeling her own anger rise.

"Not in a marriage!" He stormed toward her again.

"We're supposed to be equal partners. I know how hard it was to lose every one of those pregnancies. I was right there with you, or did you forget? You weren't the only one who'd gotten emotionally attached to each child we created."

"No, but you were the only one who could bounce back in a twenty-four-hour period, wanting to give it another whirl like I'm some freaking machine where you just drop in a deposit and wait for your baby. Well, I'm sorry to inform you but this machine is broken."

Matthew stepped back and shook his head with disappointment written clearly in every inch of his hard features. "Broken, or just giving up?" He searched her face for a true answer. "I would have supported you if you felt you needed a break or even if you wanted to stop trying. The important thing is for me to be included."

She shook her head and ignored the tears that raced down her face. "That's not true. Every time I even hinted that maybe having a child is just simply not in the cards for us, you throw up a brick wall. It's like you don't hear me!"

"Don't give me that garbage! I thought you were seeking support. You never once said 'Matthew, I don't want to do this anymore' or 'Matthew, I think I need to give my body a rest.' You made up your own mind to lie and sneak behind my back." He grabbed his clothes again and started cramming them back into the suitcase.

"It wasn't like that," she insisted.

"Then what was it like?" he challenged.

Being put on the spot like that, Chanté continued to grapple to find the right words.

"Just as I thought. You know, for a talk radio host, you're a woman of very few words."

"It's because I know what I did was wrong. But I couldn't talk to you then."

"Funny. Millions of people have no problem talking to me, but when it comes to my own wife, I'm treated like some kind of stranger." He clamped his suitcase shut and proceeded to zip it despite a few articles sticking out. "I'm out of here."

When he turned and snatched his suitcase off the bed, Chanté raced around him and tried to block his path. "You can't leave. We haven't finished talking yet."

"You had a year to talk to me. Just like you had a year to make me feel guilty that what was happening between us was my fault."

"I thought it was your fault," she said desperately. "Your obsession for a child left me with no room to breathe. It was almost as if you only wanted a child— like I wasn't enough for you. That's why I kept saying that maybe a child wasn't in the cards for us. I needed to hear that us being childless would be okay. That I was enough for you. But you never said it." Her voice cracked as she madly wiped away her tears. "And I doubt that you can say it now."

Another wave of unforgiving silence crashed through the room and Chanté could feel her heart literally tearing in two.

Matthew lowered his head and tightened his grip on his suitcase. "I have to go." He walked around, incidentally bumped her shoulder, but kept moving without an apology.

Chanté closed her eyes and remained rooted in the middle of the room long after the front door had slammed close.

On the fourth day of the retreat, Chanté remained in her private lodge, hoping that Matthew would return after he'd cooled down. However, morning morphed into the afternoon, and then faded into night and she remained sitting alone. Shortly before ten o'clock there was a knock on the door and Chanté raced to open it up, only to have her heart dive back into despair when Edie stood on the other side.

"Oh, it's you," Chanté said.

"Mind if I come in?"

Chanté cringed at the amount of sympathy dripping from her voice, knowing that there was only one conclusion to be drawn. "I take it you already know what happened between me and Matthew?"

Edie hesitated but then slowly nodded her head. "He called Seth last night," she admitted as she cocked her head. "How are you holding up?"

Instead of answering, Chanté stepped back and gestured for her friend to enter. Once she was inside, Chanté closed the door with a soft click and then wrapped herself in her own embrace. "What did Matthew say?"

Edie lowered her gaze and drew a deep breath. "I didn't hear it all. Like I said, he talked to Seth."

Chanté released a long, frustrated breath and

marched back over to the sofa. "If you're going to give me the watered-down version, then just forget it."

"That's not what I'm trying to do."

"Then spit it out," she challenged. "You're supposed to be on my side."

"I'm not on anyone's side," Edie corrected.

Her words cut like a knife and Chanté turned her back, feeling like the entire world had ganged up on her. "Fine. Don't tell me. What do you want?" She plopped down on the sofa and refused to meet her friend's gaze again.

"C'mon, don't take your anger out on me. I am your friend."

"A friend who doesn't take sides. Boy, I hit the lottery with you, didn't I?" Chanté immediately regretted her words. "I didn't mean that," she recanted.

"I know." Edie walked over and staked claim to the empty space next to her. "Do you want to talk about it?"

Chanté sucked in a deep breath and she thought the question over. "Actually, no," she said and realized she meant it. "No pity party. I'm going to be a big girl and own my mistakes."

"He's just angry right now," Edie said, determined to comfort her.

"And I'm just hurt."

"Aww," Edie groaned.

She opened her arms to embrace her friend, but Chanté held her hands up and shrank away. "I mean it. No pity party."

True to her word, Chanté didn't shed a tear that night,

or on the plane ride home. Not until she returned home and discovered that Matthew had moved out, did the dam break and tears flow.

Chapter 18

The Love Doctor to write a prescription for a divorce?

Matthew groaned at the Page Six article in the *New York Post* and then tossed it on the floor of his dressing room. In the past two months, the small room had become his primary residence, so it was only natural that the staff and crew would begin to talk. Rumors swirled fast and heavy. He'd even overheard the lighting tech and the sound engineer spinning a wild tale of how he'd walked in on his wife having an affair. Later that same day, the makeup artist and head caterer had flipped it around to be that Chanté had in fact walked in on him having an affair.

He fired the gabbing four, but that only added fuel to the rumors. So he gave up and now pretended not to hear them. In truth, he only meant to stay at the studio for a short while, just long enough for him to clear his head or rather cool down. But one day turned into two and then three. Before he knew it a week had passed and then a month and now two. And his head was just as cloudy as the night he stormed out of the Tree of Life Resort.

If he'd learned anything in his life and career: forgiving was a process. Saying "I forgive you" wasn't like a magic spell. You didn't wave a wand and abracadabra, a heart was healed. Betrayal was like being injected with poison. It could kill or traces of it could remain in your bloodstream forever.

No matter how many different ways he tried to look at it, Chanté's actions were an act of betrayal, but her words still challenged him. His gaze shifted to his reflection in the vanity mirror. He'd spent another day counseling married couples on the brink of divorce while all the while he felt like jumping out on the ledge with them.

Maybe this was why psychologists had one of the highest suicide rates.

Or was it dentists?

At the light knock against his door, he fought the temptation to shout "go away" and instead invited the person into the room.

"Dr. Valentine. Great show today," Cookie praised, sliding through the door and closing it firmly behind her.

"Oh, thanks." He leaned forward in his chair and retrieved the outline for the next day's show from his dresser. "You're here kind of late," he pointed out.

"Yeah…I, uh, left earlier and then realized that I'd left my PDA somewhere around here so I swung back by." She held up the BlackBerry in question as proof of the tale.

"Glad you found it." He returned his attention back to the outline as a way of dismissing her.

However, she didn't take the hint.

"Uhm. You're here late, too," she commented, inching from the door.

"I have a lot of work to do," he answered, not bothering to look up.

"It kind of looks like you're living here," she continued. "Are you…?"

Matthew's gaze snapped up to meet her gaze through the mirror.

"About you and your wife…" she ventured, ignoring his glare of warning. She reached the back of his chair and lightly ran her fingers across his shoulders.

"Cookie—"

"Because I was thinking that a woman would have to be crazy to let a man like you go," she purred, changing the direction of her hand to glide it through his low-cut hair. "If I was your girl, I'd make sure that you were well satisfied." She leaned forward and brushed her breasts against his back. "Do you know what I mean?"

Matthew watched her performance with a warped fascination and when he realized that she was waiting for him to say something, he did the only thing he could do.

Laugh.

The young intern froze.

He laughed harder.

Slowly, she removed her hands and stepped back. "What's so funny?"

"That you think I need a girl in my life." He swiveled around in his chair to face her. "I am forty-two years old. The last thing I need is a little girl. How old are you?"

"I'm legal," she said, jutting up her chin.

He nodded and told himself to proceed with caution. "Why would a beautiful girl like you throw yourself at a married man?"

Cookie's lips trembled like she was going through an internal earthquake. Next thing Matthew knew, the young intern was spilling every detail of her short, tragic life—an abusive, alcoholic mother, an M.I.A. father, and her one talent of always falling for the wrong guy.

As he suspected, Cookie's shortsighted flirtation with him was more about a lost little girl looking for a father figure than any real feelings of attraction. She cried, smiled and even laughed a little bit, and when it was all said and done, Matthew felt good to put Cookie, real name Cassandra, onto a path of healing.

Now, if he could just do that for his own life, he'd be in business.

"Thank you, Dr. Valentine," Cookie said, rising from the small cot in the corner of the room. "I always knew that you were one of the good guys."

Matthew rose from his chair and gave the girl a much-needed hug.

"Hey, Matt." The dressing room door swung open.

"I brought you something to eat." Seth glanced up and froze at the sight of Matthew and Cookie with their arms wrapped around each other.

"Seth." Matthew dropped his arms. "What are you doing here?"

"Hello, Shawanda. Welcome back to *The Open Heart Forum*. What's on your heart tonight?"

"I'm just calling to say that you got some nerve, Dr. Valentine," the caller said with some major attitude.

Chanté had no trouble imagining a woman with her hands on her hips and her neck swiveling like a cobra.

"How you gonna be giving me advice about how to keep my man when you can't even keep hold of your own?"

Chanté took a deep breath and tried her best not to allow herself to be bated. "I take it you're referring to Page Six of the *New York Post?*"

"Damn right, I am." Shawanda's voice rose as she hit her stride. "Here it is in black and white that your husband is gettin' ready to cut you loose. All you high-falutin pop psychologists are a bunch of hypocrites. Up here trying to tell everybody else how to live while your own lives are a raggedy mess."

Chanté and Thad shared a commiserating look through the Plexiglas. "Shawanda, first let me start off by saying that I don't know where the *Post* is getting their information. My marriage is doing just fine," she lied.

"Uh-huh. Then why is my cousin, Cookie, telling me

that your man spends every night at his studio? Hell, he's down there right now."

Chanté's heart picked up its beats and threatened to crack through her chest. It didn't bode well that this caller knew more about her husband's whereabouts than she did. "I'm sure most of you know that my husband works long hours to make *The Love Doctor* show a success—not just for the networks but to reach and inspire his audience to have healthy and productive relationships. It's the same thing I strive to do with this show."

"Uh-huh. Did I mention that my cousin is down there with your husband right now—alone—as we speak?"

Seth blinked, stared, blinked and stared some more.

"I, uh, better get going," Cookie said. Her gaze ping-ponged between the two men as she slowly made her way toward the door. "Uhm, thanks again, Dr. Valentine. I really appreciate you being there for me."

Matthew nodded and finally met her gaze again. "It was my pleasure. You just remember what I said."

She smiled, but it died when she glanced at Seth again. "Good night, Mr. Hathaway." Finally, she slipped out of the door.

Seth waited, hoping his friend and client would launch into an explanation as to what he'd just witnessed. Instead, Matthew walked up to him and reached for the container Seth held in his hands.

"Oh, good. Chinese."

"Yeah, I figured you would be hungry and that you might want to…I don't know—talk."

"Thanks," he said carrying the food over to the cot. "You're right. I'm starved."

"You're going to make me come right out and ask you, aren't you?" Seth moved toward the makeup chair.

Matthew opened the box to his sesame chicken and proceeded to unwrap his plastic utensils.

Determined to navigate through the room's thickening tension, Seth sat down and calmly braided his fingers together. "Is there something going on between you and your intern?"

A muscle twitched along Matthew's jaw and when he finally lifted his black gaze, Seth faltered a bit. "I mean, I know things between you and Chanté are still on shaky ground. But…you don't want to travel down the wrong road. You don't want to break…do something you might regret."

"No. I would never want to do something like that," Matthew said evenly.

"Then nothing…?"

"No. Nothing happened." He set his food aside. "And I'm offended you're even asking me such a question."

"First, let me ask you, are we talking as friends right now?"

Matthew looked as if he was weighing the word "friend" very carefully. "Sure. Why not."

"All right," Seth said, adjusting in his chair. "As your friend, don't give me that offended crap. We both know what the scene looked like when I walked in here. And given what you're going through…"

"Given what I'm going through?"

"Yes. What you're going through," he reaffirmed.

"Look, your marriage is a wreck. There, I said it so you can stop pretending otherwise, but it's not going to fix itself. You love Chanté. I know it and you know it. So stop trying to pick a fight with me."

The twitch made another appearance, but this time, Matt hung his head. "Yes. I love my wife...but I don't trust her." After a long silence, he finally lifted his head again. "You don't have to be a psychologist to know that a marriage without trust isn't much of a marriage at all."

Chapter 19

After *The Open Heart Forum*'s broadcast, Chanté finally made good on a rain check with Thad. After a full night of dealing with callers trying to give her marriage advice, Chanté wished she could drink something stronger than herbal tea.

"So you didn't tell him that you were on the pill?" Thad asked after she finished giving him the Cliffs Notes version to the destruction of her marriage.

"That's pretty much the gist of it."

"And now that he's gone, you're pregnant?"

"Never let it be said that God doesn't have a sense of humor."

Thad flipped his Yankees ball cap to the back and leaned over their table. "Okay. Correct me if I'm wrong, but isn't this good news?"

Chanté drifted a hand down over her still-flat belly and blinked away the instant sting of tears. "I'm eight weeks along, ten has been my average." She couldn't say it, didn't want to think it, but...

"Hey, hey." Thad pulled all the napkins out of the table's silver holder and shoved them in her direction. "No crying. I don't do well when women start crying."

"I'm not crying," Chanté sniffled, snatching up a few of the napkins and blotting her eyes. "I just have... something in my eye."

Thad nodded but he looked at her like she was sprouting a second head. When she finally managed to gain more control of her leaking eyes and running nose, he relaxed a bit and asked, "You are going to tell him, right?"

"And never know whether he's coming for me or the baby?" She shook her head. "I wouldn't want to pull him away from Cookie the Intern."

"C'mon. You didn't believe that caller, did you?" Thad asked. "Didn't that Shawanda call months ago about stealing her sister's husband and trying to keep someone else from stealing him from her? Hell, it was probably another sister."

Chanté laughed. "I just have this one image of some brother out there that's just being passed down from one family member to the next."

"Maybe it's not a good thing to teach your children how to share."

"Yeah, probably." Her laugh downgraded to a smile, and then finally a frown again.

"Look, if you're really concerned, why don't we just

drive over to the studio and see what's going on for ourselves?"

Because I'm afraid it might be true. Instead of saying the words, Chanté shook her head. "I'm not going to chase him down and beg him to come back home." She sighed pitifully. "He's got to want to do that on his own."

"So you're not going to tell him about this pregnancy?"

Chanté moaned over how many times she'd asked herself this very question. "Yeah. I'll tell him, when and if he comes home."

Edie and Seth curled into a tight spoon after another night of sweaty sex. For a long while, Edie was content to just listen to the sound of her husband's deep, even breathing, but serene thoughts soon turned troubled when they drifted to Chanté.

When they'd first returned from New Mexico, a few tabloids had picked up the story about Chanté and Matthew's stay at the Tree of Life Resort. The *National Enquirer* even had a mini-picture of Wilfred and Mable cheesing for the camera as their reliable source. As promised, Edie had the publicity department send out a press release stating that the loving Valentines' stay at the resort was for research on the West's growing fascination with tantric sex.

A half-truth.

However, Wilfred and Mable weren't the only ones who'd reported the major fight between the doctors that had Matthew storming out of the resort before the work-

shops were completed. Edie had those reports blasted
as fabrications.

A downright lie.

In truth, Edie was surprised the Valentines' split
remained quiet for as long as it did. Now that it was
out, she not only worried about a publicity nightmare
or a possible dip in book sales, but she worried for her
friend's well-being.

In the past two months, Chanté avoided Edie like
the plague. She didn't return calls, messages or even
answer her e-mail. If things continued this way, Edie
was sure she'd be reduced to sending smoke signals or
turn to stalking her friend. The bottom line was clear.
Chanté blamed Edie for what happened.

Maybe she was to blame.

"Stop it," Seth said, squeezing her tight and planting
a kiss at the back of her head. "I can hear you thinking
from back here."

Edie flittered a sad smile in the darkness. "I should
have listened to you and not gotten involved."

"Chanté and Matt again?"

She nodded. "I thought he would've gone back home
by now. I mean—yeah, they get a little crazy sometimes
when they're fighting, but this stalemate…"

"I know. When I went by to see him tonight—"

"You saw him?" Edie rolled out from the spoon and
flipped over to face her husband. "How did he look?
What did he say?"

"I've seen him look better," he confessed. "He said
he still loved Chanté."

"Well, that's great," she said, clutching his arm.

"He also said that he didn't trust her."

"Oh." She fell silent and tried to imagine her friends breaking up for good, but couldn't manage it. "She just made a mistake."

"A pretty big one."

"What? That she decided to take a break from the physical and emotional pain of losing one baby after another?" Edie said, sitting up.

Seth lazily rolled onto his back and stared through the room's sparse moonlight to meet his wife's gaze. "This wasn't another shoe shopping decision. It was a decision they both should have made."

"And we all know he would have been dead set against it. He's practically rabid for a child."

"So you knew he'd say 'no' and that makes it okay to lie about it?"

"She didn't lie," Edie reasoned.

"She didn't tell him the truth either," Seth shot back testily. "Is that how things work around here, too? Anything you know I'm against you just maneuver around me?"

Edie didn't answer.

Seth sat up. "You women."

"What the hell is that supposed to mean?"

"What in the hell do you think it means?" He snatched up his pillow. "If a man lies or manipulates a situation to get what he wants, he's a dog, a jerk or an asshole. When a woman does it, there's a perfectly good reason or rationale behind it like, 'her husband would have said no.' Who gave you the right to veto anything?"

"All right. Calm down. This isn't even our fight."

"Isn't it? You're so quick to stick up for Chanté every time you think I may agree with Matthew. Well, let me tell you so that we're perfectly clear on this. I do agree with him. He has every right to be angry and hurt."

"It's been two months!"

"So lick his wounds and get over it? Why? Because when it comes to childbearing all the decisions are left to the woman? My oldest brother, David, and his wife both decided to wait to start a family after he got his computer business off the ground. A year later, his wife grew impatient, came off the pill, without telling him, became pregnant with twins and now there is no computer company. He has to punch someone else's clock in order to provide for his unplanned family."

"This is hardly the same thing."

"Manipulation is manipulation. Dishonesty is dishonesty. Can I understand why Chanté went on the pill? Yes. Can I understand why she didn't talk to her husband, her partner, her supposedly best friend? No."

Edie and Seth came to a stalemate. Both drew in deep breaths in order to calm down.

"Maybe I better just go sleep on the couch," he said, turning for the door.

"Honey, you don't have to do that," she said and reached a hand out from the bed. "We agreed to never go to bed angry, remember?"

After a long stall at the door, Seth finally turned around. "Look, I know this isn't really our argument," he agreed. "But it would tear me up if I thought that there was something in this world you couldn't come to me about, that there is something you would purposely not consult me on. Especially something this important."

Edie climbed out of the bed and joined her husband at the door. "You're absolutely right. And other than a couple…few…some questionable shopping sprees…" She smiled to lighten the mood. "Look, you're right. All major decisions should be discussed as a single unit. I get that. I just want my best friend to be happy."

Seth finally smiled and leaned down to plant a kiss on her full lips, but when he lifted his head, his brows rose suspiciously. "Just how many shopping sprees are we talking about?"

"Oh, honey," she sighed dramatically and then batted her eyes up at him. "You would have just said 'no.'"

His laugh finally deflated the room's tension and he pulled her over to the bed. "That, my dear, just earned you a spanking."

"Ooh. That sounds like fun."

As usual, Chanté arrived home late. After two months, she expected it to get easier to come home to an empty house. Thank God she had Buddy. He actually turned out be a real companion. He was always excited when she came home. Thinking of Buddy made her think of Matthew. She thought about the times Matthew would wait up for her in the living room pretending to work.

Crazy as it sounded, she even missed the elaborate fights they had. What she wouldn't give to find him waiting for her again.

"I was beginning to think you weren't coming."

Chanté gasped and whipped around toward the voice drifting from the living room.

A light clicked on and there sitting in the center of the white couch was her miracle. "Matthew."

"Chanté," he said gravely.

Her thoughts and emotions crashed head-on and Chanté literally felt her knees weaken beneath her husband's pensive stare. Every fiber of her being was happy to see him, her heart pleaded for her to rush into his arms and beg for forgiveness.

However, there was nothing in Matthew's mannerism that suggested he was in a forgiving mood. "I take it you're not here to stay?" The question stretched between them for so long, she didn't think he'd answer.

"No."

The tears rushed down her face before she had a chance to stop them. "Matthew," her voice trembled. "I know what I did was wrong."

He broke eye contact and drew in a deep breath.

"And I'm sorry," she added, easing into the room. "I made a mistake."

"Maybe this marriage was a mistake," he said, finding her gaze again. "Lord knows we don't behave like a married couple and we fight like schoolchildren." Matthew stood up and walked toward a glass vase that was still superglued to the tabletop. He chuckled at the absurdity. "Let's be honest, if I was a caller on your radio show and I described half of the things that we've done to each other, what would you tell me?"

It was Chanté's turn to drop her gaze. "I'm not saying that we're perfect."

"Damn right, we're not."

"And I have never recommended divorce to any caller. I would urge them to get counseling."

"Ha!" He clapped his hands together and it sounded more like a thunderbolt. "We are counselors. So let's just counsel ourselves, shall we?" he shouted. "Well, Dr. Valentine, my wife and I have been trying to have children for the past five years."

"Matthew—"

"C'mon, doctor. We can do this. We're both qualified professionals from good schools."

Chanté stiffened at the slight barb. "Why do you have to be such an asshole?"

"The same reason you have to be such a bitch," he snapped back.

Her hand whipped across his face in reflex and Matthew's head hardly moved from the blow. The sting in her hand raced clear up to her shoulders and the tears continued to flow down her face. "If you're leaving, then leave."

Matthew's jaw twitched, but then he finally turned back toward the sofa and retrieved his jacket. "I'm going to give you your wish."

Chanté lifted her chin. "What's that?"

He stopped and locked gazes with her. "I'm filing for divorce."

Chapter 20

"I was such a blind, self-absorbed idiot," Chanté spat, storming through Edie's front door. "I've lost him for good now."

"Please, come in," Edie mumbled in the wake of her trail, sighed, and then closed the door. Shaking her head and tightening her belt around her plus-size figure, she stopped. Hadn't she lived this moment before?

"Well, it's good seeing you again," Edie said, following Chanté into the dining room. "I thought you weren't speaking to me?"

"I'm sorry, Edie," she said, collapsing into a vacant chair at the table. "I wanted to call, but I also wanted to hide in my own shell, too." She buried her head in her hands. "I can't seem to do anything right."

Edie slumped into her chair and pushed her breakfast aside. "What happened?"

"Matthew is filing for divorce. And please don't say anything about professional credibility or book sales."

"No. Of course not." She reached across the table for her hand. "Oh, Chanté. I'm so sorry."

"Not as sorry as I am." She sniffed and brushed away a tear before it had the chance to fall. "The thing is, I should be relieved. No more roller coasters of emotions. No more wondering when the big shoe was going to fall. Not that I have any shoes anymore."

Edie gave her hand an encouraging squeeze. "Maybe it's not too late. Have you talked to him?"

Chanté nodded and missed a few errant tears. "He came by the house last night."

"I take it that it didn't go too well?"

"We're as toxic as ever." She smiled but it looked more like a twisted frown. "Before we went to that resort, I was emotionally prepared for a divorce. When I decided to go on birth control, I did it knowing that Matthew would never understand. And I couldn't find the courage to tell him that I wanted to stop trying for a baby. I'd pick a fight for everything else, a classic case of transfer aggression. Then it became a mad race to leave him before he had the chance to dump me.

"Then something happened at the Tree of Life Resort. We connected. It was like...old times. There was no competition, no bitterness—just love. I found out that I still loved him. And I discovered I still wanted to try and give him what he desperately wants."

Edie's gaze followed Chanté's hand as it drifted

down to her belly and her brain jumped to a conclusion. "Are you pregnant?"

Chanté shared another sad, crooked smile. "Yeah. Despite the pills."

Edie was confused. "Matthew's filing for divorce knowing that you're pregnant?"

Chanté lowered her gaze.

"You didn't tell him?"

She shook her head.

"But why?"

"Because he would have stayed...and it wouldn't have been for me."

"But, Chanté—"

"Look, one of the hardest things women have to learn is knowing when to let go." She shook her head during a pathetic laugh. "Do you know how many times I've told callers that?"

"Forgive me, but sometimes there's a real fine line between letting go and giving up."

"Not in this case."

Edie pulled away from her friend and slumped back in her chair. "So that's it then?"

"Yeah." Chanté drew a deep breath and willed her courage to return.

"And what about the baby? What if this time—?"

Still afraid to hope, Chanté chose not to answer.

"Chanté, as your friend, I get to tell you that I think you're making another mistake."

"Another mistake?" she echoed.

"I didn't mean it like that."

"It's okay," Chanté assured her, standing up. "I'm a

big girl. I can take my lumps. But don't worry. If—and this is a very big if—I'm blessed to carry this child to term I have no intentions of cutting Matthew out. I just want to make sure that he doesn't stay for the wrong reasons."

Edie drew a deep breath. "I can understand that." She stood. "Don't leave. Stay and have breakfast with me. You're eating for two now. Having any weird cravings yet?"

"Well, don't laugh, but I really could go for some tomato soup and marshmallows."

Edie scrunched up her face. "I would never laugh at that. Not now anyway."

Matthew and Seth met at the International House of Pancakes for their favorite selection of Rooty Tuitty Fresh and Fruity pancakes. However, after Matthew announced his decision to file for divorce, the men fell into an awkward silence.

"I know you think I'm making a mistake," Matthew said finally. "And I know the media will have a field day with this."

"I don't care about that," Seth said. "I'll have an official press release sent out later today."

Matthew nodded and absently twirled his pancakes in his strawberry syrup. "This is the right decision, you know."

"I can't answer that for you."

"No. No. I mean, I'm just saying. Given our situation, our history and given what I know about human behavior, we're not normal. This marriage has taken a wrong turn somewhere."

"Look, one thing I can agree with you on is that you and Chanté are a few cards short of a full deck. And now what you're telling me is that cutting up cars and spiking each other's food is okay, but this…"

"Deception?" Matthew finished for him.

Seth lowered his fork. "Forget it. I—I can't help you with this. As your friend, I'll support you in any decision you make. As your agent, I'll get out whatever message you want to the press. And we'll just leave it at that."

Matthew nodded at his pancakes again. After another lengthy silence, he said, "I went to the house last night."

"Yeah?"

"I was going to be strong, lay down the facts and present my case on why I decided to file for divorce. But the minute she walked in, the words jumbled in my head and my heart ached to the point I couldn't breathe. My head flooded with all these memories of how we met, the first time I kissed her, and even the first time we—well, you know."

Seth gave him a crooked smile.

"Then I remembered how much fun we had at the resort. Rose petals on the bed, long bubble baths and body-oiled massages. I wanted to pull her into my arms one second and then in the next, I was baiting her, wanting a good fight."

"So what happened?"

"What do you think?"

"Right hook?"

"I didn't let it show, but it took me half an hour to blink the stars out of my eyes," he chuckled, but quickly grew serious again. "Fighting is a lot easier than dealing with what's really wrong."

Seth smiled. "You know, it seems I heard somewhere that 'couples tend to argue over something safe or superficial as the battlefield while the serious problems are ignored.'"

Matthew recognized the quote. "Now you know I was right."

"It's not always about being right."

"I know. I know. It's also about being able to say you're sorry. I remember."

"Yeah, but did you learn from it?"

"I thought you weren't getting involved?"

"I thought that you had more sense than to end your marriage because your wife can't have children."

Matthew exploded out of his chair. "Shut up! You don't know what the hell you're talking about."

The restaurant's diners swiveled their heads toward the television star and Seth threw his hands up in surrender when he realized that he'd hit a nerve.

"I'm sorry, man. You're right. I shouldn't get involved." But Seth knew at that moment that he was going to get involved. His wife wasn't the only trickster in the family.

Slowly, Matthew slid back into his chair, but he didn't touch his food. Seth's accusation echoed eerily of those Chanté had thrown at him at the resort. What he'd once dismissed as a ridiculous comment now gave him pause. Was he running toward the exit door of his marriage because of the possibility of no children?

Twenty minutes later, the men gave up the sham of eating their meals and requested their checks. While Matthew sank into a gloomy depression, the wheels in Seth's head churned at warp speed.

The men said their goodbyes and as they dispatched to their separate cars, Seth scooped his cell phone from his pocket and called his wife.

"Honey, it's time to throw the deer back into the water."

"Matt and Chanté?" she guessed.

"Yeah. I just finished having breakfast with Matthew."

"Well, Chanté just left here. Baby, she's pregnant again."

"What? Well, that's good news!"

"Not exactly. She's not going to tell Matthew."

"What? But—"

"Wait, before you get started, I agree with her." Edie gave him a brief rundown of Chanté's reasoning for keeping the pregnancy hidden.

"Well, all this tells me is that we need to act fast."

"I'm all ears. What's the plan?"

"We get them to do what they do best—fight."

Chapter 21

For ten weeks Chanté had grown accustomed to waking up with Buddy's butt in her face. It was just another way to fill the empty space on the other side of the bed. It was a poor substitute really, but after so much time had passed, she'd convinced herself that the trick was working.

However, when she opened her eyes this morning, Buddy was nowhere in sight. Yawning, she propped herself up on the pillows and wiped the sleep from her eyes as she glanced around.

"Buddy? Here, boy. Where are you?" When he didn't waddle out from his hiding place, Chanté groaned for having to get up and look for the adorable mongrel. But after searching every inch of the master bedroom, she grew concerned.

The bedroom door was still closed so she couldn't imagine how he could have gotten out. Also, if he had gotten out, she didn't even want to think about how much destruction the little Tasmanian Devil might have caused in other parts of the house.

"Buddy?" she called, opening her bedroom door. "Where are you, boy?" Chanté carefully combed the house and still there was no Buddy.

She heard a car's engine in the driveway and she rushed to the door to see if perhaps she had a dognapper on the premises. Bolting onto the front porch, Chanté slumped in disappointment to see that it was just old man Roger pulling into the drive.

"Good morning, Mrs. Valentine." Roger waved and shut off his engine.

"Morning, Roger." She pulled her satin robe closed and glanced around the property. "You didn't happen to see Buddy out running around when you pulled up, did you?"

"Nah, I can't say that I did." He turned and glanced around the property as well. "I, uh, did see Mr. Valentine leaving a few minutes ago."

Chanté blinked at the news. "Matthew was here?"

"Uh, yes, ma'am." Roger stared earnestly up at her. "Looked to me he was in quite a bit of a hurry, too."

"I don't believe him!" She stomped her foot and pivoted back toward the front door. "I've been the one taking care of Buddy all this time. He has no right!" She marched back into the house and slammed the door.

Roger scratched the side of his cotton-white hair,

feeling more than a little guilty for lying to the lady of the house, but Mrs. Valentine's good friend had convinced him that the lie was crucial to get the Valentines back together again—well, that and the two hundred dollars she'd slipped into his shirt pocket.

Frankly, he didn't see how kidnapping a dog was going to do much of anything, but then again, he always thought the feuding shrinks were a little off their rockers anyway.

Buddy was having a great time as far as kidnapping went. During his high-speed race across town, he was given new toys to play with and enough dog biscuits to put him in doggy heaven.

"If I get caught during this caper, I want you to tell the pet detectives that you were never mistreated," Edie said.

Buddy gave her a hearty bark and then returned his attention to the dog biscuits.

Thirty minutes later, Edie arrived at the *Love Doctor* studio, still dressed head to toe in black from her morning heist. She quickly found her husband's car and parked behind it. Seth was to meet her at exactly ten o'clock and at one minute after the hour, she was in full panic mode.

At 10:02, she truly envisioned those pet detectives screeching into the studio lot to take her away. What was the time given for dognapping? Would something like that go on someone's permanent records?

Lost in her thoughts about being hauled to jail, Edie

didn't notice the petite woman approaching from the rear of her car. At the hard tap against the window, Edie screamed and nearly wet her britches, which then set Buddy off into a barking frenzy.

After a few heart-pounding seconds, Edie placed a calming hand across her heart and rolled down the window.

"Hi, I'm Cookie." The girl jutted a hand into the car. "Are you Mrs. Hathaway?"

"Maybe," Edie said cautiously and slid her large sunglasses up higher. "Why do you need to know?"

Cookie just smiled. "Well, since I know that little fella over there is Buddy, then I'm going to assume that you are Mrs. Hathaway. Your husband is tied up with the producers of the show and he sent me out to meet you."

Edie groaned.

"Don't worry." The young woman winked. "I'm on your side."

Buddy barked and waved his short tail excitedly.

"I guess that means he trusts you. So what's next?"

"Well, I'm going to take our little friend over there and put him in Dr. Valentine's dressing room. The Valentines' groundskeeper just called and said the wife just drove off the property, so we need to get moving."

Edie was out of the car before Cookie could finish her last sentence. They placed Buddy in the box Cookie brought and then covered the top with a thin towel. In true cloak-and-dagger mode, the women stole into the studio by the back door during the taping of the show.

Once, Buddy barked as they were sneaking past the

set's caterers. Cookie, unexpectedly, let go of the box and faked a coughing fit. Edie caught the full weight of the box and kept moving—certain that at any moment someone would stop her.

"Sorry about that," Cookie said as she caught up and directed her the rest of the way to Matthew's dressing room. Once they got him inside, they removed the towel and crammed more dog biscuits into the box, and quickly got the hell out of dodge.

Chanté arrived at the studio lot, breathing fire. She received more than her fair share of stares when she climbed out of her new Mercedes and marched into the studio, mainly because she still wore her satin pajamas and matching pink robe.

She didn't care. She just wanted her dog back.

The moment she walked through the back door of the sound studio she heard the thundering applause echoing throughout the place. She had hoped to reach Matthew before taping began, now she would have to wait for the next commercial break to grab her husband's attention.

"Chanté." Seth walked up and joined her by one of the camera monitors. "What are you doing here?" He glanced around.

"I just need to speak to Matthew for a minute. I'll stay out of the way." She tapped her foot impatiently.

Seth cleared his throat and made another glance around—when he spotted Cookie a few feet away. When she gave him the thumbs-up, he relaxed and waited for the drama to unfold.

On stage, Matthew turned to address one of his

guests but caught sight of Chanté offstage. For the first time in his professional life, his mind drew a blank.

"Dr. Valentine?" His guest, a sixty-year-old man who claimed to be addicted to Viagra, waved his hand before Matthew's line of vision and brought him out of his trance. A few minutes later, Matthew cut to a commercial break and quickly exited stage left.

"Chanté, what are you doing here? And why aren't you dressed?"

"Don't play games with me! You know why I'm here. Where's Buddy?"

Matthew stared at her while he waited for her words to make sense. When that didn't happen, he ventured to ask, "Why would I know where Buddy is?"

"Don't play stupid with me. I know you broke into the house this morning and took him," she hissed.

"What? Don't be ridiculous! Plus, who ever heard of breaking into one's own house?"

"Dr. Valentine?" A stage assistant approached cautiously. "We're back on in thirty seconds."

"You don't have the right to take him. You abandoned him, just like you abandoned me!"

More heads whipped in their direction.

"Will you lower your voice," Matthew seethed. "Do you want the whole damn studio to hear you? And I did not abandon you."

"I don't give a damn who hears me. I want my dog back."

"Dr. Valentine?" the assistant urged again.

"I'm coming," he snapped over his shoulder. He returned his attention to Chanté and waved a finger at her. "Stay put. I'll be right back."

Chanté reached for his finger as if ready to snap it off, but he jerked it back in time and rushed out onto the stage.

Seth shrank back but kept his eye on Chanté as she paced around like a caged tiger.

"I thought you said this was going to help them get back together," Cookie whispered into his ear.

"Patience, my dear. There is a method to my madness."

The rest of the show went without a hitch and Matthew thanked his guests for appearing on the show with a wide plastic smile and then rushed off the stage to see what the hell his wife was babbling about.

"Unhand me," Chanté growled when he gripped her arm and proceeded to direct her away from his crew.

He ignored her and continued to tug while flashing his curious crew his famous television smile.

"I just want Buddy back," she growled.

"I don't have him."

"Liar!"

Matthew reached his dressing room and pitched her inside as fast as he could. When he entered behind her, he was sure his eyes were playing tricks on him. The entire room was ransacked and in the center of his cot was Buddy ripping the feathers out of his pillow.

"Buddy!" Chanté exclaimed, rushing over to the dog.

Matthew glanced around the place. "What in the hell is he doing here? And look what he did to my dressing room."

"Payback is a bitch." She smiled triumphantly. "Isn't that what you told me?"

"You did this on purpose?"

"Oh, will you just give it a rest. I know you were on the property this morning. Roger said he saw you."

Matthew felt like he was tumbling through the Twilight Zone. He couldn't imagine old man Roger lying on him.

"Chanté, I'm only going to say this one more time. I did not take Buddy."

"Then how did he get here? Fly?"

"You must have brought him here," he concluded.

"You're delusional." She picked Buddy up and headed toward the door. "I'd appreciate it if you'd call before you come over. No more just popping up or dropping in."

"Wait a minute. That's my house, too. I'll show up whenever I feel like it."

"I wouldn't try it if I were you." She snatched open the door. "File your damn divorce but stay the hell away from me and Buddy. You don't deserve us."

Buddy barked in agreement.

When she stormed out of the room, Matthew tried to review what had just happened. No matter how hard he tried, he couldn't make sense of it. Nor should he understand why the memory of rubbing warm body oil all over Chanté kept playing in his mind while they were arguing.

Seth and Cookie had jumped out of the way when Chanté stormed out of her husband's dressing room.

"The method to your madness isn't working," Cookie said.

Seth nodded. "I hate to say it, but I don't think these two are going to make it."

Chapter 22

"I needed to hear that us being childless would be okay—that I could be enough for you," she'd said.

Matthew tossed and turned on his pillowless cot, trying to outrun his demons of guilt, but he couldn't seem to move fast enough. Once again, he abandoned hope of a peaceful night's sleep and kicked off the covers. He couldn't go on like this, constantly second-guessing himself and being ruled by his emotions.

Every day he threw himself into his work, trying not to give his hurt or sense of betrayal breathing room to fester. But there were days when it felt like a cancer and other days when he thought he was blowing things way out of proportion.

It was a damn if you do and damn if you don't situation.

However, one question remained. *Can I give up my dream of children?*

The moment he posed the question, his heart rejected it. Why should he have to give up his dream of children when they haven't exhausted all possible avenues—including adoption?

Matthew groaned. Had he just inadvertently proved Chanté's point? He pushed himself up from the cot and paced the room. God, he missed her.

But could he ever forgive her?

He needed to, wanted to, but…

Exhaling a long breath, Matthew realized he needed a longer walk. He slipped out of his dressing room and took a stroll around the studio. In the last three months, he'd taken this walk around the building's perimeter too many times to count. Each time, he made a mental journey through his life.

Born to a wealthy African-American family was no guarantee of success. His father, an entrepreneurial jack-of-all-trades had just a high school degree and Matthew, the middle child, was not the first to go to college, but he was the first to make it into Princeton. Even after obtaining his Ph.D. in psychology, postdoctoral certification and licensing in marriage and family therapy; Matthew's life didn't truly begin until the day he broke down on a lonely stretch of highway outside Karankawa, Texas, and he walked three miles to Sam's café and met his future wife.

Matthew chuckled aloud at the memory.

After such a long walk, he'd been annoyed the small café didn't have a public phone. The sassy waitress promptly informed him they were a café and not AT&T. A few more witty banters were exchanged and Matthew found himself trying harder to impress the waitress than obtaining roadside assistance. He'd even gone so far as to pay for a sixty-cent cup of coffee with a platinum card.

Chanté was not impressed.

He never did make it to that conference, instead he rented a room in a Norman Bates-ish hotel and returned to Sam's café every day until Chanté agreed to go out with him. To this day, he loved how Chanté never took any crap and could dish out whatever he shoveled her way.

Lord, he missed her.

He took a seat in one of the empty audience chairs and stared up at the stage. In reality, his job was more Hollywood than psychology. Yes, he believed in the advice he pedaled to his guests, but problems couldn't be solved in a fifty-minute show—or during a two-month hibernation.

He stood and circled the studio once again. When he finally returned to his dressing room, it was close to midnight and he was nowhere near ready to try falling asleep. Matthew's gaze fell to the small radio on the dressing table and, despite his vow to stop listening, he turned it on and tuned in to WLUV.

"Hello, it's now midnight, this is Dr. Chanté Valentine and you're listening to *The Open Heart Forum*. Thad, who's our next caller?"

"We have Nicole on line four," Thad said. "She's having relationship problems."

"Hello, Nicole. What's on your heart tonight?"

"Hi, Dr. Valentine." A high, almost childlike voice filtered through the radio. "I'm calling because I'm ready to give up on finding a good man. I swear all the good ones are taken and the ones running around here now are brothers looking either for a sugar momma or their momma period."

Matthew's heart squeezed at the sound of Chanté's soft chuckle.

"I'm sure it's not as bad as all of that."

"Humph! I can tell you ain't been out here in a while. Every man I meet wants to run me through a five-point inspection—my weight, my size, can I cook, clean, be a freak in the bedroom, and a good girl in public? Do I have a good job, a nice car? Will I treat him like a king and not question his authority? If I pass all of that, then he'll move his tired butt into my house, prop his feet up on my coffee table, hog the remote and tell me half a million lies as to why he can't get a job."

Matthew laughed along with his wife at the woman's theatrics.

"Nicole," Chanté began. "Let me guess, you're meeting these men at a club or perhaps online, am I right?"

"How else are you going meet guys nowadays?"

"The good, ole-fashion way. Friends, neighbors, women at your church—people you can rely on to give you good, solid information on a man's character. I'm not saying that you can't meet any good men from the clubs or even online, but you can swing the odds in your favor by shopping for a man like you would shop for anything else. Put him through a five-point inspection.

If he fails, move on, don't reward him with a key to your apartment." Chanté sighed. "We'll be back after this."

While the show went to commercial, Matthew grabbed his cell phone from its charger. He held the phone for a moment, contemplating whether he should do this or not, but his fingers dialed before he'd arrived at a decision.

The line rang for a full minute and he was just about to hang up when Chanté's producer, Thad, answered the line.

"Yes, I have a relationship problem I'd like to talk to Dr. Valentine about," he said.

"What sort of problem are you experiencing, sir?" Thad asked, putting him through the screening process.

Chanté kept her eyes on the clock. Tonight's shift seemed to drag on forever and her empathy for her callers was at an all-time low. Maybe she needed a little break—finally take Edie up on that book tour she'd promised or something.

Maybe even go home for a visit. Let her parents kiss her boo-boos and make her hot chocolate.

Thad waved and gave a five-second countdown and then the On Air light lit up.

"Welcome back to *The Open Heart Forum.* As you know, I'm your host, Dr. Chanté Valentine. Thad, who's our next caller?"

"On line two, we have Buddy. He's experiencing marital woes."

"Hello, Buddy. You're our first male caller tonight. What's on your heart?"

"I'm having trouble forgiving my wife."

Chanté stiffened. "Uhm, I, uh, see." Her gaze flew to Thad who looked up from his terminal with a question in his expression.

"See, my wife and I have been together for eleven years. Nine and a half were pretty damn good. Wonderful, really. And then just when I thought we were heading to splitsville we had this…reconnection."

Chanté closed her eyes, remembering that connection all too well.

"But then I found out that she was keeping a secret from me."

Swallowing the growing lump in her throat, Chanté managed to croak, "All women have secrets. Was her secret meant to protect you or hurt you?"

Matthew didn't answer.

"There is a difference, you know."

"But one can cause the other," he said gravely.

"Intentions have to count for something." At his continued silence, she added, "My husband used to say that forgiving was a process. Maybe you just haven't processed this long enough?" Chanté held her breath.

"I wish that was true. The worst part is…the thing she accused me of…the possibility of living without… something—may in fact be true."

A tear trickled down Chanté's face. He finally said it. He couldn't live in a childless marriage. She could never be enough for him.

There was a light click over the line.

"Ma—Buddy? Are you still there, Buddy?"

"He hung up," Thad informed her and then addressed

the radio audience. "We'll be back after these messages." He cut to commercial.

Chanté snatched off her headset and grabbed her things.

"Where are you going?" Thad asked. "Was that who I think it was?"

"I have to get out of here. Stuff the rest of the hour with a repeat broadcast. I can't keep doing this. I can't keep fighting him. I can't keep begging for forgiveness. If he hasn't filed for a divorce, then I will."

Chapter 23

True to her word, the very next day, Chanté filed for divorce. A few hours later, she packed her things, grabbed Buddy and took a flight back home to Texas. Yes, she was running away from a problem—mainly Page Six of the *New York Post*—but she needed a break and she needed family.

Years ago, when Chanté "married up," as her mother called it, she bought her mom and dad a nice western ranch home—which was a considerable step up from the dilapidated shotgun house Chanté had grown up in.

The moment Chanté pulled her rented Camry into the driveway and saw her mother relaxing on the front porch swing, tears she hadn't known had built up poured down her face.

Within minutes, she was folded snugly in her mother's arms and recounting every detail of the past year.

Alice Morris listened to her only child with a loving patience only a mother had. When Chanté was through, she just continued to hold her until the tears ran dry.

Hours later, at sunset, Leonard Morris pulled his old Chevy pickup truck behind the Camry and found the women still on the porch swing with Buddy curled at their feet.

He lumbered up the stairs with a wide smile. "Is that my baby girl?" After a close-up look at Chanté's red, swollen eyes, his mood took a one hundred and eighty degree turn. "I'll kill him."

"Ain't nobody gonna kill nobody," Alice declared, and gave her daughter's shoulders an encouraging squeeze. "What you're going to do is get Chanté's bags out of the car and take them to the guest room. Chanté, go lie down for a spell while I get supper started." She kissed her daughter's temple and helped her up.

Leonard remained rooted on the porch while he watched the women enter the house. When it became clear that he wasn't going to be filled in on what was going on, he glanced down at the strange dog. "And who the hell are you?"

Buddy barked.

"Well, I guess that's about the only answer I'm going to get tonight." He turned and meandered back down the steps to get his daughter's luggage.

Matthew and the staff had just completed taping. He knew he'd made a mistake in calling into Chanté's radio show. Numerous staffers had recognized his voice and noticed Chanté's emotional response to the caller. The set hummed with rumors and speculation.

Though none of that mattered once he received a call from Chanté's attorney.

Divorce. To separate, divide—permanently.

"All right." Seth breezed into the room. "I just finished the meeting with the producers and I think you're going to like their offer for another five-year contract." He stopped and looked over at Matthew. "Are you all right? You don't look so good."

Matthew gave him a half-chuckle, half-groan response.

"You need to go to a doctor or something?"

"Chanté's attorney called."

Seth straightened.

"She filed."

The small dressing room fell silent while Matthew studied his reflection in the mirror.

"I'm sorry, Matt." Seth placed a hand on his shoulder. "I was really hoping you two would work it out."

"Yeah. I know. Kidnapping the dog was a little over the top though."

"What?" His hand fell from his shoulder.

Matthew's lips sloped unevenly. "Cookie told me this morning. She felt guilty about our fight yesterday."

Seth dropped his gaze and shuffled his feet. "Sorry. I just figured—"

"Don't worry about it. Thanks for caring so much."

"Well, it was either that or slice your car in half."

Matthew laughed. "That might have worked better."

Seth smiled, but remained silent by his friend's side until Matthew stood from his chair and reached for his jacket.

"I gotta get out of here," Matthew said. "Do you mind if we go over that offer another time?"

"Yeah. Sure. Not a problem."

"Thanks, man." He rushed out of the door and made it to his car in record time. The objective was to just drive, clear his head, and wait for the pain in his heart to ease. Instead, he found himself pulling up into his own driveway.

"Oh, hello there, Mr. Valentine."

Matthew glanced down the yard to see old man Roger lumbering up to him.

"Long time since I seen you here," he said candidly. "My wife said that she'd come up here with me tomorrow to help get more of the furniture covered, like Mrs. Valentine asked."

"What? Why would she ask you to do that?"

Roger stared at him strangely. "She said that she was going to be out of town for a few months. 'Course, I just assumed you were going to be with her."

"A few months?" The words hit Matthew like a ton of bricks. "Did she say where she was going?"

Roger blinked. "Nah, it's none of my business. 'Course I did find it strange that most of your stuff was glued to the furniture, and the amount of duct tape everywhere."

"It was, uh, just a little experiment we used to do."

Roger scratched his head as his disbelieving eyes studied Matthew. "Uh-huh. Well, like I said, it's none of my business." He turned and headed back to finish trimming the hedges.

Matthew glanced up at the house for a long time, but then decided not to go in. What was the point? That part of his life was over now.

He slid back behind the wheel of his car. Again, his objective was to just drive, clear his head, and wait for the pain in his heart to ease. Seven hours later, he arrived in Rochester and on the doorstep of his oldest brother.

"Matthew?" Scott stepped out of his palatial redbrick Colonial. The brothers were the same height and build, despite the ten-year difference between them. "What are you doing here? Do you know what time it is?"

Actually, he didn't. He glanced down at his watch and couldn't believe it was midnight. "I'm sorry. I guess I should have called."

"Are you all right?" Scott glanced over his brother's shoulder to peer at the car. "Is Chanté with you?"

Matthew's heart squeezed as if it was encased in a steel vise. "No. Chanté isn't with me." He couldn't bring himself to meet Scott's gaze.

"Oh." Scott fell silent and then seemed to remember they still stood on the front porch. "I'm sorry. Come on in." He stepped back and allowed Matthew entry and then closed the door behind him.

"Daddy?"

Matthew turned and lit up when he spotted his five-year-old nephew, Bobby, standing in the center of the staircase in his pajamas. "Oh, I'm sorry, li'l man. I didn't mean to wake you up."

"Uncle Matt!" Bobby flew down the rest of the stairs and launched into Matthew's arms.

Matthew spun his nephew around and enjoyed the soft scent of baby powder.

"All right, Mini-Me. Time to go back to bed," Scott said. "It's late."

"But I want to play with Uncle Matt."

"C'mon. You know the rules. I'd already let you stay up an extra half hour to play another game of Deadly Dragons. So say good-night."

Bobby poked out his bottom lip and looked as if he wanted to cry.

"How about if I tuck you in?" Matt said, but shot a questioning gaze over at his brother.

"Yeah! Can he, Daddy?"

Scott drew a deep breath and pretended like his son was asking for a huge favor. "All right, but you have to promise to go straight to sleep."

"I promise!"

"He's all yours." Scott slapped Matthew on the back. "I'll go start us some coffee. Something tells me we're going to need it."

"Black, no sugar," Matthew reminded him and then held Bobby over his head and pretended he was rocket blasting up the stairs.

Bobby giggled the entire way and when tucked securely into his Spider-Man sheets, he used his big, puppy dog brown eyes to get his favorite uncle to read him a story. "Are you going to be here when I wake up?" Bobby asked, yawning.

"That's looking to be a strong possibility."

"So we can play race cars?"

"Yes. We can play race cars. Now go to sleep." He leaned down and kissed Bobby's forehead. "Good night."

"'Night." Bobby yawned, rolled over and went to sleep.

At the door, Matthew stalled and cast another glance over at the bed. He sighed at the curled bundle and slid on an effortless smile.

When he finally returned downstairs, his brother awaited him at the kitchen island.

"I started without you," Scott said, lifting his half cup of coffee. "Which story did he get you to read?"

"Harold and the Purple Crayon." Matthew smiled. "You know your son well."

Scott smiled. "It's not hard. PlayStation, race cars and bedtime stories are his favorites."

"You're a lucky man, bro," Matthew said, reaching for his coffee cup.

"I used to be luckier," Scott said solemnly.

Witnessing his brother's faraway look, Matthew knew Scott was remembering his deceased wife, Barbara. It'd been nearly four years since she was killed in a car accident.

"So tell me what brings you into my neck of the woods at this ungodly hour."

Matthew drew a deep breath, wondering where he should begin.

"Maybe I should ask what you did? Forget an anniversary or a birthday?"

"I wish it were that simple." He sighed and took another sip of coffee.

"I know that sigh. This must be serious." After another beat of silence, Scott added, "C'mon. Spit it out. It's not good for us psychologists to keep things bottled up. Do you know we have the highest rate of suicides?"

"Yeah, my wife brought that to my attention." Taking a deep breath, Matthew finally spilled his guts. Scott had been aware of Matthew and Chanté's attempts to have a child, but his expression reflected his shock at hearing the shenanigans that transpired between the couple in the passing months.

When Matthew finished, Scott remained rooted on his stool, staring at his brother.

"Are you crazy?"

Matthew sighed, wondering what made him think Scott would ever understand his point of view.

"You mean to tell me that you walked out on your marriage because you couldn't have it all? The wife and the two point five children?"

"I know it sounds bad."

"You damn right it does."

"Look, Scott. It's complicated." Matthew jumped to his feet and paced. "Chanté and I planned every detail of our lives—careers, family and retirement. Then suddenly she starts making decisions without me and the next thing I know, all the plans are flying out the window."

"Plans? You want to talk to me about plans?" Scott stood and met his brother's direct gaze. "Barbara and

I planned to grow old together. We planned for Bobby to have brothers and sisters and to raise them together."

Matthew dropped his gaze and returned to his stool.

"What are you doing, Matt? You love Chanté. I can hear it in your voice when you say her name. It's in your eyes when you're thinking about her. Fine, she should have told you about the pills, but given what you told me, you didn't exactly create an environment where she could tell you.

"So you and Chanté may never have biological children. Adopt. There are plenty of children in the world who need good, stable homes with parents who'll shower them with love. If that doesn't work out then fine—it's just you and Chanté. Would that really be so bad—to be condemned to a life with the woman you love?

"I envy you. I lost my soul mate. I can't believe that you're so willing to walk away from yours."

Matthew hung his head—ashamed that that was exactly what he was about to do. There was no other woman like Chanté. No one excited his passion, or drove him up the wall like she did. For the last few months he'd tried to purge her out of his system, but nothing had worked. He had waited years to start his family when he had all he needed in Chanté. "I've been a fool."

"Damn right you have," Scott grumbled.

Matthew was on his feet again, pacing. "But what am I going to do? She's filed for a divorce. I don't know where she is. She probably won't ever speak to me again."

"You know, whenever Barbara and I had a bad fight, she would always take off to her parents', her second comfort zone."

"Texas," Matthew said, and then glanced up at his brother. "You know, I think you may be a better psychologist than I am."

"I like to think so." Scott clapped his hand across Matthew's back. "Now stop being an egotistical, self-righteous son of a bitch and go get your wife."

Chapter 24

An excited Chanté stared wide-eyed at the ultrasound monitor. At only twelve weeks gestation, she wasn't able to see much, but what she could make out filled her with an indescribable joy.

"I wish Matthew was here right now."

Her mother reached over and squeezed her hand. "You know, we could call him."

At the combination of joy and pain, a tear skipped down Chanté's face. "I will, but just not right now."

"You mean after the divorce?"

Chanté didn't answer but returned her attention to the monitor. For the past three days, her mother and father dropped more than a few hints on how they felt about divorce. The reaction surprised her, because her father once viewed Matthew as unworthy of his daughter's hand. Of course, he felt the same way about every boy who'd ever shown the slightest interest in her.

Every prom, dance or social event always fell on Leonard Morris's gun-cleaning night. When she'd finally introduced Matthew to her parents, her father had enough artillery laid out to outfit a small army. However, Matthew gained respect when he sat down, rolled up his sleeves and proceeded to help him clean the guns.

During the car ride home, Chanté smiled at the memory.

"You know, I always did like Matthew," her mother said, completing the two-mile drive back to the house.

"Really?" Chanté said, remembering the sour looks and sharp quips. "I seem to remember you saying we were like oil and vinegar."

Her mother parked the car and turned in her seat. "All right. Not always, but certainly by the time you two tied the knot. He was your intellectual match and he certainly knew how to take on your fiery temper. Two passionate people are destined to throw off sparks every now and then. So what? You made a mistake and he's hurt. He'll calm down."

"I'm not going to beg him to love me."

Her mother reached over and touched her shoulder. "Do you really think he doesn't love you? What do you see when you gaze into his eyes?"

Chanté remembered their time at the Tree of Life Resort, where they'd learned the art of soul gazing. She remembered how his eyes were like powerful magnets pulling at her. She remembered the lightheadedness, and the love. So much love.

Chanté turned and climbed out of the car. When she walked through the screen door of her parents' house, Buddy barked excitedly.

"Great! You made it back home," Leonard thundered and flashed a wide, awkward smile.

"Good Lord, Lenny. Why are you hollering? People down the street know we're home now."

"Oh." He took the chastisement. "Sorry about that."

Alice walked over to him and planted a kiss against his cheek. "We have pictures of the—"

"You know, it's almost four o'clock. We're missing that *Love Doctor* show."

"You want to watch the show?"

Chanté rolled her eyes. She knew exactly what her father was up to, and she couldn't say that she was against watching the show. She missed Matthew with every fiber of her being and now that she'd passed the cursed ten-week mark in her pregnancy, she did long to share this experience with him.

She sat down on the sofa, feeling more confused as the day ticked along. Would she actually carry this baby to term? Would it be a boy or a girl? Would it look like her or Matthew? Boy or girl, she would love for the child to have Matthew's dark, mesmerizing eyes and his smooth complexion.

Swimming lazily through her thoughts, Chanté soon realized her parents were huddled almost near the corner of the room, whispering like a nest of bees.

"What are you guys doing?" She reached for her purse to retrieve the ultrasound pictures. "Dad, do you want to see the—"

"Uh, where's the remote? We better turn that show on before we miss the end," her mother exclaimed as though everyone in the room had gone deaf. "Here it is!" she said, pulling the mighty remote out from the sofa's cushions and clicking on the television.

Instantly, Matthew, handsome as ever in a royal-blue suit, filled her father's beloved sixty-inch screen and seemed to stare directly at Chanté.

"I'd like to thank the audience and the viewers at home for tuning in today," Matthew said. "My goal has been to teach everyone about the powers of forgiveness."

"Humph!" Chanté rolled her eyes and crossed her legs.

"Shhh!" her parents hissed in unison.

Stunned, Chanté blinked and sulkily returned her attention to the television set.

"I'd like to thank my guests, Dr. Margaret Gardner and Dr. Dae Kim from the Tree of Life Resort. I only wish that I'd kept my appointment with you months ago," Matthew said sincerely.

Chanté blinked again and leaned forward in her chair. Matthew had paused and glanced off camera a bit—an uncharacteristic move for him. "I know many of you have by now heard that my wife has filed for a divorce."

The audience "aww"ed at the news.

"I want to take the last few minutes of today's show to talk to you and most importantly to my wife, my soul mate. I decided to reach you this way because I'm not interested in portraying to the world that there is such a thing called a perfect marriage. We go through our ups and downs like everyone else. Sometimes there's pain and hurt and words exchanged that you can never take back, no matter how bad you wish you could. And I wish I could.

"I've known for years through training and experience that you can't plan everything in life. But sometimes it's difficult to get your head and heart aligned. All we can do—all anyone can do—is their best and then just hope for the best. We may never have everything we want in life, but I do want you and only you for the rest of my life. I love you. Won't you please take me back?"

"Oh, my God." Chanté jumped to her feet just as the audience released a thunderous applause. "He said it." She glanced over at her parents. "He loves me! Did you hear that?"

Buddy joined in on her excitement and started barking.

"Yes, baby. We heard. Now what are you going to do?"

"I—I gotta go." She glanced around and snatched up her purse. "I have to get back to New York."

"Are you sure, baby?" her mother asked, walking over to her. "Is this what you truly want?"

"Oh, yes!" Chanté grabbed and hugged her mother. "I love him. I've always loved him."

"I can't tell you how happy I am to hear that."

Stunned, Chanté turned toward the hallway and saw her husband, still dressed in the same blue suit from the day's show and holding a long box. He opened it and inside was a replacement pair of Manolo Blahnik alligator boots.

"What? How?"

"I caught the first plane out of New York after this morning's taping," he said, walking toward her. "Your father was kind enough to hide me in the back room and get you to see the show. Did you mean what you just said? Do you still love me?"

Chanté eased out of her mother's arms and walked on trembling legs toward her husband...and her future. "How could I ever stop loving the father of my child?"

Matthew opened his mouth to speak, but then his wife's words penetrated his brain. The boots fell to the floor. "Child? Do you mean...you're about to...we're about to have a baby?"

"Twelve weeks."

Tears sprang to Matthew's eyes and his arms opened in time to catch his wife when she launched toward him. "Oh, my God. Are we really about to do this?"

"I don't know. But I think we're off to one heck of a start."

Alice and Leonard slid their arms around each other and continued to beam at the loving couple.

He nodded but then added, "No matter what happens, we're in this together for the long haul. Right?"

"Right. No more secrets, duct tape or spiking your breakfast."

"Deal."

Chanté lifted her brows. "You don't have anything to add?"

"Oh." He cleared his throat. "No more chainsaws, cutting up shoes or unwanted dogs."

Buddy barked.

"Except for you, Bud."

"In that case, Dr. Valentine—" Chanté wrapped her arms around Matthew's neck "—I think we're going to make it just fine."

Epilogue

Three years later...

"Welcome back, Mr. and Mrs. Valentine," Dr. Gardner greeted the moment the couple walked through the doors of the Tree of Life Resort. "The Hathaways are already checked in. They informed me you've had another baby since your last visit. Congratulations. Your third, right?"

"Right. Our first girl. Now it's Matthew Jr., Leonard Scott, after my father and Matthew's brother, and the new baby is Victoria." Chanté blushed as she curled into her husband's embrace. "We like to think this place is lucky for us."

"We're here to try for baby number four," Matthew boasted.

"I certainly wish you luck. And I also want to express my gratitude for promoting our resort on your shows. We stay pretty booked throughout the year. We even have a couple of new teachers I believe you know."

"Look, Willy. It's the Valentines," Mable gawked from across the lobby.

The elderly couple rushed over. "Hey, you two love-birds. I hope you are joining our classes in Tao sex." Wilfred beamed his pearly white dentures. "There are quite a few new positions I think you'd get a kick out of."

"New positions? Then count us in." Matthew winked, and then he looked down at his wife. "Maybe we'll get twins this time."

"Honey, I love you, but don't press your luck."

* * * * *

TO LOVE AGAIN

Who can know the
human heart,
a fragile thing at best?
And love, that supernal
spirit forever fuels our quest

As...
Slowly wisdom colors
Memories, clears away
the smoky glass.
Broken dreams restored,
hearts mended, vision
crystal-clear at last.
—*The Book of Counted Joys*

Prologue

"Darling, I'm back!"

Alana Calloway stared, mouth agape, at the tall immaculate figure of her late husband, Michael. Dressed completely in white—an expensive linen suit and Italian loafers to match—one moment he hadn't been there and the next, there he was, smiling at her, displaying dimples in both clean-shaven, pecan-tan colored cheeks. His dark brown eyes held an amused glint and a luminous aura surrounded him.

"I must say," Alana murmured, still awestruck, "you look good for someone who's been dead for a year. What kept you?"

I know I'm losing my mind, she thought, but in case this is real, I want to be able to say I asked at least one intelligent question.

It was in the middle of the night and they were standing in the bedroom of their Daly City home. The hardwood floor gleamed. The furnishings were Scandinavian: spare but artistically pleasing to the eye. A breeze tossed about the sheers at the windows and the piquant fragrance of jasmine filled the air.

Michael walked toward her with his large, brown hands outstretched. Alana's heart skipped a beat. Would he be able to touch her or would his spectral hand pass through her solid form the way they depict ghosts in films? Or would his caress be cold, dead and horrifying?

"I would have been here sooner but it's difficult to get a visa unless you died a saint." He grinned infectiously as he grasped both her hands in his. He was warm, real, alive!

"You've lost weight," he observed, concerned. He looked down into her cognac-colored eyes. "But you're still my beautiful butterfly."

Alana continued to fix him with a disbelieving stare.

"How is this possible?" she cried. "Are you a ghost?" Her eyes devoured him. This may prove to be her last chance to see him. She reached up and touched his face, her hands moving down to his muscular arms, felt through the fabric of the linen suit.

Benevolence shone in his dark eyes.

"I suppose you could say that," he told her lightly. He brought her right hand to his lips, gently kissed the palm. "I don't have much time. These things are tricky at best—visitations, I mean—so I must be swift."

He looked her in the eye, his expression grave.

"Much will be revealed to you in the next few days. Through it all, try to remember that I love you, Lana. I always loved you. But I was only human…"

Suddenly, Alana could no longer feel his touch. It was as though his body had become insubstantial, vaporous. She could still see him although his form was transparent and steadily fading.

"Michael, what's going on?"

Michael shrugged helplessly. He apparently had no control over the occurrence and was as shocked by it as she was.

"My time is up," he said resignedly. His voice sounded as though he was speaking to her from down a well. "Your time is only beginning. Remember me fondly, Lana."

With that, he vanished, leaving Alana standing alone in the middle of the room. Her voluminous nightgown whipped about her slim legs as the formerly light breeze became a gale and the aroma of jasmine grew stronger, over-powering.

"What's happening?" she shouted, her voice's volume small and ineffectual against the howling intensity of the wind-storm.

Chapter 1

Turning over in bed, Alana Calloway looked at the lighted dial of the alarm clock through half-open eyes. She had to get up or she'd be late for her meeting with Margery Devlin. Two days before the Annual Valentine's Day Charity Ball and Margery would be on pins and needles, fussing with last-minute details: making certain her San Francisco mansion was sufficiently replete, being critical of every little transgression, being sure that the appearance of the household staff was immaculate.

Alana wasn't in a festive mood. The one year anniversary of her husband's death was yesterday and she could think of a million other places she'd rather be on Friday, February fourteenth, but Margery was her surrogate mother, and she felt honor bound to be present.

Judging from the sunlight streaming in through the slits in the draperies, the day promised to be bright and clear. That alone buoyed her spirits. She stood and went into the large walk-in closet. Grasping the lapels of a man's navy sports coat, she lovingly fingered the material, then bent her head to breathe in the lingering scent of the woodsy aftershave that permeated it.

Taking the coat off the hanger, she put it on and wrapped her arms around her body. The coat's hem practically fell to her knees because Michael had been at least seven inches taller than Alana. With her eyes closed, she could almost feel his two strong arms holding her against his broad chest. If she concentrated, she could remember the deep timbre of his voice whispering, "Good morning, Lana."

Tears filled her eyes. "Michael," she cried morosely, "what were you doing in an Oakland neighborhood in the middle of the night? And when they ordered you to hand over your money, at gun-point, why didn't you just give it to them and not try to fight them. Couldn't you forego your police training for just one instant? No. You had to fight back. Why couldn't you think of me and how miserable my existence would be without you? Couldn't you think of me? I hate you for leaving me alone like this!"

With a sob, she replaced the coat. Her daily ritual completed, she slowly walked to the kitchen to put on the coffee. While it perked, she took a hot shower. The phone rang as she lathered up. Unwilling to leave the warm shower, she let the machine answer it. She could hear the anxious voice of the caller from the bathroom.

It was Genero, her assistant. "Alana," he said, sounding as though he had been sprinting, "would you please tell your mother that your people perform better when she isn't breathing down our necks? Little-Miss-Hollywood is getting on my last nerve and sister doesn't want to go there."

Alana smiled. Genero and Margery were both high-strung. No wonder they were getting in one another's hair. Genero was the coordinator in her catering business. She was owner and the supervising chef, but Genero made certain her instructions were carried out to the letter. Meticulous to a fault, he was easily flustered and turned into a tyrant when excessive pressure was put on him. Margery knew exactly which buttons to push.

Quickly rinsing off and toweling dry, Alana sat on the bed as she dialed Genero's cellular phone number.

He answered at once. "Hello!"

"Well, *you* sound pleasant," Alana said, laughing.

"Alana, thank God," Genero breathed, his voice softening. "You can't get here fast enough to suit me. Margery is making our lives miserable. Changing recipes. Questioning the staff's abilities. Clovis is wielding his cleaver menacingly. If you love your mother, you'll speak with her at once."

"Put her on," Alana said calmly.

"Alana, where did you ever find this, this person?" Margery demanded imperiously. "I think you ought to—"

"Margery," Alana cut in, "I want you to leave Genero to his work. He knows what he's doing. I would not have left him in charge if he didn't'."

"But—" Margery began.

"Please, Margery. I would like this affair to be the most highly praised fête of the year. Unless you put your trust in me, I don't think we'll be able to pull it off."

"Oh, very well," Margery conceded. "I'll let the little man win this go-round."

"Little!" Alana heard Genero exclaim hotly before Margery hung up.

Sighing heavily, Alana rose and went to the kitchen to pour herself a large cup of java. She had a feeling she was going to need it.

Wrapped in a white terrycloth robe, she stood at the sliding glass door that led out to the balcony of her Pacific Heights apartment. The reflection in the glass was that of an attractive young woman with flawless café-au-lait skin, wavy, coal-black shoulder-length hair, large, wide-spaced, sable-colored eyes with golden flecks in them, a short, pert nose under which was a full mouth with sensual contours.

She occupied the entire top floor of a stately Victorian home owned by a retired University of California English professor, Jonathan Crenshaw. She had lived there for about a year, having taken the converted apartment shortly after Michael's death. She'd been lonely rattling around in their large Daly City home.

Daly City had been ideal for them because it wasn't very far from San Francisco, where Michael worked as a police detective, first class, and Alana had her fledgling catering business. Margery had wanted Alana in San Francisco, where she would have been able to see her on a daily basis. But Michael had balked at the idea, saying that newlyweds needed their space. Alana had felt bad about the decision because since her parents' untimely demise in a head-on car crash ten years ago, Margery was the closest thing she had to kin.

The balcony overhung Jonathan's backyard and offered an unobstructed view of their neighbor's orange clay tile roof. She glanced down and thought she spied Jonathan's silver head below. Opening the sliding glass door and stepping onto the balcony, she placed her coffee cup on the weathered redwood railing and bent over it to call out to him.

"Good morning, Jonathan."

The still handsome septuagenarian beamed at her, revealing dimples in both suntanned cheeks. He removed his big straw hat as he returned her greeting. "Good morning. You look particularly well rested and lovely today. Is there a reason…?"

Eyebrows arched in confusion, Alana said, "What?"

"Someone sent you a beautiful bouquet of red red roses," Jonathan informed her, smiling. "Not wanting to disturb you in case you were sleeping in, I left them outside your door. Is there a new beau in your life?"

"If there is, this is the first I've heard of him," Alana said jokingly. "Roses you say? I can't imagine who would send me roses. No one has sent me flowers since…" She stopped. She was about to say, Michael sent me those orchids on our first anniversary. "Since Godzilla was a lizard," she said instead. That was one of Michael's favorite sayings, meaning a great length of time had passed.

Jonathan laughed and replaced his hat. He squinted

up at her. "Make sure you tell the eternally gorgeous Miss Devlin that her number one fan sends her his best. And I want to hear all about your new beau, my dear." Then as an afterthought added, "Oh, yes, your mail arrived. I put it through the slot in your door."

As Alana went back inside, she glimpsed Jonathan's tall, fit figure bent over his beloved roses, pruning away the unwanted growth which would in turn leave room for the flowers to thrive.

She went into the living room to scoop the mail up off the floor. There were a couple of bills, a lingerie catalog, a magazine and a letter written on fine linen stationery. There was no return address on the letter and her own address had been typewritten. Tearing it open, she gingerly unfolded the letter, expecting to read a short missive from a close friend. Instead, the note read:

My darling Butterfly... It's time you learned to love again... It's time you learned to love again.

Alana's hands trembled as she reread the note. The breath caught in her throat, and she found her legs wouldn't hold her up. She gratefully sat down on the Shaker bench which stood near the front door. This is some cruel joke, she thought, it has to be. She looked down at the paper, then in a fit of anger, balled it up and tossed it into the wastebasket next to the bench. Who would want to hurt her this badly? Reading Michael's personal endearment for her evoked bitter sweet memories. No one, absolutely no one on this earth, called her "butterfly" except her dead husband.

A chill ran down her spine. She stood and retrieved the piece of paper. She would make a detour before driving to Nob Hill. She'd phone Margery from the Caravan and tell her she was going to be delayed; but first, she had to get dressed.

Ten minutes later she was heading out the door attired in a midnight-blue raw silk pantsuit. Tailored to fit her slim, slightly muscular figure, it accentuated her trim waist and nicely rounded derriere, but she had not chosen it because she knew it heightened her sex appeal—she'd chosen it because it had been within easy reach when she'd gone into the closet in search of something to wear. In the last year Alana hadn't put much thought into ways in which to attract the opposite sex. As far as she was concerned, she was still in mourning.

Just outside the door she nearly tripped over the huge bouquet of roses. She'd completely forgotten Jonathan had told her they were there. She bent to scoop up the fragrant gift. Inhaling the sweet aroma, she sighed. She hoped that whomever had sent them wasn't connected to the letter. She needed something positive to attach her emotions to today.

Removing the card, she read: *Love is a spirit longing to be free. Fear is the jailer and faith holds the key.* It was signed, Your Secret Admirer.

Alana held the roses close as though they were a loved one she was giving a warm embrace. A satisfied smile brightened her features making her heart-shaped, brown face appear childlike, almost ethereal. The flowers had to be from Nico. Who else could make her feel so wonderful with just a few words written from his heart?

She turned on her heels to take the flowers into the apartment. She was glad she'd made up her mind to go see him this morning. Not simply because she needed his help but because she also needed his strength.

Sunglasses on, purse firmly in hand, she stepped back out of the house on Lombard Street into another beautiful San Francisco morning. As she approached the champagne-colored Caravan with her company's Vesta insignia on the side: a painting of a lovely black woman dressed in a toga, a few grains of golden wheat in one hand and an egg beater in the other, she pointed and pressed the remote keyless entry button.

She slipped onto the leather seat, fastened her seat belt and turned the key in the ignition. She sat there a moment as the engine warmed up.

Reaching down for the cellular phone, she absently dialed Margery's number. What could she say to her that would not make her worry needlessly? Margery, being an actress, was given to reacting dramatically to any sort of change in plans. Alana was going to be delayed? Why? She was going to drop by the police station to see Nico? Why?

Alana found herself wishing anyone other than Margery would answer the phone. She was relieved when Maria, Margery's personal assistant, answered in her Spanish-accented voice. "Hello, Devlin residence. Maria Martinez…"

"Hi, Maria."

"Alana, where *are* you? You know how Margery

gets when things don't go her way and right now she's arguing with Genero about the menu. He tried to tell her that all the food has already been purchased for the menu you all settled on months ago but she doesn't want to listen."

"I'll be there in about forty-five minutes. I have to swing by the police station for a few minutes first. Hang in there, Maria."

"You know me," Maria said, laughing suddenly. "Margery can growl all she wants to. I'll keep my cool. Are you certain nothing's wrong, Alana? You sound peculiar."

Alana supposed since she and Maria had been friends a long time, the other woman could detect subtle changes in her tone of voice. They were around the same age, Maria having recently turned twenty-eight. At the age of eighteen, Maria had come to work for Margery soon after her family came to the United Stated from Mexico. Alana had just moved in with Margery during that time period and the two became fast friends. Alana had been a bridesmaid in Maria's huge Catholic wedding in Santa Clara and had held her hand when Maria had been in labor with Mariana, now five. Carlos, Maria's husband of seven years, had been out of town on business and hadn't been able to make it back home on time.

"I'll tell you all about it when I see you," Alana promised her friend. "I should be there at around eleven."

"Okay," Maria reluctantly agreed. "I'll give Margery your message. See you later."

"All right. Thanks, Maria."

* * *

Eight-fifty Bryant Street was bustling with activity, even at nine fifty on a Wednesday morning. The San Francisco Police Department never closed. Keeping the peace in a city that spans one hundred thirty square miles and was the home of over seven hundred thousand people was a daunting task.

Nicholas Setera, one of the city's finest, was busy taking down the statement of a drug addict he and his partner, Jack Pullman, had arrested twice before. It wasn't the junkie they wanted, it was his supplier. Pete Bodis, alias Peanut, committed burglary to support his drug habit. He was arrested this time for a smash-and-grab. He threw a rock through the window of a pawn shop and stole a portable TV.

Nico cleared his throat and looked at Peanut over the computer monitor. His brown eyes were stern as he shoved the arrest form across the desk for the addict to sign. "You must like our accommodations, Peanut. You keep coming back for more."

Peanut was slumped down on his chair. His brown, pockmarked face wore a sullen expression and he looked like he hadn't had a decent meal or a bath in weeks. He sat up, preparing to sign the form.

Nico slammed his hand down hard on the desk, atop the form. "You're pitiful. Don't you give a damn about anything anymore?"

Peanut's eyes widened with fear and his hands dropped to his lap. Oh God, he thought, Setera has that look in his eyes. He knew he wasn't going to be taken to his cell without a sermon. He'd gladly spend twice the allotted time behind bars if only he didn't have to hear what a mess he'd made of his life. That was cruel and unusual punishment.

The muscles worked in Nico's strong, square jaw as he eyed Peanut. "How long have you been on that crap? Three, four years? Your first arrest, not by yours truly, was in ninety-four. Before that you were an orderly at San Francisco General. You had a wife and two kids. Whatever became of them? Do you ever see your kids?"

Peanut didn't reply. His eyes were riveted on his hands.

"You're twenty-nine and you look fifty-nine," Nico stated flatly. He ran a hand over his short, curly, jet-black hair. His heart wasn't in this. He knew Peanut was just as much a victim as he was a criminal. Nine times out of ten if a man hadn't become an addict, he would have been a law-abiding citizen. Who knew what circumstances in his life had induced him to try narcotics as an anesthesia to his problems. However, Nico also knew he'd be remiss if he didn't try to reach the addict on some level. A life wasted is one life too many.

"It's too late for me," Peanut said in a voice so low that Nico had been unable to hear him.

"What?" Nico asked evenly.

Peanut met Nico's gaze. "I'm a dead man." He tried to moisten his cracked lips. "Ain't no hope for me."

"There's always hope, Peanut. I've known addicts in worse shape than you are who turned their lives around. You can do it. It will be the hardest thing you've ever done in your life, but it's not impossible. I'll help you as much as I can. I have friends who work with addicts. They can help you get clean, if you really want to be clean."

Nico's last statement hung in the air. He waited, hoping that the decimated human being sitting across from him would respond positively. Even a nod in the affirmative would be a step in the right direction.

"How?" Peanut asked plaintively, his voice cracking. Unshed tears sat in his bloodshot eyes.

Rising, Nico bent over the desk and grasped Peanut's hand, firmly shaking it. "One step at a time, my brother, one step at a time."

He grinned as he sat back down and began typing a message to John Goldman, director of the South Market Rehabilitation Center. John was a good friend, and though it was difficult to find space for all the addicts who needed a place to dry out nowadays, he felt certain John could pull off a miracle. Nicholas Setera was a man who believed in miracles.

By the time Alana reached Bryant Street, she had almost talked herself out of seeking Nico's help. The last time they'd been together, about a month ago, they hadn't parted on the best of terms. In fact, Alana had thrown him out of her apartment.

It had begun innocently enough. Both Alana and Nico were free for the evening. He was off duty and she didn't have any parties to cater, so she'd invited him over for a home-cooked meal.

Before Michael's death, Nico was a frequent guest in their home. She and Michael and Nico and whomever the woman of the hour was would often double date.

They liked to dance and on weekends went to some of the trendier San Francisco night spots, sometimes closing the places. But they were also the type of people who could enjoy a quiet evening at home barbecuing steaks and playing bid whist.

Michael and Nico had been partners for five years. They worked Vice. Their personalities were complementary: where Michael was hotheaded, Nico was a calming force. When Alana met Michael, she was welcomed into their group. So it wasn't surprising that she grew to love and admire Nico like the brother she'd never been blessed with.

Alana had prepared arroz con pollo, Nico's favorite main course. When she opened the door to greet him, the aroma of the Cuban dish assailed his nostrils. As if under a spell, he handed her the dozen red roses he'd brought her and headed straight back to the kitchen.

Alana shut the door, a smile on her face. She was always pleased whenever someone reacted favorably to her cooking. In the kitchen, she placed the flowers in a vase as she watched Nico examine the contents of the pots.

"Mmm..." he said rapturously. "Are you hiding my mama somewhere on the premises?"

His downward sloping, velvety-brown bedroom eyes regarded Alana with newfound respect.

"I'm innocent, Officer," Alana told him, grinning.

Placing the top back on the pot, Nico turned to take her into his arms. He danced her around the tiny kitchen.

Alana laughed happily. "Okay, I admit I *did* get the recipe from Mama Setera."

"I knew I smelled Cubano magic in those pots," Nico told her triumphantly.

Nico was Cuban-American of African descent. He and his parents were among the hordes of Cubans who, because of poverty and political persecution, fled the island nation in the early eighties. He had worked hard to claim his share of the American Dream, earning a bachelor's degree in criminal justice, serving two years on the Greater Miami police force.

Five years ago, when he was thirty, he joined the San Francisco police department. He made detective two years later.

Now, he reached for the vase that Alana was still holding in her arms and placed it on the counter. He then hugged her with gusto. "You have made me so happy," he said, his deep voice lapsing into a Spanish accent as it did when he was angry or excited, or in this case, ecstatic.

Their eyes were locked. "It only took a phone call," Alana said. "Mama Setera was pleased to know that her baby boy is being well fed so far away from home."

Alana should have known something had changed between them by the passionate expression in Nico's warm brown eyes. However, in the heat of the moment, she misread his signals and shrugging out of his embrace, she pleaded the need to get back to preparing dinner and pressed him into service by asking him to set the table. Something to keep his hands busy.

The dinner conversation was warm and animated

as always. Nico declared that the arroz con pollo was *"Muy delicioso."*

After dinner, as they stood side-by-side at the sink washing dishes, Alana suddenly felt the fine hairs on the back of her neck stand at attention. Admittedly it was a singularly erotic sensation, but it unnerved her to realize her close proximity to Nico was causing the reaction. She glanced at him sideways. He was watching her intently, his sexy eyes speaking volumes. Her heart thumped excitedly. He smiled. She flushed. Her golden-brown skin was tinged red from her neck to her ears.

She looked away first, going to the pantry to get a clean dish towel. She didn't really need one, but the trip afforded her a few seconds' respite from his overpowering sexuality.

When she turned back around, Nico was still watching her. She wondered if it was possible for a man to seduce a woman with just his eyes. She felt herself weakening under his gaze.

"Would you excuse me?" she said a bit breathlessly. She handed him the dish towel. "You start drying. I'll be right back."

In the bathroom she splashed cold water on her face and neck, hoping it would cool the embarrassing heat that threatened to consume her. Her big brown eyes held a frightened expression in them. She was *attracted* to Nicholas Setera. Her husband's best friend. *Her* best friend, for God's sake.

Okay, to be honest, she'd always been attracted to him. The man was a splendid specimen. But that was simply aesthetics. She could admire a work of art without becoming emotionally attached to it. Couldn't she?

She sat on the toilet seat and tried to reason her way through her dilemma. She missed intimacy. It had been nearly a year since Michael was taken away from her, and hence it had been a very long time since she'd been with a man. Not that she missed sex so much. It was just that she and Michael shared a very passionate sex life, and once you've had that, to be totally bereft of it makes one even more aware of what you were no longer getting.

Being in Nico's presence was a constant reminder. He exuded sensuality. No, the man fairly reeked of it. It was present in the shape of those bedroom eyes and the sooty lashes that framed them. It was in the way his wide, mobile mouth turned up at the corners when he smiled. The play of the muscles in his back when he was walking out her door. The symmetry of his long tanned body. The strength of his hands. Even his feet with the neatly manicured nails and graceful arches were sexy. She made a mental note not to go to the beach with him anymore. In warm weather the beach was one of their favorite places to frolic. Now, however, she didn't think she had the willpower to watch him come out of the water, his trunks clinging to him. What was wrong with her? She had to gain control over her thoughts before she returned to the kitchen and Nico's scrutiny.

"Alana! Are you all right?" Nico asked, knocking on the door.

"I'm fine. I'm just reapplying my makeup," Alana lied, attempting to stall for time.

"Don't do that on my account, I think you're beautiful without it," Nico said innocently enough.

Beautiful? He'd never called her beautiful before. Wasn't there a law against using that word to describe a pal? "You look…decent" or "You won't frighten small children," were acceptable. But beautiful? Nah. He'd definitely crossed the line of decency.

Livid, Alana quickly dried her face, came out of the bathroom and plowed right into Nico, who was standing in the hallway. Nico reached out to steady her on her feet, and she angrily jerked her arm free of his hold.

"You should be ashamed of yourself," Alana said accusingly, storming past him.

Puzzled, Nico placed a hand on his chest as if to say, "Who me?"

"You know what I'm talking about," Alana tossed over her shoulder.

"Ay!" Nico exclaimed in exasperation as he caught up with her in the middle of the living room.

They faced one another. Nico stood with his arms crossed at his chest, looking down into Alana's upturned face. He sighed. She impatiently tapped her right foot on the carpet, awaiting his apology.

Nico's voice was low and controlled when he spoke. "You are…" rolling his r's, "upset with me because I think you're beautiful?" he said incredulously.

Alana tried to discern whether he was actually oblivious to his effect on her or if he was being obtuse. His eyes raked over her, sending her temperature skyward once more.

"That's what I'm talking about," she said, backing

away from him. "You've got to stop looking at me like that."

Nico had grinned at her. His sexy eyes looked her up and down. "Like what?"

"Like you're the Big Bad Wolf and I'm Little Red Riding Hood, that's what."

Nico closed the space between them in a couple of steps. Grasping her by the shoulders, he pulled her hard against his chest. For a millisecond, Alana thought of resisting him, but although her mind was strong, her body was decidedly weaker.

She fit easily in his embrace. At that moment she could have been convinced that she'd been born to be in his arms.

"Don't be afraid of your feelings, Lana. It's me, Nico. I would never hurt you," Nico said in her ear. *"Querida. Mi corazon."*

Alana, being fairly fluent in Spanish, knew what those words meant: Darling. My heart. She didn't want to think about what his words would portend though. For the time being, she was giddy with happiness, completely lost in the sensual quality of their bodies touching.

One of his hands was at the base of her spine, igniting sparks of sexual longing that she'd held in check for far too long. His other hand was in her hair, at the back of her neck, gently massaging her there.

"Te quiero, Lana," he murmured huskily. I love you. I want you. They meant the same thing in the midst of passion. Nico bent his head to kiss her, and she met his mouth with the full force of her emotions. A little gasp

escaped from between her lips as they parted to allow him access.

He was gentle, not wanting to be too aggressive. Yet he was thorough, exploring her with the intensity of a lover with more than kissing on his mind. It was foreplay on the most intimate level.

The hand that had been caressing the back of her neck moved downward to the hem of her blouse, then, to rest on her hips. Their bodies pressed closer, and Alana's five-feet seven-inch frame wrapped itself around his six feet. Without missing a beat, they walked crablike over to the couch and fell onto it, Alana on top of him.

That's when she felt his arousal, and her feverish mind registered what she was doing: making out on her living room couch with her husband's best friend. She hastily got up off of him, straightening her blouse as she did so.

"Oh, my God, Nico. This can't happen. We can't do this. It isn't right."

Nico got to his feet. After tucking in his shirt, he looked into her eyes. "Lana, this may not be the best time to tell you this, but I've been in love with you for a very long time. At least two years before Michael was killed. I would never have told you if Michael had lived, God rest his soul, but Michael is no longer with us."

He stood close to her, his hand on her arm. His warm brown eyes were pleading as he continued, "I know you love me, Lana. I've seen it in the way you look at me. And tonight, when we touched as lovers do, I felt the power of your desire. Please don't make me wait any longer. I need you."

"I need…" Alana began, but couldn't finish. What *did* she need? To make love to Nico with such abandon that all the pain of the last thirteen months would be forgotten…if only for one night? That wouldn't be fair to either of them.

"I need time to think this through," she said at last. Her large brown eyes were filled with remorse. She knew she was hurting him, but it was better to give herself time to decide what her true feelings for him were than to jump into a relationship and find out later that he'd only been a convenient stand-in for Michael. She was too fond of Nico to use him in that manner.

Sighing, Nico allowed his arms to fall resignedly at his sides. He walked over to the door and placed his right hand on the doorknob. His eyes were on her face. "Are you throwing me out?" There was a glint of humor in his brown depths.

"I'm throwing you out," Alana confirmed, unable to hold back a gentle smile.

"Forever?" he said. A dimple appeared in his left cheek.

"You're the best friend I have," Alana replied honestly. She frowned. "Of course not forever."

Nico opened the door and turned to look back at her as though he was trying to commit her present facial expression to memory. "I won't phone you until you contact me," he promised. "I love you, Lana."

"I love you," Alana returned.

He left without another backward glance.

Chapter 2

After Peanut was taken to a holding cell, Nico went to the officer's lounge to get himself a cup of decaffeinated coffee. He didn't drink the real stuff because, at the end of a long day, it left his nerves jagged around the edges—hence making it nearly impossible to get a good night's rest.

As he walked back into the outer office, a large, open room that was the workplace of the dedicated men and women who comprised the Vice squad, he saw Alana coming through the door. He nearly spilled his coffee as he spun on his heels and went back into the lounge. Another officer, Eric Bilkis, a big, burly redhead was coming out of the lounge at that instant and collided with Nico.

"Hey, man, haven't you ever heard of turn signals?" Eric joked.

"Sorry, Red. There's a lady out there I'm not keen on seeing, if you know what I mean," Nico told him.

"You bachelors," Red said, grinning. "Now if you treated a lady like a lady should be treated, you wouldn't be hiding in lounges."

He craned his neck, looking out over the office. "Which one is she? The blonde at Gardner's desk? The brunette talking to Brewster?"

"No," Nico replied, his eyes on Alana's face. She didn't look happy. She was probably there to tell him to stay out of her life. He couldn't bear to hear those words coming from her mouth. "It's the beautiful lady in the blue suit."

"You need your head examined, my man," Red said as he watched Alana with admiration. Then, "Hey, she looks familiar. I know I've seen her before. Wait a minute. Isn't she Michael Calloway's widow?"

"Yes," Nico hesitantly admitted.

"You dog!" Red guffawed. "You need to be hiding."

"Get your mind out of the gutter, Red," Nico warned through clenched teeth. "I hold that woman in the highest esteem and would be willing to fight anyone who doesn't."

Eyebrows arched in surprise, Red said, "Oh, it's like that, is it? Well, okay, it's about time you took the plunge, Setera. No more making us married guys looks like wimps because we jump when our wives say jump. Now you've got a ring through your nose. I'm liking this. Maybe I should go tell the little lady where you are. You'd have more privacy in here than out there."

"That's quite all right," Nico said. "I'll go to her."

He took a good swig of his coffee, poured the rest of it down the sink, then tossed the empty container into the trash. Mentally steeling himself, he left the lounge with a smiling Red looking after him, giving him the thumbs-up sign.

That was the problem with being friends with so many of my co-workers, Nico thought. They're always giving me unsolicited advice. Not that he wouldn't have had the nerve to face Alana without the prodding. After seeing the expression on her face, the blatant fear, he wouldn't have made it through the day without finding out what was on her mind.

A modicum of his own anxiety dissipated when Alana turned, saw him, and smiled at him. Perhaps she hadn't come to lower the boom after all.

She approached him in a rush and fell into his open arms. Her full mouth was turned up in a sensual smile. "I was beginning to wonder where you were. I thought that maybe you'd gone undercover."

Her brown eyes were searching his face. "You wouldn't do that without informing me, would you?"

"No, Alana," Nico said quietly. His voice, alone, assured her.

Relieved, Alana sighed. "Thanks for the roses. They were beautiful and the poem, too." She looked deeply into his eyes. "I missed you."

"I missed you," Nico returned the sentiment. He hugged her tightly, not caring that they'd become the center of attention in the busy office. "How have you been?"

"Lonely. There were many times I'd pick up the

phone to call you and replaced the receiver because I still have so many unanswered questions. And now this…"

Alana reached into her shoulder bag and retrieved the letter she'd received in the morning's mail. She handed it to Nico, who read it.

"Butterfly was Michael's pet name for me," Alana explained. "He called me that because of—"

"A butterfly shaped birthmark you have on your bottom," Nico supplied effortlessly.

Alana's smile faded. She felt her cheeks grow hot. "He told you something that personal?" she whispered.

"You'd be surprised by what partners talk about on a stakeout," Nico said, taking her by the hand. "Let's take a walk, shall we?"

As he passed his desk, he paused to remove his jacket from the hat tree near it. As a detective he wasn't required to wear a uniform, and today was wearing a tailored blue suit with a crisp, white, long-sleeved, buttoned-down shirt that he'd rolled up at the sleeves. He unrolled the sleeves, buttoning them at the wrists, and slipped into the jacket with a little assist from Alana.

They went outside, around the side of the building, and found a wooden bench in the shade of a palm tree. Sitting down, Nico regarded her with a concerned look in his eyes.

"When did you get this?"

"It was in today's mail," Alana replied.

"It has a Los Angeles postmark. Whom do you know in L.A.?"

"I have a few acquaintances in the business in Los Angeles," Alana said. "And then there's Bree…"

"No," Nico said with conviction. "Bree wouldn't do this."

"I agree," Alana said. "If this had come from Bree, she would have signed her name with a flourish. She and Georgie have both told me they think it's time I started seeing someone." Twins, Briane and Georgette Shaw were Alana's oldest and dearest friends. They had grown up together.

"The L.A. postmark doesn't have to mean it came from someone in Los Angeles, just that it was mailed there. Someone close by could have had a friend mail it from L.A.," Nico observed.

"So you believe it's meant to frighten me, and that we should be looking for someone with a sinister agenda?"

"No, no," Nico said quickly. "First of all, who but an acquaintance of yours or Michael's would know his pet name for you? I believe it's a practical joke. Their using Michael's endearment for you was a tad much, but maybe it was simply an attention-grabbing device."

Alana agreed with Nico's reasoning, but something else occurred to her and she wondered if he'd also thought of it.

"Nico, those unanswered questions I referred to earlier, maybe you can help me answer a few of them."

Nico knew where she was going. They'd discussed it before, and he'd always steered her away from it. But now, after everything that had happened between them, he wasn't so inclined to protect his dead partner from Alana's probing questions. He couldn't hide the truth from her forever. And now he had a stake in the outcome.

He frowned as he glanced down into her upturned face.

"You're not going to bring up your suspicions about Michael being unfaithful again, are you?"

"The events leading up to his death just do not make sense to me, Nico. What was he doing in an Oakland neighborhood at three o'clock in the morning? Also, why did he tell me he was going to a poker game? I haven't met anyone yet who could corroborate that lie. And another thing: for months before his death Michael was drawing away from me. He was cold, abrasive. He was like a man with a lot on his mind, things he definitely didn't want to share with his wife. I swear, Nico. I think he was cheating on me."

Nico grasped one of her hands, squeezing it gently. "Alana, I know Michael loved you." Looking into her eyes, he continued. "You say he was secretive, distant, he snapped at you for no reason at all. Maybe he was involved in something he shouldn't have been, but it didn't have to be an illicit affair. He could have been doing something illegal."

Michael being on the take was more difficult for Alana to believe than his having an affair. The Michael she knew was honest and steadfast. The product of a broken home, he seemed to value his home life all the more for it. A man who had never known his own father, he often talked of being a parent, a good parent, to his and Alana's future children. He was a handsome man. She imagined women threw themselves at him. His resolve could have weakened.

"Do you have any evidence to back up these allegations?" Alana asked of Nico's comment about her husband.

"Do *you* have any evidence to back up your suspicions?" Nico countered.

Standing, Alana took the slip of paper with the message on it out of his hand. She shoved it deep into her shoulder bag. "No, but I plan to get some," she replied, looking down at him, her dark eyes determined.

Nico rose also. "And how are you going to go about doing that?"

"Using photos of Michael, I'm going to canvass the neighborhood until someone comes forward and talks to me," Alana informed him. "A cop got killed in their neighborhood. Maybe someone saw something and was afraid to talk to the police about it. Maybe they won't be as reluctant to talk to me."

She slung her bag on her shoulder, preparing to leave.

Grabbing her by the arm, Nico turned her around to face him. "Sweetheart, that's a bad idea. That neighborhood has seen its share of violence. There is no way I'm going to let you do something so foolhardy."

Sending him a challenge with her eyes, Alana said, "And how do you suppose you're going to stop me?"

"I'll handcuff you to your bed if I have to," Nico answered. The image proved too enticing. Clearing his mind, Nico frowned at her. "I'll help you," he said at last. "If you have to know what Michael was doing before his death, I'll find out for you."

Smiling, Alana was pleased Nico hadn't called her bluff. There was no way she would have done what she'd threatened to do. Thank God she knew him so well. She had been counting on his deep sense of honor and duty to come to her rescue. "I'd appreciate your help," she said, meeting his gaze. "But I'm coming along for the ride." She offered him her hand to shake on it. Nico reluctantly took it. "I'm your new partner, Detective," she told him.

Nico held on to her hand as he pulled her close against him. "Not so fast, there are a few rules the junior partner must abide by because if she doesn't, the boss—and that's me—will call the whole thing off."

"I'm listening," Alana said, her warm breath against his cheek.

"We're in this together. We make decisions together. You have to promise me that you won't do anything without thinking it through. No going off half-cocked. You got me?"

"Yes," Alana said softly. She wished he would release her because his nearness was doing crazy things to her libido. Their eyes met and held.

"Now that you know the rules, here is my stipulation for offering my help. When this is over and you know, once and for all, why Michael was behaving strangely just before his death, you and I will settle things between us, Alana."

"Agreed," Alana breathed.

On tiptoe, she planted a sisterly kiss on his cheek. Nico, however, caught her by the shoulders and soundly kissed her on the mouth. "I didn't promise to play fair," he murmured against her ear.

He released her and Alana stumbled backward, turning the heel over on her right pump. Straightening up, she grinned at him. "I'm fine," she assured him. "Okay. Call me when you're ready to get started. The sooner, the better. If I'm not at home, I'll be at Margery's."

"I'll do that," Nico said, smiling. "Drive carefully."

"I don't know," Maria said, exasperated. "She wouldn't say. She just said she was going by the police station, and she'd explain everything when she arrives. *El fin.*"

She turned and walked out of the room, leaving her inquisitors looking at each other with questioning expressions on their faces.

"What do you suppose Alana is up to?" Margery asked of her best friend, romance novelist, Antoinette Shaw.

Toni frowned, causing wrinkles to appear in her smooth brow. "You worry entirely too much about Alana. She isn't a child any longer."

"I agree. If left to her own devices, Alana will get over her grief soon enough," Genero spoke up. He sat back on the overstuffed chair in Margery's elegantly appointed bedroom. The three of them had gone upstairs to question Maria about Alana's message, away from the prying eyes of the myriad workers downstairs.

"She could be dropping by the police station to make up with Nico after their misunderstanding," Toni offered reasonably. "Alana isn't one to hold a grudge."

"That would be fabulous, wouldn't it?" Margery enthused, rising from her comfortable position on the bed. She was wearing one of her silk jogging suits. It was aquamarine with one bold fuchsia stripe down the front of it. Petite at five-three, she always wore three-inch heels. Today she was wearing a pair of white leather backless sandals by her favorite Italian designer. On a woman of lesser style and panache, the outfit would look ridiculous, but on Margery the combination was stunning. She wore her black hair in a short style, swept away from her lovely heart-shaped face.

"That they should finally succumb to their feelings for one another would be ideal," Toni readily agreed.

Antoinette Shaw was quite the opposite of Margery where physical attributes were concerned. They were both forty-eight, however, Margery, who was in the limelight, never discussed her age. If pressed, she'd say, with complete sincerity, "Thirty-nine and holding." Whereas, Toni, who was an ex-activist, being involved in the Civil Rights Movement in the sixties and a vocal opponent of the Vietnam War, was a realist and approached aging with both eyes open. Personally, she thought she'd never looked or felt better. She was statuesque, at five-eight, and had a voluptuous figure. Not overweight but definitely not under. She had high cheekbones, large, very dark, almost black eyes and a full mouth which she'd always used to full effect. She got her skin coloring, a creamy golden brown, from her mother who was of French Creole and African-American ancestry.

"Love will prevail," Genero said, smoothing a shiny lock of hair from his face. He had the indigo skin of his forebears, who had been West Indian born. He never discussed his lineage. It wasn't that he was ashamed of being Jamaican. On the contrary, he was quite proud of his people. It was just that he'd found, since coming to America, that people responded more positively to the mystery that was Genero. Only his closest friends—and he counted Margery, Toni and Alana among them— knew where he came from and what he was about. All others were left to wonder, oftentimes in awe, about him. He liked it that way. What mattered was that he was one of the best chefs in California and one day he would own the most popular restaurant in Beverly Hills. At twenty-seven he had plenty of time to work toward his goal. He considered his stint with Alana as a stepping stone. He respected her prowess as a chef, and he liked her as a person.

"I hope they do make up," Margery said prayerfully. "My darling Alana has been mourning a man who doesn't deserve her loyalty. However, I couldn't come out and tell her what sort of person he was, I'd only succeed in alienating her. I couldn't bear that. She's my daughter. But I know several things have been nagging at her these past few months and if things work out as we wish, she and Nico could make me a grandmother by next year."

"Don't get carried away," Toni cautioned her with a grin. "A wedding first, then we'll think about grandchildren."

Toni and Genero went to sit next to Margery on the big, four-poster bed, flanking her.

"It'll all work out," Toni consoled her.

"Of course it will," Genero added brightly. He got to his feet. "I should get back down there," he announced. "God knows what Clovis has added to the vichyssoise. For some reason, he seems to believe substituting onions for leeks is acceptable. I keep telling him that leeks have a milder flavor than onions. One must not overpower the taste buds."

Alone, Margery and Toni looked at one another and burst out laughing.

"I love that boy," Margery said confidentially. "But we have got to get him interested in something other than cooking."

"First things first," Toni said, wiping the tears from her eyes. "We need to find out what's going on with Alana before we can think of turning our attention to Genero."

Standing, she paced the room, looking quite regal in her African-inspired caftan. "Little did we know, thirty years ago, where a small promise would take us…"

Toni was referring to the pact that three eighteen-year-old college freshmen had made one night as they sat, cross-legged on their dormitory beds.

It was December, nineteen sixty-seven. The three friends had been too poor to afford to go home to their respective southern states for the holidays, so they'd decided to keep each other company.

Antoinette Shaw and Constance Moore were roommates, and Margery lived down the hall. They'd become fast friends when they'd met in June and when they found out that all three were southern belles: Antoinette hailing from New Orleans, Margery from Tupelo, Mississippi and Constance, from Birmingham, Alabama—the coincidence only cemented their friendship all the more.

So as they sat, bemoaning their difficult state of affairs, they began to talk, as young girls will, of how much better their respective futures would be.

Anyone looking on would have spied three lovely women-to-be dreaming impossible dreams. Making promises they would not be able to keep. However, if they could have peered into the hearts of those three, they would have been pleasantly surprised for Toni, Connie and Margery possessed a strength of will that would propel all of them to greatness.

Constance had been blessed with a voice only the gods could have bestowed upon her. She was a voice major who was already making a name for herself. Dame Judith Iverson, the lead soprano with the Metropolitan Opera, having heard Connie sing during a visit to California State, had written the aspiring opera singer a letter expressing interest in becoming her mentor. Connie had gratefully accepted, and Dame Iverson had responded by insisting that Connie spend the summer with her in New York City, where Connie could study voice alongside some of the most promising singers in the country.

Antoinette was a born poet. Already published by a small literary house at eighteen, she saw the world as a place to be schooled and took every opportunity to learn something new. This attitude sometimes got her in trouble though. If not for that mind-set, she might not have become involved with Charles Edward Waters, the son of a wealthy Boston businessman, and wound up expecting twins by the end of her freshman year in school. A Catholic, she didn't even consider not having her girls, even when she found out she could not depend on Charles Edward Waters for support.

Margery, the petite bundle of energy from Mississippi, would be the next Dorothy Dandridge even if it killed her.

As the youngest child in a family of eight other siblings, she was used to being ignored. But the way Margery looked at it, that simply meant you had to try harder. So try, she did. As she would tell countless reporters later in life, her career began in church. Sundays would find the Devlin family in St. John Baptist Church, praising God and tiny Margery waiting for her chance to shine. From the age of three, she recited poems that left the congregation genuinely moved. By the time she reached puberty, she was director of the Christmas pageant. No one else had Margery's flair for the dramatic. She could take the meager props the destitute church could ill afford and turn them into a magical wonderland. Churchgoers often filed out of one of Margery's productions with tears streaming down their contented faces. It wasn't surprising to anyone in Tupelo when Margery Devlin won a scholarship to study acting in far off California.

That night, in sixty-seven, they made three promises to one another. Number one: to always be there for one another when they were needed. Number two: to be supportive of each other's careers wherever possible. And lastly, to take care of each other's offspring should anything happen to one of them, God forbid.

As the years passed, Constance became a principal singer with the Metropolitan Opera. She married Dr. Garth Shelby and gave birth to Alana Margery Antoinette Shelby. With hard work and determination, she'd made all her dreams come true. Then on a stormy October night in 1987, while leaving a party, she and Garth were killed by a truck driver who had swerved to avoid hitting another car that had stalled on the highway.

Both Margery and Toni had been at the apex of their careers. Margery was the most sought-after African-American actress in Hollywood, having won an Oscar for her role as a long-suffering mother in the drama, *The Living Is Easy.* She was at the much dreamed of point in her journey where she could pick and choose roles and be paid an exorbitant amount for doing something she loved. Unfortunately her personal life wasn't going as well for she was in the process of divorcing her husband, actor Daniel Lincoln, for adultery.

Toni, an award-winning novelist, was the darling of the San Francisco literary world. The mother of twin teenaged daughters, Georgette, a superior student, and Briane, another Margery who was following in her auntie's footsteps by becoming an actress. Toni had chosen singlehood, being unable to give her heart to another man after having it trampled on by Charles Edward Waters, who had never tried to be a part of his daughters' lives.

Following the loss of Alana's parents, Margery and Toni agreed that she should go to live with Margery in San Francisco. It helped that Connie and Garth had left very clear instructions in their wills that Alana should be taken care of by Margery and Toni, the particulars to be decided by the two friends. So for the first five years after her parents' deaths, Alana was the charge of her two doting aunts. Then five years ago, Toni moved back to New Orleans where she could keep an eye on her elderly parents.

"I feel so guilty, having to resort to subterfuge," Toni said, turning to look at Margery.

"There is nothing wrong with looking out for your child's best interests," Margery said stoically. "We won't *do* anything per se. We'll simply observe and see what develops. Watch and hope."

"It's already been over a year and she's still having those dreams. I know because she told me about the last one. What I don't know is why the guilt? What reason does Alana have for feeling guilty?"

"Who knows?" Margery shrugged, sighing. "Maybe they argued just before he went out and got himself killed. Widows often experience guilt associated with their husbands' deaths. It isn't uncommon."

"I wish she would confide in us more," Toni said wistfully. "She needs someone to talk to. When I suggested she see a therapist, she just laughed. 'Aunt Toni,' she said, 'I'm not a basketcase. I'm simply grieving in my own way. Can't you respect that?'" Toni mimicked Alana's voice almost perfectly. "Of course I can respect that."

"She's always been loyal to those she loves," Margery reminded Toni. "Losing her parents like that was hard on her and then to lose her husband to a violent death. He was the only man she ever considered herself in love with. She may never be fully over him." She glanced over at Toni, her eyes filled with amusement. "Remind you of anyone?"

"I am not still in love with Charles Edward Waters," Toni disavowed. She turned away, going to stand at the French doors and peer out at the hills behind Margery's home. "If anything, I'd like to get my hands around his scrawny neck and squeeze. I didn't need him, but the least he could have done was to be a father to his daughters."

"The last time I saw him," Margery said, coming to join Toni at the French doors, "he wasn't a bit scrawny. He was as vital and handsome as he was nearly thirty years ago, maybe even better looking. You know how black men tend to grow into their own after a certain age? Well, the man is ripe, darling. And now that he is no longer married, maybe…"

"Maybe nothing," Toni said with finality, her dark eyes flashing fire. "Girl, you'd better control those matchmaking tendencies of yours because if Charles Edward and I were ever *accidentally* thrown together again, someone would be dead in a matter of minutes and it wouldn't be yours truly."

"All right," Margery placated her. "I'm sorry I even brought it up."

The intercom on the wall near the bedroom door

buzzed, and she walked over to it and pressed the TALK button. "Margery here."

"Red alert," Genero said cheerfully. "Alana has arrived and is presently giving Maria the four-one-one."

"We'll be right down," Margery replied crisply. Then to Toni, "Come on, let's go see how far the game is afoot, my dear Watson."

"After you, Sherlock," Toni said, smiling.

"We're going to have to let you go, Karen," Miss Ekert said, looking down her bifocals into Karen Robinson's stricken face. "I'm sorry, but the company is downsizing. I'm afraid your position has been eliminated."

Karen hadn't been cognizant of a word past the phrase "let you go." She was mentally calculating the cost of the gas she'd used to come to work this morning only to be fired. Let go. Such a pleasant-sounding euphemism. Why didn't she call it by its true name? Fired, canned, eviscerated. God knows, her gut felt like someone had just stuck a knife in it.

"But you told me only last week, that I was doing an excellent job," Karen said hopefully.

"You are a good receptionist, Karen," Miss Ekert said, her voice sympathetic. "But that isn't the point. The company's losing money, we've got to unload unnecessary luxuries and unfortunately your position is a luxury. Anyone coming into this real estate office can be greeted by any available agent."

"I'll take a cut in pay," Karen offered, close to desperation. "But I need this job."

"We thought of that option," her boss said sadly. "We still couldn't swing it. I'm very sorry. I'll give you the best letter of recommendation I can compose, Karen. I'm truly sorry."

"Sorry" doesn't put food in my son's mouth, Karen thought with acrimony. But what do you care? You come to work in a Benz, dressed in designer outfits every day.

Miss Ekert placed a sealed number-ten envelope in Karen's outstretched palm.

"We were able to provide you with two weeks of severance pay, plus this week's check. I hope that helps," Miss Ekert said, sounding as though she'd been more than generous. She managed a weak smile. "You are not required to work the rest of the day. Unless, of course, you want to." There was a hopeful tone to Miss Ekert's voice that enraged Karen.

"No," Karen said, barely able to contain her anger. She got her purse from the lower drawer of her desk. Two years. Two years and this was how they treated her? She'd given her all to this job. She never wore a sour expression. Her voice was always pleasant and professional. She was the first person customers saw when they walked through the door, and she made certain they were not put off. On several occasions, she had overheard customers praising her because of her cheerful attitude. Now she looked at Miss Ekert with lackluster eyes. "I'll just get out of your way. There are a few hours left in the day. I should put my time to good use by looking for another job."

"I haven't had time to write your letter of recommendation," Miss Ekert said regrettably. "I'll do it right now."

She began walking toward her office, which was in the rear of the building.

"That's all right," Karen called after her. "I have an up-to-date resumé. I'm sure that if whoever hires me is interested in my previous place of employment, they will phone you."

She had forced back the impending tears and was more composed as she stood in front of Miss Ekert and reached for her hand. She smiled as she shook Miss Ekert's thin, pale hand. "I've enjoyed working here the past two years. Good luck with the downsizing. I hope it keeps you afloat." About as well as a dingy with a hole in it the size of a watermelon, she thought.

That image must have brought an elated glint to her brown eyes because Miss Ekert breathed a sigh of relief and pumped her hand enthusiastically. "I'm so happy we could part friends, Karen. It pains me so to let you go."

"Yes, I'm sure it's hard for you. But don't worry about me. I'm young and smart. I'll find another job."

A couple of the agents, both attractive blondes, came over to say their farewells.

"I'll miss you, Karen," the taller one said, but her smile didn't reach her eyes.

"Take care of yourself," said the other.

Karen simply smiled and turned to leave.

Her vision was blurred by tears as she walked around the building to her car. As she got behind the wheel of the 1980 Toyota Corolla, she hoped it would start. It needed a lot of work done on it. For the last few months, she'd been driving on a wing and a prayer. She turned the key in the ignition. It started right up. She laughed hysterically. At least she would be saved from one more indignity today.

Chapter 3

When Alana arrived at the house on Nob Hill, she was met at the door by a curious Maria who dogged her steps all the way to the kitchen. Alana knew Margery's kitchen as well as she knew her own, so she went directly to the pantry, where she hung her purse on one of the hooks provided for the kitchen staff's belongings.

She had removed the letter with the intention of showing it to Margery and Toni.

She unfolded it and gave it to Maria to read. "I received that this morning. Some prankster thought it would be amusing to send me a message that would remind me of Michael."

Puzzled, Maria looked up at Alana after reading the note.

"Who would do such a thing? Even if you don't take

it seriously, what kind of person would think of sending you such a message, and why?"

"Someone who's bitter?" Alana proposed, meeting Maria's eyes. "Suppose you were in love with a man, then he gets killed, and you read in the paper that he's survived by a wife. How would that make you feel?"

"Angry, used, humiliated," Maria replied disdainfully. "I would want to dance on his grave."

"Yes, but what good would it do?" Alana said, keeping her voice low. "He's already dead."

Maria smiled. "I see what you mean. He's gone but his wife is very much alive and probably living it up on his death benefits. Why not share some of your misery with her?"

As they talked, Alana walked around to the various posts in the kitchen where her employees were busy preparing the cuisine for the upcoming party.

She paused next to Clovis, who was chopping up leeks.

"Hello, Clovis, how are you today?" she said.

Clovis, a tall, dark-skinned native Californian, grinned at her, revealing large white teeth in his mustachioed face.

"I'm doing well, thank you. You're just in time to witness the fact that I'm using leeks and not onions in the vichyssoise. For some reason, Genero accuses me of doing otherwise."

"You're doing beautifully," Alana praised him. "I'll be sure to mention to Genero that I saw the leeks with my own eyes."

She kept walking, but before she could pause at another workstation, Maria grasped her by the arm. "Wait a minute," her friend began. "Why do you suppose she waited so long to start in on you? Why wait over a year?"

"It will soon be Valentine's Day," Alana said, sounding quite sure of herself. "The holiday for lovers. It's the time of the year when people all over the country turn their attention to romance. Maybe she has no one in her life. Maybe Michael was the man she thought she'd be with for the rest of her life."

"You're making a lot of assumptions," Maria said, looking serious. "What if you're wrong and Michael was never unfaithful to you? Then what?"

Before she could answer, Margery and Toni came into the room and descended upon Alana.

"Darling. There you are, finally," Margery exclaimed. Alana had concluded, years ago, that it was impossible for Margery to enter a room without seeming as though she was walking onto the stage of a packed theater.

Alana kissed her proffered cheek. "Don't get your pantyhose in a bunch, Little Momma. I'm fine. I just needed to talk to Nico before coming here."

"About what?" Margery asked petulantly. "What could be more important than my party?"

Don't lay it on too thickly, Toni thought. Margery really could be a ham when she wanted to be.

Alana looked over at Maria, who handed Margery the letter.

The color drained from Margery's face when she

read it. She silently passed it to Toni, who, untrained in the dramatic arts, managed to retain her coloring.

"And what did Nico make of it?" Toni asked.

"He believes it's harmless. A reminder from a friend that I need to get on with my life," Alana replied, watching Toni's face. Her aunt wasn't one to hide her emotions. If she was afraid for Alana's safety, Alana would be able to read it in her facial expression.

Toni's placid features revealed nothing aside from curiosity.

"How exciting," Genero put in as he walked up and took the note from Toni. "A mystery. We'll help you solve it, Alana. It'll be fun. Sort of like that scavenger hunt we did for the Morrissey party last year. Who will find the culprit in the least amount of time?"

"No, no," Alana said, shaking her head. "May I remind you that we have two hundred guests arriving in a little under forty-eight hours? Someone must be here to make sure our plans are carried out, and that someone, dear Genero, is you. That's why I hired you. I know how much you love a mystery, but your services are required right here."

Twisting his handsome face into a frown, Genero handed Alana the note and turned away. "I never have any fun."

"Back to my question," Toni said. "Does Nico think anything needs to be done about this?"

"As a matter of fact," Alana began, "Nico and I are going to investigate the matter together. He promised to phone me as soon as he gets some free time."

Alana could have sworn she saw Margery give Toni

a meaningful look and then the two aunts smiled at each other. Of course, they could have been pleased because she and Nico were back on speaking terms. They were aware that she had not seen him for over a month.

"Well," Margery said, clapping her hands, "then that's settled. Genero will remain here and oversee the party, while you and Nico reenact an episode of 'Murder, She Wrote.' Although how you could leave me alone with that little man in my hour of need, I'll never know. Haven't I been good to you? Or do you harbor some secret resentment of your dear aunt?"

Sighing, Alana placed a protective arm around her diminutive surrogate mother. "Little Momma, have I ever let you down? I have everything planned to the last detail. Genero is a godsend. My people are thoroughly professional. And I promise you, I will be in and out of here at least twice daily until the night of the party. And I will be the first to arrive when the festivities begin."

"All right," Margery conceded, sounding like a child who was being coaxed out of a temper tantrum. "But you have to promise me that once you find the person behind this, you will put forth your best effort to go forward with your life, my love."

"That's why I'm doing this," Alana said, reasonably. "I realize it's time I did something positive about my suspicions instead of letting them fester. So, yes, I do promise."

She stood patiently while first Margery, then Toni, hugged her hard enough to almost require CPR afterward, then she continued her rounds, making certain the party preparations were being executed satisfactorily.

"Alana and Nico spending time together will make them realize how much they need each other," Toni said to Margery once they were alone. "So far, things are going beautifully."

"She's definitely headed in the right direction," Margery agreed happily.

As Nico maneuvered his black vintage 1966 Stingray through the afternoon traffic, heading toward the ocean, his mind was on Alana and how he was going to handle their makeshift investigation. Foremost in his thoughts was the conviction that he had to be totally honest with her. Which meant he had to confess to knowing about Michael's affair.

That knowledge had been eating away at his insides for some time now. He'd found out about Michael's indiscretion quite by accident.

One night after signing out at the station, Michael suggested they go grab a bite to eat but Nico had made other plans, so he begged off. By happenstance, they were both going to Oakland, and as Nico crossed the San Francisco–Oakland Bay Bridge, he spotted Michael's car up ahead. At that moment he decided to follow him. Michael had recently started bringing up other women in their conversations. Michael was big on hypothetical situations. He'd often begin his sentences with, "What if…"

Nico didn't think Michael would have the nerve to come out and tell him he was having an affair because he knew Nico adored Alana. Nico was continually telling Michael how fortunate he was to have Alana. Deep down, Nico felt that Michael got a kind of perverse pleasure out of telling him all about his marital woes. Shortly before his death, his major complaint about Alana was that she wanted to wait another year before conceiving a child. She didn't feel her business was on a good enough footing and wanted to concentrate on her work before becoming a mother.

That night, Nico played a hunch through to the bitter end. Staying several car lengths behind Michael in order to avoid detection, he trailed him to an apartment complex in Oakland.

Sitting in his car, he watched with fascination as Michael was met at the apartment door by a young, attractive woman who threw her arms around his neck and kissed him on the mouth. Nico recalled thinking how domestic the scene looked. She could have been Michael's wife greeting him after the close of a busy workday. The smile on Michael's face was warm and inviting. Like he had every right to be kissing a woman who wasn't Alana.

Nico knew then that his partner had a secret life. In Daly City, he had Alana who, in Nico's estimation, was the perfect wife. In Oakland, he had that pretty woman who'd enthusiastically fell into his arms. Undoubtedly neither woman suspected what Michael was up to. It took an unusual type of woman to willingly share her man with another woman. No. Michael was furiously juggling two lives. As with all secrets, it was just a matter of time before the truth came into the light. Nico's sole concern was how long he could protect Alana from the knowledge and when she learned of Michael's infidelity, how he could lessen the blow for her.

When Michael was killed, Nico saw no reason to tell Alana of her husband's proclivities. He thought her grief would take a natural course and she'd eventually go on with her life. Not being able to get inside her head, he had no way of gauging her true feelings. So all he could do was bide his time and be there for her should she need him.

Sometimes, Nico found himself wishing he could turn back the clock to the moment he'd met her.

He and Michael had been club-hopping that night, nearly four years ago. They'd been sitting at the bar in a blues club drinking cold beers when Nico heard a delightful feminine laugh. He thought it odd that he should be able to distinguish that sound from the cacophony of the band and the many other voices around him but he had and he followed the sound until his eyes rested on a lovely golden-brown skinned woman with shoulder-length tresses that reminded him of a raven's wing. She looked up suddenly and their eyes met. She smiled at him. He smiled back, automatically coming up off his chair. Her smile was all the encouragement he needed.

So entranced by her was he, that he hadn't even noticed his partner, sitting right beside him, had also made eye-contact with her. Michael was already across the room before Nico was out of his seat.

By the time Nico reached Alana's table, Michael had pulled up a chair next to her and proceeded to charm the three women seated around it.

In a matter of minutes, Michael and Alana were up

dancing and Nico was left at the table with Bree and Georgie Shaw.

"He doesn't waste time, does he?" Georgie had commented dryly. She'd told him she was an attorney. She'd just passed the California bar examination. "On her first try," her sister, who was an actress, had added proudly.

"No," Nico said regrettably. "Michael isn't one to let grass grow under his feet."

"Is he nice?" Bree inquired sweetly. Nico had been somewhat taken aback by that question. How was he supposed to reply? Michael was his friend. "No, frankly, he's a womanizer of the first order." At least that would have been closer to the truth. However, they were out for an evening of fun and not armed with the gift of divination, Nico had no way of knowing that months later, Michael and Alana would be married. "He's the best," he'd said then.

Later, as the evening waned, he'd gotten his chance to dance with Alana. However, by that time, it was obvious she was smitten with Michael.

It was difficult for her to draw her eyes away from Michael's handsome face as Nico pulled her into his arms for a slow dance.

"Are you two good friends?" she asked, her voice husky.

"We've known one another since the police academy," Nico had told her. "That was almost two years ago."

"You're both great-looking guys," she'd said, looking up at him with those clear brown eyes. His heartbeat thundered in his ears. Could she be interested in him?

"Why aren't you in a relationship?"

Nico had gone on to explain the life of a cop to her: the long hours, the imminent danger that had a way of making you hesitant to bring another person into your life. She'd listened intently and her next words told him everything he needed to know about her. "It takes a special kind of person to do what you do and retain your innate humanness," she had said, her voice low.

"Stop that," he'd joked. "Or you're going to make a grown man blush."

She'd laughed a deep, throaty laugh that he'd found altogether delightful. He'd lost his heart there on the dance floor.

In the intervening years, he'd simply fallen more in love with her. He thought of transferring to another city more than once but realized he couldn't bear to be away from Alana for any great length of time. So he made up his mind to be the best friend to Alana that he could possibly be. When Michael showed his true colors, he would be there to look after her. He was helpless to do anything other than wait for the inevitable.

Michael's death had shocked them all. Nico had certainly never imagined such an abrupt conclusion to Alana's marriage. A whole new set of rules applied here. He vowed to remain silent about Michael's other life. When not on duty he comforted Alana, listened to her curse the Fates for putting her husband in the line of fire of murderous carjackers.

Months after Michael's death she was still trying to rid herself of his ghost and now that someone had created a mystery for her in the form of the letter she'd received this morning, Nico had only one option: to confess everything.

Chapter 4

"What are you doing home so early?" Geraldine Robinson asked of her daughter as Karen walked through the door of her apartment. She'd dropped by the grocery store on the way home because Michael needed milk for his cereal in the morning.

Her mother was sitting on the sofa, folding clothes. Michael was playing with his toy soldiers a few feet away. Geraldine dropped the towel she was folding back into the laundry basket and went to her daughter. "Karen?"

Karen continued into the kitchen, where she placed the bag on the small table and began putting away the foodstuffs: the milk into the refrigerator, the green beans into the cabinet next to the stove. Finished, she faced her mother.

"They fired me, Ma," she said. Her bottom lip trembled as she fought back tears.

Geraldine, a stout woman in her early fifties, enfolded her only child in her arms. "My poor baby," she cooed. "Tell Momma everything."

Karen looked up into her mother's clear, compassionate brown eyes and silently thanked God for her.

"Miss Ekert said that the company is losing money so they had to cut back, which meant they could no longer afford to keep me. She said they could do without a receptionist," she told her mother, her voice listless.

Holding her at arm's length, Geraldine looked up into her eyes. "You had outgrown them anyway," she said positively. "A few more credits and you'll have your business degree. I have a little money set aside. We can make it until you find something else. Don't think of this as the end of the world, baby. Think of this as an opportunity to expand your horizons."

"It just came at a bad time," Karen replied, sniffling. "I was counting on that job to help pay my tuition for my last semester in night school. Now I'm going to have to postpone school for a while until I can find another job, a job that pays well enough so that I can afford to continue going to school. Sun Realty really messed with my plans, Ma."

"A little setback isn't going to do you in, child," Geraldine prophesied. "You've had disappointments before..." She glanced lovingly at Michael. "But look how far you've come. When you got pregnant with Michael, you could have gone on welfare like any number of other women, but instead you stayed in school and kept working, knowing that in the long run, fending for yourself was going to help you provide a better future for your child." She gently squeezed one of Karen's hands. "I was proud of you then, sugar. And I'm still proud of you. What that man did to you…" She blew air between her full lips in an exasperated gesture. "Well, some women would've just up and died from the humiliation, but not you. You survived. You're strong, baby. That's how I raised you to be." Her eyes held a humorous expression in them. "Remember when Michael was born, and you wanted to give him up for adoption, for all of fifteen minutes, and I talked you out of it? Have you ever regretted your decision?"

"Not for a minute," Karen answered, looking at her son with her love for him glowing in her eyes. "He's the best thing that ever happened to me."

"And you're the best thing that ever happened to me," Geraldine said with conviction. "Momma will be here for you. The Lord will provide."

Karen burst into tears then, but they were not tears of regret at losing her job, or tears of anger at an unfeeling system, but tears of relief at knowing she always had someone whom she could talk to when she was at her lowest.

"Go ahead and let it out," her mother advised her. "Then I want you to go wash your face and come back out here wearing a smile. We've got work to do."

Karen felt something tugging on her dress's hem and looked down to see Michael with a worried look in his large, golden-brown eyes. Eyes just like his father's. "Why are you cryin', Ma?" he said in his small voice.

Karen knelt and pulled him into her embrace. "Mommy's a little sad because she lost her job today, sweetie. But it's nothing for you to be sad about because everything's going to be all right."

At two years of age, Karen knew there wasn't much Michael understood about the grown-up world. He knew a job was the place his mommy went every day except on the weekend. And he knew that on the weekend, he had his mother all to himself. She made pancakes for him Saturday and Sunday mornings. They would sleep late and watch cartoons in bed and when they got up, she took him to fun places like McDonald's and the zoo where he saw all sorts of wonderful animals. His favorite were the monkeys. They always made him giggle.

"Can I have pancakes in the morning?" he said, looking up at her expectantly.

Karen laughed happily. "Yes, sweetie. I'll make pancakes for you tomorrow morning."

By late afternoon Alana was becoming a bit anxious to hear from Nico. Following Margery and Toni's brief interrogation, she'd rolled up her sleeves, put on an apron, and pitched in with the food preparation. When it was at all possible, she liked working alongside her staff. More often than not, however, her expertise was needed wooing the clients and in the initial planning of an event.

She was helping Gina, a young single mother who'd been with Vesta for a couple of years, stuff eggrolls. Gina was telling about the latest adventure in her daughter, Laura's life. "Just before I left her at the day care center, she turned to me and asked, 'Mommy, do you know why boys like to hit me and pull my hair?'" Gina's dark brown eyes were animated as she continued. "No, I told her. No, honey, I don't know why. Then she looked at me with a thoroughly innocent expression on her tiny face and said, 'Miss Stephens says it's because I hit them first.'" Gina laughed. "Well, I didn't know what to say to that. My three-year-old, a bully? I didn't realize she had an aggressive bone in her body."

"Maybe it would be a good idea if you visited the day-care center one day, just to observe," Alana suggested, stifling laughter. "It could be she's defending herself. Have you had a chance to talk to Miss Stephens about it?"

"No, I'm going to do that this afternoon," Gina said as she wiped her hand on a dish towel. She picked up the large baking sheet they'd been placing the finished eggrolls on and passed it to Clovis, who covered it with plastic wrap and carried it to the walk-in freezer. The day of the ball, they would be removed from the freezer and deep fried.

"When you've got kids, it's one thing after another," Gina complained, turning back around to face Alana.

"Still," Alana said, smiling at her, "I envy you. You have a beautiful child, and you're engaged to one of the nicest men I know. You're a fortunate person, Gina."

"Yeah," Gina concurred, her full lips curved in a wistful smile. "I guess I am at that. But it sure has taken me a while to get here. You know what a living hell my first marriage was. The one good thing that came out of that was Laura. The experience also taught me to stand on my own two feet. It was a hard lesson but one I needed to learn." She laughed. "I lucked out with Gary, but still, I'm never going to depend on another person to support me."

"Girl, you are fierce!" Alana said proudly.

"No, girlfriend," Gina said seriously. "You are the one. You have been my role model."

"Get out of here," Alana said, hands on her hips.

"When you hired me two years ago, I thought I'd be here maybe four, five months. But when I saw you in action, I said to myself: I could learn something here because this woman has her stuff together." Gina cleared her throat. "Uh-huh. I sure did. And I was right. I've learned more about catering from you in two years than I could have working in a restaurant in twice as much time."

"That's because you applied yourself," Alana politely informed her. But she was grateful for the compliment, which she knew to be genuine. Gina Evans was not the kind of person to kiss-up to the boss. She was a straight shooter who would rather incur your wrath than bite her tongue.

Hearing a collective sigh from the four women in the room, Alana looked up and saw Nico coming through the swinging doors.

He had gone home between there and work and had changed into a pair of black jeans, a blue denim shirt and a maroon T-shirt underneath. Alana glanced down and saw he was wearing his favorite black motorcycle boots. I am not riding on the back of his Harley Davidson tonight, she thought briefly.

"Hello, Nico!" said the chorus of feminine voices.

"Hi, ladies," Nico said. He blushed.

Alana quickly washed her hands and dried them on a towel.

"I'm leaving now. I'll see you tomorrow morning," she told Gina. "Give that little bully of yours a kiss from me."

Walking toward Nico and taking him by the hand, she led him out of the kitchen. "You know," she said jokingly, "you really should have someone announce you before you come into a room full of women. Hunk alert, hunk alert!"

Nico grinned at her, showing perfect white teeth in his golden-brown, square-chinned face. His downward sloping, warm brown eyes regarded her with keen interest. "Do I detect a note of jealousy in your voice?'

"Who, me?" Alana said noncommittally. She wasn't about to fall into that trap. "Besides, you're supposed to be using your detecting skills to locate the person behind that rather cryptic note."

They were alone in the hallway, and Nico took the opportunity to pull her into his arms. "You smell like ginger," he said as he caressed her back. Alana felt her body relax in his embrace. There was no use fighting it. She was growing ever fonder of his nearness. She looked up into his eyes.

"How was your day?"

Nico laughed. "I've longed to hear you ask me that. Only I wanted it to be when I came home to you."

Alana's stomach muscles tightened at the sound of the unconcealed longing in his voice. Her heartbeat speeded up. She pressed her face against his muscular chest. He smelled of soap and water and sandalwood.

There was no adequate response to such an intimate comment. She reached up and gently touched his cheek, then she wiggled out of his hold. "Hang on, I forgot my shoulder bag."

She left him standing there while she went back into the kitchen to get her purse, which she'd left hanging in the pantry.

The clamor immediately ceased when she walked through the twin swinging doors of the kitchen. A sure sign that she was being talked about in her absence. "Forgot my purse," she said to no one in particular. All eyes were on her as she retrieved the purse and quickly walked back out. The voices resumed as soon as the door closed behind her.

That was strange, she thought, then shrugged it off. A handsome man came by to pick her up. People were always intrigued by romance. There was no harm in their thinking that she and Nico were an item.

Nico, with Margery and Toni keeping him company, was waiting for her in the foyer.

"Oh, there you are, darling," Margery said, coming to take her by the arm. "Nico was telling us that you and he are in the middle of an investigation. You *will* tell your aunt all about it tomorrow, won't you?" She kissed Alana's cheek. In a lower voice she said, "You can always change your mind about going through with this. Let it go, dear. What good would it do you to find

out something you'd rather not know? Haven't you endured enough heartache?"

Alana returned her kiss. "I need to know, Little
Momma. I'm sure you can understand that."

Margery nodded, keeping any further comments to
herself.

"You take good care of our girl," Toni demanded of
Nico after having pulled him aside.

Nico had long admired and respected Toni. He remembered reading about her exploits as a boy in high
school. He never imagined he would actually meet her
one day. But about three years ago Alana had invited
him to Thanksgiving dinner with them. He was amazed
when Antoinette Shaw strode into the dining room carrying the turkey. He had been enamored of her ever
since.

"Don't worry, Toni," he said now. "I'll guard her
with my life."

"That's all I expect," Toni said lightly. But she meant
it and he knew it.

Alana came to claim him then, and they left.

"I hope my aunts weren't putting you through the
third degree," Alana said as they descended the front
steps.

Nico placed a protective arm around her. The weather
had turned chilly, as San Francisco afternoons do in
February. "I brought an extra leather jacket for you,"
he told her. Alana's gaze went to the Harley Davidson
waiting in the driveway.

"And why, pray tell, did you bring that machine?"

"It's good for getting in and out of afternoon traffic," Nico said, defending his beloved motorcycle. "And it's small and not as noticeable as your van or my car would be. Afraid your 'do' won't survive the night air?"

He got on the motorcycle and put on his helmet, fastening it under his chin. Ignoring his comment, Alana quickly slipped into the aforementioned jacket and straddled the seat behind him. "The only thing missing is my biker-chick outfit."

"Complete with the leather chaps?" Nico said, smiling.

"And the removable 'Mom' tattoo on my right forearm," Alana added, her grin infectious.

"I'd like to see that," Nico returned easily. "But for now, hold on to me."

"Where are we going?" she asked as she donned the helmet.

"Someplace where we can talk. I have a few confessions to make."

"Oh goody, confessions," Alana said in a playful mood. She put her arms around his waist, locking her fingers. "I can't wait. What, you use foreign coins in the drink machine at work?"

"It's much more serious than that," Nico said as he kick-started the huge Harley.

Nico took Van Ness Avenue all the way down to Geary Street, then turned onto Park Presidio Boulevard. At that point Alana had no difficulty discerning that they were headed into Golden Gate Park. The Japanese Tea Garden was one of their favorite destinations. The serenity of the intricately landscaped garden made it one of the most visited points of interest in San Francisco.

The park itself covered one thousand acres that, over the years, had been divided into recreational fields, picnic areas, paths for walking and museums.

After parking, Alana and Nico walked through the beautiful, painstakingly carved gateway and strolled hand in hand past pools filled with giant goldfish.

Deciduous trees grew all around them. Footbridges over pools of water. Paths bordered by dwarf trees and large stone statues that stood like sentinels at Shinto shrines.

Alana always felt at peace in these tranquil surroundings. She wondered, however, why Nico had chosen this particular place to make his confession. Perhaps the quietness of this garden would cushion the blow of his revelation?

They chose a bench near the entrance to one of the shrines and sat down.

"Make it fast," Alana said. She had the feeling this was not going to be something she wanted to hear, and she wanted to get it over with as swiftly as possible.

Nico bit his bottom lip. He narrowed his eyes as he regarded her, opened his mouth to say something, then shut it again. Sighing, he reached for one of her hands and held on to it as though he gained strength from her touch.

Alana arched her eyebrows in an impatient gesture. "Come on, tell me, Nico."

"Oh, God," he began. "Alana, this is the hardest thing I have ever had to do." He took her other hand, and Alana had the feeling that he was holding on to her in order to prevent her from fleeing once she heard what he had to tell her.

"First, let me tell you about the Michael Calloway I knew," he prefaced. "When we first met, in the police academy here in San Francisco, I liked him right away. He was gregarious, the life of the party. People flocked to him. He became my best friend, and I was proud to call him my partner. But almost immediately after you two were married, he grew frantic. Something was eating him. It was like he'd changed into a whole different person." He paused and glanced down at their clasped hands. "But I knew that wasn't true. Michael hadn't changed. I had. He was still the man who loved women." Alana flinched and he held on to her more firmly. "You knew that about him before you married him, did you not?" His Spanish accent was surfacing now. Alana gave an almost imperceptible nod. She knew. "As I was saying," he continued, "Michael hadn't changed his spots, but I was no longer tolerant of his behavior because I was..." He looked her straight in the eyes. "Because I was in love with his wife."

Tears sat in Alana's big brown eyes. "Nico, don't."

Nico brought her right hand up to his mouth and kissed her fingers. "Let me finish, please." He looked down again, unable to see those tears in her eyes without wanting to take her in his arms and kiss them away. "One night, Michael and I were out getting a sandwich and, as it often did, the topic of conversation turned to your marriage. I was uncomfortable talking about your problems. Now, you know why. He was upset because you wanted to postpone having children."

Alana nodded, remembering. "Yes, he wanted to start a family right away."

"I sided with you," Nico told her. "Michael blew up and accused me of being in love with you, and I didn't deny it. That's when he shoved me and the fight began. At any rate, he told me that he was cheating on you and that you were too naive to realize it."

"Why didn't you come to me?" Alana asked, her voice low, controlled. "Maybe I could have salvaged my marriage."

"Come to you with what?" Nico said. "It would've been my word against his, and whom would you have believed? Besides, I had a hidden agenda: I wanted you."

"Okay," Alana said. She breathed in deeply and exhaled. "You've confessed. But really, Nico, you have nothing to feel guilty about. Michael told you he had other women but you didn't have proof, so you really don't know whether he was telling the truth or just being a blowhard."

"I *do* know," Nico said quietly. "I followed him to her door. I watched as she greeted him, they kissed, and he went inside."

Alana felt sick to her stomach. She wrenched her hands free of his grasp and got to her feet. Looking down at him, she shouted, "Who is she?"

"I never pursued the matter," Nico said truthfully. "What was I supposed to do, come to you with an address and you go over there only to have your heart torn to shreds? He's dead now, Alana. Let it rest."

Seeing all the curious eyes turned their way, Alana

sat back down and lowered her voice considerably. "So why tell me all this now?"

"Because you came to my office and threatened to find her on your own if I didn't help you," Nico reminded her.

Alana bowed her head sadly. "True enough."

Nico moved closer to her and placed his arms around her shoulders. "He loved you in his own way," he said in his calm manner. "Just not the way a husband should."

"Well," she said after a long pause. "We've come this far, we'd just as well go all the way."

Nico's bedroom eyes bespoke his confusion.

"I want her name and address. I want to talk to her face-to-face," Alana announced.

Nico stood, picking up his helmet as he did so. Seconds passed as he simply looked down at her, then he turned and calmly walked away from her. Alana gathered up her purse and her helmet and followed him. "You can't deny me, Nico. You owe me."

Nico's expression was thunderous when he faced her. "I owe you?"

"For keeping all of this secret for so long," Alana explained.

He quickened his pace. He was already through the gate and heading toward the parked motorcycle.

"Nico!" she called.

He was on the motorcycle and turning the key in the ignition when she caught up with him. She quickly got on behind him.

"Are you a masochist?" she heard him say as he gunned the motor. She held on tightly as he sped out of the parking lot. "I will not give you her name and address," he said with finality.

Alana rested against him, letting the pain of his revelation wash over her.

As he drove, Nico could feel her body tremble in the throes of a crying jag. God knew, there was very little he would deny her, but how long was he expected to watch her being consumed with the loss of a man who didn't show her the respect she deserved? Maybe he was missing something here. It was impossible for him to put himself in her place. What could possess her to want to talk to the woman who had been her husband's lover? He didn't understand it. Perhaps he never would.

He pulled into the parking lot of a Mexican restaurant and shut off the engine.

Alana slid off the seat and waited for him to join her.

"I'm sorry," she said before he could even utter a word. "You don't owe me a thing, Nico. You've been a prince throughout this whole sorry mess." Her soft brown eyes were contrite as she looked up at him. Her hand went to her face to wipe away the residue left by her tears. "I'm such a fool. It's not as if I didn't suspect Michael had someone else. I mean, a woman knows these things. But to actually have my suspicions confirmed. Well, that's a whole different ball game."

"Don't apologize to me," Nico said, his voice harsh.

Alana stepped backward. "You're angry—"

Nico quickly caught her by the arm. He smiled. "No. I'm not angry with you. I'm angry with myself. I don't know what I was thinking, coming to you with the proof you've been looking for and then refusing to go a step further because I don't agree with your line of reasoning." He let go of her. "I can't know what you've been going through since Michael was killed. I only know what I've observed. And my perceptions have been colored by my love for you. So you tell me, Alana. Tell me why you feel the need to meet with this woman."

People were going in and coming out of the restaurant around them, and there was a brisk winter breeze making its presence felt. Alana had been growing cold standing out in the open, but now she felt a warmth from within. To be loved by a man of Nico's caliber was an unexpected pleasure. It was funny—up until a few minutes ago, she had thought Michael had been the love of her life. As it turned out, what they had shared was built on lies and illusions. His lies. Her self-delusion. But here was a man who was offering her his heart and soul, with no excess baggage attached.

"I think it's because I feel the need to be totally rid of him," she said softly. "It's like being immersed in ice water. It's a shock to the system, and it numbs you. I don't want to wonder about them any longer. Once I meet her, and if she's willing to talk to me, I know I'll be able to put everything associated with Michael behind me."

They had removed their helmets and their gestures were dramatic as they talked. To anyone looking on, they appeared to be arguing. Ultimately, a Mexican gentleman with a handlebar mustache, wearing a large, white apron with the words, *El Jardin Abundancia* emblazoned across the front, came outside and called, "Hey, lady, is that guy bothering you?"

Alana paused in mid-sentence and smiled at the man. "No. Everything's fine here. Thanks for asking."

"All right," the fellow said. "You coming in to eat? Today's special is the tortillas."

Turning to Nico with a wry smile on her lips, Alana said, "Were you planning on feeding me tonight?"

Nico eyed the small restaurant with skepticism. "I was going to take you someplace nicer," he said in a low voice.

"We'll be right in," Alana told the proprietor.

The man grinned at her and went back inside.

"Okay," Nico said grudgingly as they began walking toward the restaurant's entrance. "But don't blame me if you have a sudden attack of Montezuma's revenge and spend half the night in the bathroom."

Laughing, Alana put her hand through his arm, urging him forward. "Some of the best cooks are found in the most unlikely places," she said from experience.

The decor of El Jardin Abundancia—the abundant garden—restaurant consisted of original oil paintings on the walls of beautiful flower and vegetable gardens, red tablecloths on the tables and hanging plants. "It's clean," Nico observed. "I'll give them that much."

"And the air smells good," Alana said as they claimed a booth near the picture window.

They sat down opposite each other and deposited their helmets on the seat beside them. Nico reached across the table and playfully traced the outline of Alana's jaw. He sighed. "They say good things come to those who wait," he murmured, as though he was talking to himself. He raised his gaze then, his liquid brown eyes caressing her face. "Do you want to know when I first knew I was in love with you, Alana?"

Alana lowered her eyes, her sooty black lashes resting above high cheekbones. Moistening her lips, she looked directly into his eyes. "Let me guess. Was it the time we went to Lake Tahoe and your date, the supermodel, refused to go into the water and Michael was glued in front of the TV watching basketball, which left the two of us?"

Leaning forward, Nico grinned at her. "What makes you think it was that time? As I recall, you wore that white one-piece, and by the time we finished one game of water polo, you, and it, looked like something the cat dragged in."

"Is that right?" Alana said, feigning hurt feelings. "Well, if *I* remember correctly, you and Sheena—"

"Shana," Nico corrected her.

"You and 'Shana' went for a stroll in the woods and returned covered with poison oak. I've spent many a spare moment wondering how you managed that in a vertical position."

"You thought about that, huh?" Nico asked, his left eyebrow arched in amusement. "Actually it was all quite innocent. She picked up a leaf, admiring its beauty. The girl was used to limousines and champagne. What did she know about the woods? I took the leaf from her. You know how quickly poison oak spreads."

"Yeah." Alana laughed. "By the time you two got back to the cabin, you were covered in red welts and scratching like crazy."

"We've gotten off the subject," Nico said seriously.

"Which, I think, was your intention. Why does my telling you I love you make you so uneasy?"

Alana grasped one of his big hands across the tabletop. "You mean so much to me, Nico. I think you know that. I definitely couldn't have made it through the last year without you." She gently held his hand and met his gaze. "I'm afraid that if we take our relationship a step farther, that we'll end up spoiling what we already have. You know how it is between couples who've become intimate and something goes wrong. Chances are, they are *not* going to continue being friends." Cocking her head sideways, she placed his hand on her cheek. "I want you in my life forever, Nico. Not just for a moment."

"Don't compare me to him, Alana," Nico told her evenly. His dark, hooded eyes bored into hers. "I knew it was inevitable, your reluctance to allow yourself to fall in love again after your experience with Michael. But I'm not like Michael, Alana. We were total opposites. His not knowing his father did something to his psyche. I, on the other hand, have a great relationship with my dad. We love and respect one another. My papa taught me the most difficult lesson a father can teach his son. He taught me to love the woman I choose to spend my life with. My father has never been untrue to my mother, not after forty years of marriage. Not after six children, a mortgage and the ups and downs of life, in general. They remain as in love today as they were when they were first married at the base of Cuba's highest mountain, Pico Turquino, forty years ago."

"Good evening," the waitress, a pretty Mexican girl in her late teens said, as she stopped next to their booth.

"My name is Lucy, and I'll be your waitress tonight." She paused, her broad smile revealing straight, white teeth. "We're happy you could join us. The special to-night is—"

"Tortillas!" Alana and Nico responded in unison to the delight of Lucy who laughed happily.

"I see you've met my uncle Rudy," she said.

Chapter 5

The City by the Bay was awash with light and brimming with activity as Alana and Nico made their way across town on the Harley Davidson. Alana was content to sit behind Nico, her arms wrapped around him, her cheek pressed against his back. For the moment she had given up the idea of seeking out Michael's mistress. She was tempted to let it go, as Nico and Margery had urged her to do. What would she accomplish anyway? Michael was beyond redemption. And the woman, whoever she was, would probably be hostile toward her, especially if she had known Michael was a married man and had still opted to be with him.

But what if she was also a victim? Michael could have deceived her, too. They could have both been his unsuspecting dupes. That possibility hadn't previously occurred to her. If there was a chance that they had both been played for fools, she wanted to know about it. Logically, the only way to find out was by meeting with the other woman.

So when Nico walked her to her door, she gave him a hug and said in his ear, "I know you don't want me to pursue this, but I've decided I'd like to meet her."

Holding her at arm's length, Nico peered down into her face. "I had a feeling you would," he said, his voice low. He smiled at her. "How do you want to handle it?"

Frowning, Alana considered it. "Let me get back to you on that, okay? Bree's flying in from L.A. in the morning, and I promised Georgie I'd go with her to pick her up at the airport." She smiled at him, her eyes bright. "Have you picked up your tuxedo yet? You do remember that you're my date for the ball?"

Nico grinned. "That date was made before we, well, you know," he said, referring to the first time they'd kissed and the subsequent results of their actions. "Do you still want me?" He stepped closer to her. "It would be my pleasure to escort you. Do you want me, Alana?"

Alana's pulse rate accelerated, and she felt the heat beginning to rise somewhere in the vicinity of her lower regions. Want him? Yes, she wanted him. She wanted him with a ferocity that alarmed her.

She inhaled silently and exhaled with a groan. Their eyes met, and seeing the humor in his told her he'd chosen his words specifically to get a rise out of her. He smiled. She rolled her eyes. "You are the biggest flirt, Nico Setera," she said accusingly as she stepped backward. "Yes, Setera. I'd like you to take me to the ball. I want you to be dressed to the nines. I want you to be on time. And I want you to drive the Stingray, not the Harley. For now, that's all I *want* of you. So say good night."

"Good night," Nico responded, still smiling at her expense.

Alana tiptoed to plant a kiss on his cheek, and Nico kissed her on the forehead, his mouth lingering there for a moment longer than necessary. "Things have a way of changing," he said.

The next morning Alana rose from her comfortable bed, went into the closet, removed Michael's jacket from its hanger, threw it onto the floor and stomped on it. Then she found a cardboard box and dumped everything belonging to her dead husband (that she'd formerly been reluctant to part with) into it and hauled it to the curb. Thursday was garbage pick-up day.

She was just completing her task when Georgette Shaw, one of her dearest friends, pulled up in her 1965 powder blue Mustang convertible. Georgie, with her long braids flowing behind her, walked up to Alana and gave her a brief hug. "Hey, girlfriend. What in the world are you doing? Why are you jumping up and down in that box?"

Stepping out of the box, Alana smiled at Georgie. "I was just getting rid of some of Michael's things, that's all."

"And having fun doing it," Georgie observed with a grin. She placed an arm about Alana's shoulders as they walked to the house. "What happened? Did you and Michael argue in one of those too-vivid dreams you have about him? Do you want to talk about it?"

They climbed the stairs to Alana's apartment side by side, and once inside, Alana retrieved her shoulder bag and came back out to the living room where she'd left Georgie.

"We can talk on the way to the airport," she said. "If the flight is on time, Bree and Pierre will be wondering where we are."

"The dog or the man?" Georgie said as they left the apartment.

Turning around to look at her, Alana said, "What do you mean, the dog or the man? I'm talking about her poodle."

"Then you haven't heard," Georgie said with a scowl. "My sister's latest Don Juan happens to be named Pierre St. Martin. He is a wannabe who has latched on to her in hope that some of her good fortune will rub off on him."

"She's bringing him?" Alana asked. She wanted to meet him. Bree's relationships were always interesting even if they were invariably short-lived.

"She is," Georgie confirmed with a grimace. "We spoke last night. She says she can't bear to be away from him for two whole days. Love's in full bloom. I tell you, Alana, I don't think anything Mom tried to teach that girl about self-respect ever sank in."

"Well, we'll just have to make the best of it," Alana said in her role as mediator. "Believe me, Aunt Toni will have him running back to La La Land, with his tail between his legs, in a matter of seconds if she gets one inkling that he's mistreating Bree. So don't worry about it."

In the car Georgie turned to smile at her. "You're right. The Terminator will handle that situation. What's going on with you? Have you experienced satori concerning your husband?"

As Georgie pulled away from the curb, Alana fastened her seat belt and relaxed. "You could say I've experienced a sense of sudden enlightenment about my husband." She went on to tell Georgie everything she'd learned about Michael over the last twenty-four hours.

"I can't say I'm surprised," Georgie said once Alana was finished. "But I am sorry to hear it, girlfriend. My sympathies are with you. I just regret Michael isn't still with us so that we can plot a proper form of punishment for him. Now that would be good therapy for you."

Alana smiled at her friend who, as an attorney with the public defender's office in San Francisco, was well versed about crime and punishment.

She and Georgie and Bree had known one another all their lives. Georgie and Bree were two years older than Alana so they'd always regarded her as their baby sister. The sisters were fraternal twins. Georgette was born three minutes before Bree which, throughout their formative years, was the catalyst that made her the leader, and instigator, in their relationship. Her rule often made Bree resent her sister, however not to the extent that their bond became irreparable. They loved each other and remained loyal sisters in every sense of the word.

Alana envied them their closeness because she had no siblings. And on several occasions she'd used that argument to shame the sisters into settling disputes. They were lucky to have one another, and she made sure they remembered it.

As they approached San Francisco International Airport, Alana admonished Georgie to be nice to Bree's new beau. "Who knows?" she said. "Your first impression of him could have been flawed."

Georgie gave her a knowing look and laughed. "Okay. We shall see what you think of him."

After leaving the car in short-term parking, they entered the terminal and spent ten minutes trying to locate Bree among the crowd of travelers. San Francisco International Airport is one of the world's busiest airports, so they were fortunate when they heard Bree calling to them from across the room.

Alana had to admit Georgie had been correct about Pierre St. Martin. He and Bree were standing near the luggage carousel awaiting the arrival of their bags. They were both dressed casually—Bree in jeans and a golden-hued silk blouse and her favorite pair of Doc Martens. He was also wearing jeans, a T-shirt and a leather jacket with leather boots, all in black. He wore dark glasses and his long, natural black hair in dreadlocks. There was something innately cocky about his stance as he stared off into space, a look of utter boredom on his handsome face.

The sisters hugged fiercely, then Alana gave Bree a hug and a peck on the cheek. "Hi, sweetie, you look gorgeous as always," she said.

She wasn't exaggerating. Bree was beautiful with her large light-brown eyes, unlike her mother's or Georgie's, who had very dark eyes. Alana supposed Bree inherited her eye color from their long-dead father, killed during the Vietnam War.

Bree had the pecan-tan skin that paler women burned themselves on beaches in hope of acquiring. Her mouth was full and her nose long, well-shaped. She wore her thick, black luxurious locks in a short, tousled style that was all the rage in Tinseltown. She was extremely popular as an actress in Hollywood, being one of the most sought-after performers in television. She jokingly referred to herself as the queen of the small screen. She'd made several television movies and was well-known as the black detective, Jody Freeman, who always got her man. The Jody Freeman movies were action-packed comedy-dramas that always drew a large viewing audience.

That wasn't to say that her sister was plain. Georgie held her own in the looks department. They were opposites in how they perceived beauty, however. Bree was more glamorous—it was her job to look good, after all. Georgie adopted a business look for the courtroom and had a more casual approach to apparel for everyday. She fancied jeans and loose tops and her hair was invariably in braids. She'd worn it in that style since college, and now it hung down her back, almost to her hips.

They were both five feet, eight inches tall, Bree being rather slim and willowy, Georgie, more voluptuous, like her mother. They were both athletic. Bree enjoyed running and swimming. Georgie also ran and had a third-degree black belt in judo, an interest introduced to her by her friend, Sammy Chan, who owned a dojo there in the city.

"Georgie, you remember Pierre…" Bree said, her well-modulated voice enthusiastic. She was praying her sister would also remember her manners.

"Yes, how are you, Pierre? Welcome to San Francisco, I hope you enjoy your stay," Georgie said politely.

"Hello again, Georgie," Pierre said. He had the southern twang of a Texan. Alana couldn't imagine him growing up with the name Pierre St. Martin in West Texas. The other kids would have ridiculed him mercilessly. Pierre St. Martin had to be a stage name. Bree used Briane Miller when her true name was Briane Marie Shaw.

"And this is my dear friend, Alana Calloway. Alana owns a catering service here in San Francisco," Bree explained.

Alana offered her hand in greeting. Pierre removed his glasses as he smiled at her. His eyes were a pale shade of green in his dark brown face. "Hello, Alana. Bree has told me so much about you, I feel as though we're already friends."

Charming *and* handsome, Alana thought. No wonder Bree is enamored of him. Who wouldn't be?

Bree was busy taking Pierre, her ebony-hued toy poodle, out of his traveling cage. Pierre possessed a pugnacious nature and was extremely protective of Bree. The only people he'd taken a liking to over the years was Alana, on whose lap he was known to curl up on and take a nap; Toni, who, he'd learned, had no patience for his imperious moods, and Toni's mother, Marie Shaw, who had such an angelic aura about her that all creatures tended to be drawn to her.

Now as Bree held him in her arms, he was wiggling his tail and pushing out of his mistress's arms, eager to go to Alana. Alana took him, and he immediately began licking her face. "I've missed you, too," Alana said with affection.

"I don't believe it," the human Pierre said. "He actually likes someone other than Bree. That dog hates me."

"You and I *do* have something in common, after all," Georgie said as she reached down and picked up one of Bree's many bags. "Head 'em up and move 'em out, you guys. Mom and Margery are waiting."

"We're staying with Aunt Margery?" Bree asked. "I told you we had reservations at the Fairmont."

"Yes, well, our little Margie wouldn't hear of it," Georgie told her. "She insisted that you stay with her. She and Mom are in hog heaven having all three of us home."

"Oh, dear," Bree said worriedly. Then to Pierre, "But don't you worry, darling. They're really wonderful women and you have been dying to meet Aunt Margery."

Alana wondered if Bree made it a habit of stroking Pierre's ego or if she was truly nervous about his meeting her mother and aunt. Over the years Bree had played at relationships. Could it be she was serious about Pierre St. Martin? As they crossed the terminal, she decided Bree's anxiety was real. She wanted them all to like her new paramour.

Pierre put up a valiant effort to assure Bree everything would be all right. Even Georgie seemed impressed by his sincerity. Maybe I was wrong about him, she thought.

Bree's apprehension was unfounded, however, because when they arrived at the house on Nob Hill, Toni and Margery were on their best behavior.

Hugs and kisses were the order of the day. Margery even gave a pat to the head to the canine Pierre who had been most unkind to her the last time he'd visited.

"Hello, you little rug rat," she said happily. "Left any presents in anyone's shoes lately?"

"Auntie," Bree said. "He only did that because he senses that you don't like him."

"Then he's very intuitive for a birdbrain," Margery returned good-naturedly. She then relinquished custody of the dog and gave her undivided attention to his human namesake. "I'm very pleased to meet you, young man. Where did you get those interesting eyes?"

Pierre blushed profusely. Margery had a way of reducing full-grown men to whimpering babes. They were putty in her hands. She'd worked years at perfecting her craft.

"I, I," he stammered.

"Don't worry, darling," Margery said as she took him by the arm and led him out of the foyer into her home. "With a face like yours, you don't need to speak."

"I'm sorry, Miss Robinson, but we haven't any job openings at the moment. I'd be glad to take your application, and if anything opens up, we'll call you back for an interview," the human resources manager at the fifth business office Karen had visited that morning, regrettably said. "Our company has had to put a freeze on hiring."

Sighing, Karen nodded. "Okay." She placed a neatly filled-out application form on the woman's desk. "Thank you for your time. Have a nice day."

The older woman looked after her with sympathy. "Good luck with your job hunting, dear," she called.

Karen turned to briefly smile at the woman before pushing the glass door open and stepping onto the sidewalk in front of the travel agency's office.

Her fifth rejection. It wasn't that she'd believed all she had to do was apply for a job in order to get one, it was just that she hadn't observed even the prospect of being hired yet.

She tried to maintain a positive attitude as she quickly walked to her parked car. She had one more place to try: a small architectural firm across from the Civic Center was looking for a secretary. She could type and knew shorthand and was schooled in WordPerfect, a computer program which proved helpful to secretaries in the performance of their jobs. She'd never worked as a secretary before, but she was qualified nonetheless.

She liked the cool ambience of the architectural firm the moment she stepped into the office. The walls and floors were done in muted tones of gray and maroon. A pretty African-American receptionist greeted her and invited her to take a seat. One of the architects, Mr. Prentice, the partner who needed an assistant, would come out and take her back to his office for the interview shortly.

Karen sat down on a gray leather upholstered chair facing the entrance. She was wearing her best business attire: a two-year-old navy-blue suit whose skirt fell just above her knees. She had not wanted to wear it because having it on evoked bad memories. The last place she'd worn it had been to Michael's graveside memorial service.

Not wanting to be seen, she'd stood apart from the others amid a copse of trees. Her mother had tried to talk her out of going, but she was unable to stay away. Even with the realization that Michael had used her, her love for him compelled her to say goodbye to him.

It was a chilly, overcast day in February. There was a long line of cars at the L.A. cemetery: limousines, privately owned cars of family and friends and the service vehicles of the San Francisco Police Department. Michael had been one of their own, and they'd shown up in droves to show their respect.

When Karen arrived, in her beat-up Toyota, she had had to park at the very end of the processional, and by the time she was close enough to see and hear the service, her shoes were mud-splattered.

She'd stood about thirty yards away and observed as the minister talked about Michael Calloway. She heard him describe a man she was not familiar with: a pillar of his community, a devoted husband. Her Michael had been a confirmed bachelor who, although he loved her, did not propose to her even after she conceived his child. They had met in a club in Oakland. He told her he lived in nearby San Francisco and worked as a security guard. He never mentioned the San Francisco Police Department. He most definitely never mentioned his wife.

Karen had learned his true identity when she had read about his murder in the *San Francisco Chronicle.* The paper did a touching tribute on the young cop who'd been gunned down by would-be carjackers. The killer had been apprehended three days later. The police were not about to let anyone get away with killing a brother in uniform.

Karen followed the whole morbid tale with fascination. She cut out every article the paper ran about him, pasting them in a scrapbook. When Michael's obituary appeared in the paper, along with the time and place his service was to be held, she knew she would be there.

So as she stood among the trees in the drizzle, her tears intermingling with the rain, she watched as the chief of police handed a folded American flag to Michael's widow.

The woman stood and was immediately embraced by a tall man in dress uniform. From her vantage point, Karen could see that Michael's wife was beautiful. She was wearing a designer suit and was smartly coiffured. All those around her were especially solicitous of her, and when the tall man in dress uniform was not at her side, she was flanked by two attractive older women— one of whom bore an uncanny resemblance to Margery Devlin, the movie star.

Suddenly, Michael's wife looked up and stared in

her direction. Karen knew she had seen her. She felt incapable of moving, however. Then the woman who resembled Margery Devlin put her hand on the widow's arm and whispered something into her ear. Karen took the opportunity to leave. She'd seen enough.

"Miss Robinson?" a deep male voice inquired.

Karen slowly raised her eyes to the smiling face of a tall, trim, dark-skinned, ruggedly-handsome man in his mid-thirties.

He reached for her hand. She hastily rose to her feet and grasped his hand. They shook, and he laughed deep in his throat. "You were daydreaming. What's the matter, aren't you having a good day?"

He indicated the way to his office with a courtly gesture. They began walking down the hall. "The reason I ask is it's my theory that people daydream more often when they're worried about something."

He talked easily to her, as though he'd known her all her life. Karen was instantly at ease in his presence.

"I'm not exactly worried," she said. "A little apprehensive, maybe."

"About the job?" Scott Prentice asked.

He opened the door to his office and allowed her to precede him. Karen stepped into a large, airy work space with plenty of light filtering in through the over-sized windows.

There was a large oak desk near one of the windows, and a few feet away from it stood a huge drawing board with several rolled-up blueprints sitting atop it. Karen assumed that was where he did most of his work.

Scott sat down behind his desk, and Karen took the chair directly across from him.

"Don't worry about the job, Miss Robinson. It's yours if you're willing to work hard and learn as you go."

"Oh, I am," Karen said enthusiastically, leaning forward in her chair. "I'm a hard worker. I'm smart. I'm completing my bachelor's degree in business administration. I know I'd do an excellent job for you, Mr. Prentice."

"Business administration," Scott Prentice said, a smile causing crinkles to appear at the corners of his brown eyes. "You're overqualified for this job, Miss Robinson."

"I'm in a catch-22 situation here, Mr. Prentice. I don't have a degree yet. I'm paying for my education, and I'm a single mother. I have a two-year-old..."

"The terrible two's, huh?" Scott said. He turned around the eight by ten photograph whose back had been to Karen atop his desk. Karen looked into the face of a cherubic girl-child with her father's skin color and eyes the exact shade of roasted almonds. The face elicited a smile from her.

"Cute, isn't she?" Scott said proudly.

"A heartbreaker," Karen agreed.

She saw no reason why she shouldn't feel free to display her photos of Michael, so she whipped one out and handed it to Scott.

"He looks like a scrapper," Scott said. "Who keeps him for you during the day?"

"My mother," Karen replied.

"You're lucky," Scott told her. "I get to see Danielle

only on weekends and holidays. My ex got custody of her in the divorce."

Karen was pleased to hear no irritation in his voice when he mentioned his ex-wife. She didn't think much of men who maligned the mother of their children. Her experience with Michael had inadvertently taught her that lesson.

"I know that having to see your daughter on weekends and holidays isn't like seeing her every day, but whatever time you spend with her is good. My son never sees his father."

Embarrassed at the thought that she'd carried the conversation to a much too personal level, Karen looked down.

"I agree," Scott said, smiling. "I should be grateful for the time I have with Danielle instead of grousing about the time I don't have with her."

He liked Karen Robinson. She seemed honest, and she wasn't afraid to say what was on her mind although there was a reticence, a shyness, about her that made him wonder. He'd take a chance on her.

"You're hired," he said with confidence. "When can you start?"

"Right away," Karen said, her brown eyes flooded with relief.

"Don't look so thankful," Scott said teasingly. "I may be an ogre to work for."

They rose and shook on it. When his hand touched hers this time, Scott knew he'd had an ulterior motive for offering her the position: he was attracted to her.

Karen continued to smile at him. "You don't look

like an ogre to me, Mr. Prentice. At this point, you look like a lifeline. I'll have no problem working for you."

"Then it's settled," Scott said. "Can you really start right away, because I have a proposal that needs to be typed up."

"Yes," Karen replied a little breathlessly. "Just point me to my desk."

Alana lay her head on the inflatable tub pillow and closed her eyes. The soothing sounds of jazz artist, Cassandra Wilson, playing on her portable CD player came through the earphones she wore and the scent of Orange Flower wafted up from the warm, foamy bath water. She sighed. Nico would be coming over in two hours so that they could discuss how best to approach Michael's mistress. For the present though, all she wanted to do was relax and let the world recede into the background.

She felt her muscles loosen up as she sank further down into the fragrant water. The sensation was like floating. She drifted off to sleep, buffeted in a cocoon of seeming euphoria.

Then, she was in the water at Lake Tahoe. The day was sunny and bright and she and Nico were tossing a beach ball back and forth. She looked around, wondering where Michael was and she remembered he was watching basketball.

Nico threw the ball over her head. As she leapt out of the water for it and came back down with it, she slipped and went under. She swallowed water and panicked. She couldn't get her breath. The next thing she knew, Nico was pulling her out of the water onto the bank. He gently lay her upon the grass and she was coughing and spitting up water as he straddled her and massaged her lungs from behind, forcing the water out.

Soon, she was fine and sitting up, offering him a wan smile. She went to say something and he silenced her with a raised hand. Then he pulled her into his arms and held her close to him. Not a single word passed between them, however, she could feel his love and his relief at not losing her radiating from him. She had never been more content and in her dream-state, thought, "Don't let me wake up for a while, just let me enjoy this."

A hand was on her bare shoulder, nudging her awake.

"Alana, Alana."

It took a moment for her to realize that she was no longer dreaming. With a start, she sat up, splashing water onto the bathroom floor. Nico squatted beside her, smiling at her. "Girl, what are you doing sleeping in a tub full of water? You could drown like that."

Alana was grateful there were plenty of bubbles that served as a blanket to cover her.

"Nico, what are you doing here?"

Nico rose, reached over and selected a large, fluffy white oversized bath towel from the shelf opposite the tub. He handed it to her. "I arrived early and rang the bell. You didn't answer. I knew you were here because I saw Jonathan downstairs and he told me you were. Thinking something might be wrong, I used your spare key. Once inside, I called to you, you still didn't reply so I searched the apartment and found you here snoozing." He bent down. Their faces were only inches apart. "Let me wash your back for you while I'm here." When he placed one muscular arm, up to the elbow, into the bath water, close to Alana's backside, she hastily slid forward in the tub.

"Where *is* that sponge," Nico said, his downward-sloping brown eyes alight with amusement. Alana grabbed his hand and held on to it.

"Out," she ordered sternly, looking him in the eye. "Get out now or in a moment, you'll be drenched. You only get one warning."

"That could be fun," Nico told her. He stood and began removing his shirt, revealing a washboard stomach and highly developed pectorals.

Alana stared at him. "You're playing while I'm rapidly turning into a prune."

"No one's stopping you from getting out," Nico said. He turned his back to her. "Okay, go ahead and get out."

"The second I rise, you'll turn back around," Alana accused him. "No. You've got to go, Setera."

"Oh, all right," Nico said at last. He walked out of the room and closed the door behind him.

Alana carefully stood and began toweling dry. The door came back open and Nico stuck his head in. "By the way, I brought take-out."

Alana quickly wrapped the towel around her and stepped out of the tub. Angry, she slipped and slid on the wet tile. Nico came forward and pulled her into his arms, thereby preventing her from falling. She threw her arms around his strong neck and held on.

"You are a relentless prankster," she breathed. He smiled at her and she was unable to maintain an angry frame of mind.

The feeling that came over her then was reminiscent of the spiritual sense of contentment she'd had in the dream Nico had awakened her out of. I love him, she thought. I'm in love with Nico. It had taken a jolt from her subconscious in the form of the dream to make her face up to it. That's why she had felt as if she couldn't let go of Michael. While he was alive, she had been in love with his best friend. It had happened at Lake Tahoe. If she had known Michael was seeing someone else, she would have left him then. Consequently, she wouldn't have punished herself with guilt-feelings the last year. Deep down, she had told herself: My husband's dead. He loved me but I didn't love him as I should have. I don't deserve to be happy.

Hindsight, she thought sadly. If I'd known then what I know now, I would've chosen Nico the night we all met.

"What's that frown for?" Nico asked, breaking the silence between them.

Alana brightened. "I adore you."

Nico responded by softly kissing her lips. When the kiss ended, Alana dreamily gazed up into his eyes. Then she felt a draft. Laughing nervously, she firmly grasped him by the shoulders. "Don't move." The towel hung loose between them. Any sudden movement on his part and she'd be standing before him in all her glory. She reached down for the towel and re-wrapped it around her body. "Okay, you can move now."

Nico gave her an enigmatic grin. "I don't think I want to go just yet. You've just said you adore me. If we stand here a while longer maybe you'll admit that you're in love with me."

Alana lay her head on his chest and smiled contentedly.

Soon, she thought.

Chapter 6

Nico waited patiently outside of apartment 306 of the Royal Arms Apartments in Oakland. The group of buildings were government subsidy housing, with a difference: the residents had taken it upon themselves to maintain their homes in a decent, respectable manner instead of relying upon bureaucrats to run things. Therefore the grounds were manicured, the walls and hallways were clean and free of graffiti, and there were no drug dealers hanging on corners plying their goods anywhere in the vicinity of the Royal Arms.

Nico had read in the papers that the neighborhood had had some assistance from Muslims in keeping the criminal element out of their complex—a fact that made certain politicians unhappy, but then they didn't live in the Royal Arms. The residents had welcomed any help they could get since, in their opinion, the authorities weren't doing an adequate job.

The door remained closed; however, a gruff female voice called, "Who's there?"

Nico calmly placed his badge in front of the peephole. "My name is Nicolas Setera. I'm a detective with the San Francisco Police Department."

"Badges don't mean nothin' round here," the woman said through the door. "What else you got?"

Nico wasn't in the least perturbed by the woman's cautious attitude. It was a dangerous world, and nowadays being a cop didn't garner the trust in your average citizens' minds and hearts the way it used to.

He gave her the number of the police operator. "Call that number," he suggested. "And ask them to describe me, then if you still don't want to talk with me, I'll gladly leave."

The woman was away from the door for five minutes as Nico stood on the front stoop, observing the activities of her neighbors. Children were playing on the lawn, a man half-heartedly washed his car two doors down. A teenaged couple was apparently walking home from school together—they both had backpacks slung over their shoulders as they held hands.

Hearing the door being unlocked, Nico returned his attention to apartment 306. A plump, middle-aged woman, a smile on her round, dark brown face ushered him in. "Okay," she said lightly. "You check out."

Nico stepped into a neat, modest living room. A toddler was sitting in the middle of the room in front of a television set, watching "Sesame Street." The little boy looked up, saw Nico, grinned, and said, "Hi!"

"Hello," Nico said, smiling.

"Pay attention to the Count," the woman admonished the boy. "You need to learn your numbers."

She looked expectantly at Nico. "What can I do for you, Detective?"

Nico was still focused on the child. He reluctantly looked away from the tyke and gave the woman his undivided attention.

"Mrs.—"

"It's Miss. Geraldine Robinson. Won't you have a seat, Detective?" She continued to eye him suspiciously.

Nico sat on a multifloral armchair, and Geraldine sat across from him on the matching couch.

"Do you recall hearing about the murder of a San Francisco police officer in this neighborhood about a year ago?"

Geraldine Robinson sat with her back stiff, her brown eyes never leaving Nico's face.

"Yes, I do remember when that happened. What a shame. A nice young *family* man like that," she said in mock sympathy.

Nico heard the note of sarcasm in her voice and it made him wonder if Geraldine Robinson knew more than she was letting on. His eyes narrowed. "That officer was my partner, Miss Robinson," he said sharply. He watched her face.

Geraldine flinched noticeably. "What exactly do you want from me, Detective—"

"Setera," Nico supplied.

"I'm a busy woman," Geraldine said defensively. "I was in the middle of preparing dinner when you rang my bell."

It occurred to Nico that she was protecting someone. "Did you, or anyone else living here know Michael Calloway?"

Geraldine sighed. All she wanted was to get this police officer out of her house. "No, Detective. No one living here knew Michael Calloway."

Geraldine rose. "I'll show you to the door, Detective. I'm sorry I couldn't be of more help to you."

Suddenly, she froze, a horrified expression on her face. From across the room came the sound of a key being inserted into the front door lock. Geraldine glanced up at the clock on the living room wall. Not *now,* she thought frantically.

"Momma!" Karen called as she walked through the door, her arms filled with packages. "Michael!"

Karen spotted her mother standing, like a mannequin, in the center of the room, her mouth open in shock.

"Momma, what's wrong?" she asked as she approached her. "Mr. Prentice had to go out of town for a couple of days, so he told me to take the afternoon off…"

As she passed the étagère, she saw Nico. Her eyes were panicked as they searched the room for Michael, who had gone into his bedroom to get his stuffed Big Bird. "Michael, Michael, come to Mama, baby!"

Sensing her mother's level of anxiety, Karen was

almost beside herself with worry for her son. She ran from the room calling to him.

Nico was on his feet, following her. "Miss Robinson? Nothing has happened to your son, believe me. I'm a cop. I'm not here to cause you or your family any harm."

By the time Nico got midway down the hall, Karen was returning with Michael in her arms. The packages she'd been carrying were strewn down the hallway. Nico had to step around them to reach her.

"Miss Robinson, there's no need for you to be upset. I just want to ask you a few questions about Michael Calloway."

Standing in the hallway, Karen regarded him with angry eyes. She covered her son's right ear with her left hand. "Why are you questioning us about him?" she asked belligerently. She turned and continuing walking until she'd reached the living room where she sat on the couch, still cradling Michael in her arms. Geraldine had gone into the kitchen to resume dinner preparations, but her ears were strained to hear anything going on in the living room.

"Who are you?" Karen asked, her tone wary.

Nico introduced himself and produced his badge and picture ID. Karen perused them then met his gaze once more.

"Why are you asking questions about Michael?"

"He was my partner," Nico replied. He sat down next to her on the couch, turning toward her. "The thing is, his widow wants to know why he was found in this neighborhood. He wasn't on duty that night, and he'd told her he was going to be elsewhere. You understand?"

"Yes, I understand," Karen said as she rocked Michael in her arms. She looked down into Michael's upturned face. "Would you go into the kitchen with Grandma, sweetie? Ask her to give you a cookie and some milk."

Michael climbed out of his mother's lap and did as he was told.

"He seems like a great kid," Nico complimented her.

Karen smiled. "He is a great kid." Their eyes met and held. "How well did you know Michael?"

"Not as well as I thought I did," Nico said cautiously. "Although, we were best friends for a number of years."

"For months after he died, I expected someone to come here asking all sorts of questions. When no one did, I figured Michael had done a good job of keeping us a secret."

Nico sat back as well. He wasn't going to push her. Karen seemed to want to talk. It was as if she'd been waiting for the moment when she could talk to someone about Michael. He was grateful he was that someone.

She laughed self-consciously. "I didn't know he was married until after I read his obituary. I'd known him for three years. I read in the papers that he'd been married for only two. I often wonder which of us he met first and why he chose her to marry over me. Can you answer that?"

"No," Nico said softly. He didn't know what he'd expected to find in Michael's mistress. Someone cold and detached? This woman was neither of those. She appeared intelligent, and from everything he'd observed since stepping into apartment 306, he judged her to be an honest, hard working young mother trying to build a better life for her son.

"I can't tell you why Michael did what he did," he told her honestly. "All I can tell you is that you came as a surprise to his wife. That's why I'm here. She sent me to act as a sort of intermediary between you two."

"So Alana has just found out about us?" Karen asked, her eyes a little sad.

"You know her name?" Nico said, astonished.

"I was at the memorial service. I heard the minister call her name. That was you next to her throughout the service?"

Nico nodded. "Yeah, that was me."

"You care about her," Karen said matter of factly.

"Very much," Nico admitted freely.

"That's good," Karen said. "At least *she* has someone to help her get over that creep."

"She wants to meet you," Nico told her, watching her face for a surprised reaction.

Karen merely frowned. "I don't know," she said in a low voice. "What if she wants to pull my hair out?"

"Alana's not that kind of person," Nico said reassuringly. "She says she wants to meet you so that she can finally purge him from her system. Maybe you can help each other. From your comments about him, it doesn't seem as though you're completely over him yourself."

"Oh, I've been through all the stages of grief," Karen told him. "At first, I was in denial. Then I blamed myself. Now I'm putting the blame where it should be, on Michael."

"Then you're a little farther along than Alana is," Nico said. "She lived with the hope that she'd been mistaken about his infidelity for over a year. Now she

knows he was cheating on her and is experiencing feelings of inadequacy. She thinks that if she'd been a better wife, Michael would not have strayed…"

"That isn't true," Karen said forcefully.

"I know it isn't true," Nico said, looking her in the
eyes. "Maybe you can convince her."

"All right," Karen said, having made up her mind.
"I'll meet with Alana. When?"

Nico reached into his jacket pocket and retrieved
the hand-written note Alana had given him to give to
Karen if she proved to be amenable to their meeting.

Karen tore it open and read:

*It's not my intention to disrupt your life, Karen.
And if you choose not to meet me at Le Petite Café
tomorrow afternoon at one-thirty, I'll respect
your wishes and not try to contact you again.
But if you do decide to come, know this: I don't
hold any grudges against you. I won't judge you.
I won't seek revenge for wrongs done me, either
verbally or physically. I simply want to talk to you.
Alana Shelby Calloway*

Karen knew Le Petite Café, she'd been there for
lunch on a number of occasions. The restaurant was
always crowded at around one. So there would be plenty
of witnesses if Alana Calloway decided to attack her.
She'd feel relatively safe in that environment.

"Okay," she told Nico momentarily. "Tell her I'll
be there."

* * *

"That's it," Alana said as she concluded Thursday morning's staff meeting. "I officially declare that all major preparations are complete, and I'm giving you all the rest of the day off. Thank you for a job well done."

Clovis raised his hand to get her attention.

"Yes, Clovis?"

"Alana, about your suggestion that we join the party after the buffet has been set up. Were you serious?"

Alana smiled at him affectionately and glanced at the rest of her crew scattered about the kitchen.

"Of course I was serious. Margery has contracted with another service to provide waiters and waitresses. You guys worked hard to prepare all the food, you deserve to get out there and enjoy yourselves. So, please, wear your best party outfits and bring a loved one. It's Valentine's Day!"

"I'll definitely be there," Gina put in, her brown eyes sparkling with excitement. "I'd never turn down the opportunity to rub elbows with the rich and famous. Maria told me Whoopi is coming. I love her. I've seen all her movies."

"There, you see?" Alana said, hoping Gina's enthusiasm was catching. "Come and have a good time."

"I'd feel out of place," Clovis maintained. "I'm just a cook."

Alana stepped forward and grasped one of Clovis's big, dark hands in both her hands. Looking into his eyes, she said, "Don't you ever let me hear you deride your profession again." She smiled. "Ours is an honorable calling. Everybody has to eat, and few people have your talent for making food appetizing. So never say, 'I'm just a cook,' say instead, 'I'm the best damn cook on the planet,' then you'd be closer to the truth."

The gentle giant smiled benignly. "You always have a good comeback prepared, don't you, Alana?"

"That's my job," Alana said. "I'm the coach, you're the team. I have to keep my team fired up." She looked around the room. "Any more dissenters?"

There was a general consensus that everyone would be attending the ball. "Very good," Alana said finally. "Then go home and get some rest, you're going to need it tomorrow."

After everyone else had gone for the day, Alana made one last round, making certain everything was put away properly; then she gathered her belongings and left the kitchen. She needed to go home and work on Vesta's books. She'd named the company after the Roman goddess of the hearth, since the hearth in the past was the center of the home. She'd vowed that her company would reflect good, wholesome qualities. Vesta would always produce nutritious, delectable food for a fair price, and she would treat her employees like family.

Her cellular phone rang as she began ascending the stairs in search of Margery and the others. She knew that Georgie and Bree, along with the two Pierres, were gone to Fisherman's Wharf to purchase crabs. Bree wanted to have a crab boil tonight. But Margery, Toni and Daniel, Margery's contrite ex-husband who'd arrived shortly after Bree and Pierre, were somewhere in the house.

"How's everything going?" Nico asked, his voice husky.

"Everything's going so well, I just let everyone go home for the day," Alana answered, smiling. She paused on the stairs and leaned against the wall. "How are things with you? Did you catch up with the infamous other woman?"

Nico laughed on his end. "Karen Robinson isn't your run-of-the-mill home wrecker. She seems…nice."

"Nice?"

"She claims she didn't know Michael was married until she read it in the papers."

Alana considered that and said, "You're a good judge of character. Do you believe her?"

There was silence for several seconds as Nico weighed his response. He didn't want to be precipitous. Plus, there was the matter of Michael's child. Should he tell her or wait for Karen to do so? "Is there any way we can get together sometime today?" he asked quietly. "I had the early shift so I'm no longer on duty. Besides, I'd like to see you."

Hearing the concern in his voice, Alana felt butterflies forming in the pit of her stomach. What could be so important he couldn't tell her about it over the phone?

"Sure. I'm leaving Margery's in a few minutes. I have to go home and work on the books. Tomorrow's payday."

"I'll meet you there in a half hour," Nico said.

After they'd hung up, Alana ran the rest of the way upstairs and went to Margery's study, which was adjacent to her bedroom. As she'd guessed, Margery, Toni and Daniel were in the book-lined room talking about old times. They looked up when she entered the room.

"I just came up to say goodbye," Alana said. "Nico's meeting me at my place in a few minutes..."

"Has he had any luck?" Margery wanted to know.

"He found her," Alana announced. She didn't know why, but she felt relieved by the thought. If everything went as she hoped, Michael's ghost would be exorcised by Valentine's Day. "Her name's Karen Robinson, but that's all I know so far. I'll keep you posted."

Margery and Toni had crossed the room to wrap their arms around Alana in a group hug.

"It's almost over now, my love," Margery cooed as if to a small child.

"When it's done, you'll be the stronger for it," Toni predicted. "You will have gone through the fire and survived." She planted a motherly kiss on Alana's forehead. "I'm proud of you for pursuing the matter. It shows a strength of character I've always known you possessed."

"Yes," Margery agreed.

She and Toni glanced at one another, and after a silent form of agreement between them, she continued. "Now, my love, there is something your aunt Toni and I must confess."

Alana looked expectantly at her aunts. Guilt was plainly evident on both their dear faces. She frowned. It was all coming together for her. The suspicious manner in which Margery and Toni had been behaving recently. The knowing looks. Their apparent relief that she and Nico had reconciled.

Nico had not raised the subject of Karen Robinson

being the culprit behind the note. Then that left only...
"I don't believe it. You two sent that note, didn't you?"

"Only because you were pining away for a man who clearly did not deserve you," Margery said quickly. "We tried everything to make you snap out of your depression. But you refused to listen to reason..."

"A person must grieve at her own pace," Alana said.

"You didn't have all the facts," Toni said, her dark eyes appealing to Alana for sympathy. "Our only concern was for your well-being."

"What facts?" Alana asked, looking from Margery to Toni. "Exactly how did you acquire these 'facts'?"

Margery and Toni looked at one another.

"Well, don't be silent now," Alana said, her voice taking on the imperious tone Margery was known for. "Spill it."

They did. However, they were talking so fast, their words so closely juxtaposed to each other's, that Alana found the narrative difficult to follow.

"You remember you came to me crying about Michael's many excuses. You said you were certain he was cheating..." Margery intoned.

"So we called a friend of a friend who recommended a private detective," Toni said, picking up the ball. "This detective, Dean Ray, Joe Bob..." Flustered, she looked to Margery for elucidation.

"Robert Dean," Margery provided. "He went by Bob Dean. Anyway, Mr. Dean found out that Michael was seeing Karen Robinson."

There were tears in her eyes when she turned to clasp one of Alana's hands in hers. "That's not all, my love."

"There is a child," Toni spoke up, seeing that Margery was about to collapse into tears. "Mr. Dean was able to obtain a copy of the child's birth certificate. Michael is named as the father."

Momentarily shocked into inactivity, Alana simply stared into space. Then she realized she was holding her breath and began sucking in lungs full. It felt as though the room was closing in on her. Breaking Margery's grip on her hand, she ran blindly toward the door.

Daniel blocked her exit. She almost made him lose his balance when she collided with him, but he was a big man and outweighed her by at least seventy pounds.

His strong arms went around her and held her in a vise of steel. Looking over at Toni and Margery, who were holding on to one another, he said, "Phone Nico and tell him to get over here."

When all the players were assembled in the study, Daniel rose from his place beside Alana, allowing Nico to take over for him. Fixing Margery with a look of compassion, he began:

"From what I've been able to glean about this situation, you, Margery, were trying to prevent Alana, whom you love as you would a daughter, from being hurt."

Margery nodded vigorously. A fresh tear rolled down her mascara-streaked face.

"And you, Toni," Daniel continued, "acted as an accomplice because, as we all know, you two stick together like glue. And then there was the matter of the promise you made to Connie all those years ago..."

"A promise?" Alana said, leaning forward.

Her eyes were dry. She figured she'd shed enough tears over Michael to fill the Pacific Ocean. She was cried out.

Toni informed her about the promise three eighteen-year-old girls had made to each other thirty years ago, her voice breaking with emotion.

"We meant well," Toni said, near the end. "I'm afraid we sometimes do foolish things in the name of love."

"Yes, we do," Daniel said, looking lovingly into Margery's eyes. He turned his attention back to Alana. "What your dead husband did to you will never be fully explained. But what these three did: the hiding of secrets, well, they did out of love. Toni and Margery, as your surrogate mothers, and Nico, as the man who loves you more than your husband ever did." He smiled at Nico. "I hope I'm not embarrassing you, my man."

With his arms wrapped protectively around Alana, Nico looked into her beautiful face. "Not in the least," he said, smiling at her.

Alana reached up and gently touched his cheek, her eyes meeting his. "I love you too," she said, her voice a whisper.

Daniel felt his throat tighten as he witnessed this spectacle. True love. Such an elusive thing.

Margery and Toni were hugging each other, tears streaming down their faces.

Daniel walked over to them and took each of them by a hand. "Shall we give them a little privacy?" he suggested.

Alone, Nico pulled Alana more fully into his embrace. She rested her head on his broad chest, listening to the strong, steady rhythm of his heartbeat. She was finally at peace in her soul. It was over. Everything she needed to know about Michael had been disclosed. She could catalog him along with every other mistake she'd ever made in her lifetime: in the dark recesses of her memory bank.

They sat on the couch, not speaking, for a long while. Then, Nico broke the silence with, "Say it once more."

Lifting her head to place her mouth over his, Alana kissed him soundly. Parting, she smiled at him. "I love you."

Nico grinned, his downward-sloping, velvety brown bedroom eyes taking on a passionate light. He bent his head and taking her lower lip between his teeth, gently pulled on it. Then he covered her mouth with his, her lips parted and their tongues danced seductively until they fell back into Margery's overstuffed, ivory-colored couch, oblivious to everything except one another.

Chapter 7

Karen felt her palms grow damp with moisture as she watched Alana Calloway cross the crowded restaurant, making her way to her table. Alana was smartly attired in a dark copper-toned Donna Karan pantsuit and flats to match. Her thick, dark hair was flawlessly done in an upswept style, one lock falling over the right side of her high-cheekboned face. To Karen, she looked as though she'd just stepped off the cover of *Essence*.

What further unnerved her was how Alana had made a beeline for her once she'd entered the restaurant. Had Nicholas Setera's description of her been that detailed?

"Hello," Alana said, standing next to her. "You must be Karen."

Karen got to her feet and hastily shook Alana's proffered hand. "Yes," she replied, nervously looking around them. "How did you know?"

Alana laughed shortly as she sat down opposite Karen's chair. "In case I was held up, I asked John to seat you at my favorite table."

"Oh," Karen said as she settled back into her chair.

Alana decided that Nico had been correct in his estimation of Karen Robinson's appearance. Perhaps three inches shorter than Alana's five-seven, Karen was trim, almost to the point of being reed thin. Her dark brown eyes were almond-shaped and at the moment held an expression of apprehension in them. Her face was heart-shaped and quite pretty in spite of her lack of makeup. She wore her black hair in a short fashion that was shorn close on the sides.

Face to face with the other woman, Alana thought. The experience wasn't what she imagined it would be. Karen Robinson didn't look like a cold-hearted man stealer to her. Under different circumstances, Karen was probably someone she'd choose for a friend.

"Would you like to order something?" Alana asked.

"No, no," Karen hurriedly replied. "I couldn't eat a thing." Her stomach growled. She'd missed breakfast.

"Well I could," Alana said, motioning to a passing waiter. "Oh, David!"

Seeing Alana, David stopped in his tracks, a tray of drinks suspended in the air as easily as if it was attached to his wrist.

"Gotcha, Alana. I'll be right there."

He continued to another table in his station, deposited the drinks in front of the patrons with a flourish, and turned to head back to Alana's table.

After a quick buss to Alana's cheek, he grinned at

her, his green eyes shining in his California-suntanned face. He absently smoothed his blond ponytail back.

"Girl, you look good enough to be on the menu," he said, his smile bringing out the dimple in his left cheek. "Vesta keeping you busy?"

"As ever," Alana told him. "David, Karen."

"Hello, Karen. You look wonderful, too. First time here?"

"Yes," Karen said shyly, unwilling to be more forthcoming.

"Well then, may I suggest the crabmeat salad? It's fresh, it's fine, it's divine."

"I'll take it," Alana replied at once. She'd had a craving for crabmeat since last night when she'd missed out on Bree's crab boil. She and Nico had gone to her apartment where they'd spent most of the night talking.

"Okay," Karen acquiesced.

"And what would you like to drink?" David asked, order pad poised to take down their requests.

"A cola?" Karen timidly said.

"Are you asking me or telling me?" David joked.

"Lay off, you rascal," Alana warned him good-naturedly. "She'll take a cola and I'll have iced tea. Go do your job, or I'll hire you away from John, then you'll really be sorry."

"Slave driver!" David retorted, grinning at her.

David went to get their salads, and Alana smiled at Karen. "Don't mind him. He was just trying to include you in our usual give and take. You see, this was my first gig after graduating from the California Culinary Academy. I was here for over a year, working under the head chef. I got to know several of the staff quite well. David remains my favorite."

Karen knew she must appear simpleminded, sitting there like an idiot with little to say, but she felt so out of place, it was difficult to think.

Sensing her discomfort, Alana reached across the small, round table and placed her hand atop Karen's.

"I meant what I wrote to you in that note, Karen. I'm not here to heap blame on you. Truly."

Their eyes met and they smiled at one another.

Alana removed her hand and sat up straight in her chair. "I thought we could sort of compare notes, try to piece together the secret life of Michael Calloway. Starting with when each of us met him." She paused, clearing her throat. "I met Michael in ninety-four. June, I think it was. Two friends of mine and I were out dancing at a club here in San Francisco. He walked over to our table and introduced himself. The next night we had our first date."

Karen's demeanor experienced a metamorphosis as she leaned forward. Her eyes were no longer timid. They were somewhat angry.

"I met the b...*him* in ninety-three," she said, her tone barely under control. "In December. I remember because Christmas was just around the corner. He gave me a gold bracelet for Christmas."

A little surprised by this revelation, but not completely nonplussed, Alana pursed her lips and said, "Mmm...huh." She had come there to get answers to her questions and no matter what Karen Robinson said, she was going to listen.

"We met in a club in Oakland," Karen said. "He liked to dance."

"I would say that's an understatement," Alana remarked dryly.

They looked at one another and laughed uproariously at the absurdity of it all. They'd both met him while out dancing.

Bringing their salads and drinks, David smiled pleasantly.

"Now that's more like it," he said approvingly. "Enjoy your lunches, ladies." He left them to their meals.

"Oh, God," Alana said, coming down from her laughing jag and wiping the corners of her eyes with the white cloth napkin provided for Le Petite Café's customers. "I wonder how many other women he picked up in clubs."

"You think he had time for more than two?" Karen asked, dabbing at her tears with her napkin as well.

"No," Alana said, looking at Karen. "I mean he was already seeing you, and then he meets me, courts me, and convinces me to marry him all in the course of three months."

"You married him after three months?"

"I'd never been in love before. I led a rather sheltered life. I went to an all-girl high school in New York. Then my parents were killed, and I moved here to live with my aunt. I attended California State, then found my true calling: the culinary arts. My mind was totally on getting ahead. Then I met Michael, and he blew me away."

"Me, too," Karen agreed. "I was struggling to get

through my first year of college when we met. I came from the projects. In Michael, I saw my way out."

"He seemed so sincere," Alana said, sighing. "I never doubted he loved me. Not until the end."

"Me, either," Karen said. "And the thing is, I avoided men whom I thought to be bad influences: drug dealers, men with no direction. Then to be deceived by him. I was mad as hell when after I got pregnant, he made it plain to me that he had no intention of marrying me. But, as it turned out, my son has been a blessing. He's the only thing I don't regret."

Nodding sympathetically, Alana took a sip of her iced tea.

"What kind of father was he? Michael always raved about what a great father he'd be. He never knew his own father, you know."

"I have to give credit where credit is due," Karen said magnanimously. "He paid the hospital bill and he provided for Michael's needs. I didn't have to hassle him about that." She laughed. "The only time he appeared really happy was when he was holding Michael. The last few months he was alive, he was like a man possessed. Now that I know about you, I can see why."

"Yes, I noticed that as well," Alana told her, meeting her gaze. "It couldn't have been easy for him. Juggling work, two women. Providing for his son. I almost feel sorry for him."

"Almost," Karen put in. "But not quite."

She sat up straight in her chair and regarded Alana with clear, determined eyes. "I know he's dead and we'll never know why he did what he did, but why do *you* think he married you instead of me?"

Alana didn't reply right away. Since learning of Karen's existence, she had assumed Michael had met her after their marriage. However, if what Karen said was true, he'd known the other woman at least five months before they'd met. Did Michael love her more? Was that the reason he'd married her?

Unfortunately, only Michael could answer that question. She recalled the last dream she'd had of him. "Remember me fondly," he'd implored.

"Who knows why he chose to marry me?" Alana said at last. "I think maybe he was in love with us both and couldn't decide whom to give up. But it seems to me that if he'd been forced to make a decision, he would've chosen you. You gave birth to his child. Michael never got over being abandoned by his father. I can't imagine his doing the same thing to his son."

"But he lied to me about everything," Karen said, unwilling to attribute such a noble trait to Michael. "It's true enough, he loved his child. However, I think he would have gone on deceiving everyone if he'd lived." She tossed the napkin she'd been nervously twirling between her fingers on to the table. "I should have known he was married by the way he behaved. I don't know why I was so blind."

"You loved him," Alana said simply. "We didn't *want* to believe the worst. It would have destroyed our perfect illusions."

Nodding, Karen smiled. "You're right. I wanted to believe he'd break down and marry me someday. I'd given him a beautiful child. If I could simply be patient, maybe he would eventually do the right thing."

Alana's gaze was steady as she smiled at Karen. "Whatever you do, Karen, don't give up on finding someone who will truly love you. Sometimes finding him is as easy as turning around and looking at the person standing next to you."

"You're talking about Detective Setera, aren't you?"

Alana laughed. "Nico said you were smart."

"It doesn't take a genius to see that he cares for you a great deal. The way he stood by your side the day Michael was laid to rest. His tracking me down so that you would have a sense of closure. You're a lucky woman, Alana."

"I am," Alana agreed.

She bent down and picked up her purse. She rummaged through it for a moment, coming out of it with a long manila envelope. She handed it to Karen. "I feel like passing a little of my luck along."

Karen appeared reluctant to accept the envelope. She looked at it as though Alana was offering her a bomb.

Laughing, Alana placed the envelope on the tabletop. "I promise you, it won't explode."

Karen gingerly touched the envelope, then picked it up. Pulling up the flap, which wasn't glued on, she opened it and removed the contents. Her eyes grew larger with shock and disbelief. "Oh my God!" she exclaimed. "Oh my God!"

"Consider it Michael's inheritance from his father," Alana said, a contented smile on her lips. "That is the full amount of Michael's death benefit…"

"But you don't even know for a certainty that Michael is really his son…" Karen protested.

"I am certain," Alana assured her. She looked directly into Karen's eyes. "I know what I'm doing, Karen."

She didn't want to go into how Margery and Toni had acquired a copy of Karen's son's birth certificate. For one thing, the story was too long to get into at the moment and for another, she was sure the detective, Bob Dean, had employed illegal practices to obtain the document.

"This is too much," Karen said, her eyes misty. "You don't even know me. What if I'm a disreputable person and I use this for selfish purposes?"

Alana set about eating her crabmeat salad. Between mouthfuls, she said, "You're the mother of his child. You deserve that money. Do whatever you wish with it. It was only sitting in the bank earning interest."

Karen stared at the cashier's check. She had never seen so many zeros in her life. She could finish college, put a down payment on a house. Send Michael to a good college when the time came. For once in her life, she wouldn't have to live from paycheck to paycheck. She felt as if she'd just won the lottery.

"This isn't some kind of mean-spirited joke?" she said. "You're actually giving me nearly a hundred thousand dollars?" She leaned forward, looking into Alana's eyes. "I don't know what to make of you. Are you crazy? Why? Why would you do this?"

Sighing, Alana placed her fork on the tabletop and drank some of the iced tea. With both elbows on the tabletop, she rested her chin in her palms. She smiled slowly.

"That check represents the last of Michael Calloway," she said. "He's gone from my life forever."

"And my son gets a better life," Karen said, catching on.

She laughed, her brown eyes clearing up considerably. The time for weeping was past. A celebration was in order.

"David!" she called.

David, in the middle of serving swordfish to an elderly couple, finished with his unique flair and then hurried to Alana and Karen's table.

"Did I hear one of you goddesses beckon me?"

"I did," Karen said happily. "Champagne, David. The best you have and make it ice cold."

"You're a woman after my own heart," David said, beaming.

Amused, Alana watched as David made haste to do Karen's bidding. Then her eyes rested on Karen's face.

"You're not anything like I imagined you would be," she told Karen.

"You aren't, either," Karen said. The apprehensiveness was now replaced with self-confidence. "But I need to say this, even though I know we have come to an understanding: I'm sorry. I'm sorry for the pain I inadvertently caused you. For the sleepless nights. Worrying where your husband could be. I wouldn't wish that kind of hell on anyone."

"Thank you," Alana replied sincerely.

David returned with the champagne. After placing a

crystal wineglass in front of each of them, he pulled out the cork. The sound reverberated around the room, and diners applauded. There was something about champagne that put everyone in a festive mood.

He poured the golden liquid into the glasses, pausing to allow the bubbles to settle, then he placed the bottle in ice, moving the ice bucket close to Karen. "Don't let it tickle your noses," he said, as he departed.

Karen raised her glass. "To the future," she said.

"Without Michael," Alana added.

"May we all live happily ever after."

"And to your son," Alana said, smiling.

"May he grow up to be nothing like this father," Karen declared prayerfully.

"Amen," Alana intoned.

They touched glasses and drank deeply.

"Can we eat now?" Alana said afterward. "I missed breakfast this morning."

Karen laughed as she picked up her fork and dug in. "My mother's going to have a heart attack when I tell her what happened today."

Chapter 8

With a macabre sense of humor, Alana realized that if the house on Nob Hill suddenly blew up she would lose everyone she loved in one fell swoop.

She was standing in the alcove between the kitchen and the ballroom, watching the festivities, which were in full swing. Margery, with Daniel at her side, was laughing at something the mayor had said. Alana smiled. She was sure Margery was warming to Daniel in spite of her protests to the contrary.

Couples danced to the melodious tones of a twelve-piece orchestra. Bree and Pierre, standout performers, were the center of attention. Georgie, with Brian Chandler, her attorney boyfriend, took the spotlight off the thespian couple with their version of a hip hop tango. The crowd cheered.

Feeling a hand at the small of her back, Alana leaned into Nico's warm embrace. His arms went around her trim waist, and he bent his head to plant a kiss on the curve of her fragrant neck.

"What are you doing back here?" he said. "You should be out there with me, putting Bree and Georgie to shame."

Turning to face him, Alana smiled. He looked so handsome in his tuxedo. "Let them have their fun," she said, more than content to remain where she was: in his arms.

Admiring the silver lamé gown she was wearing, which fell three-inches above her knees, had spaghetti straps, soft folds at the bustline, and plunged downward in the back all the way to her waist, Nico sighed. "Everyone should see you, just once, in this."

Turning to wrap her arms around his neck, Alana clasped her fingers together as she kissed his chin. "I wore it for you."

"And I'm a grateful man," Nico told her seriously. He kissed her lips. "But you're not getting away with being a wallflower tonight."

Taking her by the hand, he led her into the ballroom.

"Alana," Georgie, wearing a red beaded gown in honor of Saint Valentine, called from the dance floor. "Get over here, girl, and show us how to salsa. Miami style."

"You've been challenged," Nico said, his warm brown eyes looking at her with such sensual vibrancy that Alana felt her body tingle with excitement.

They assumed the stance, her right foot sliding forward on the hardwood floor. Nico removed his coat and flung it into the audience. He saw Toni catch it in midair and smile gleefully at him.

The band went into an upbeat Latin number, and Nico executed a movement which reminded Alana of a matador. Then his hand was reaching for her, and they moved with sensual fluidity as they made the dance their own.

"Oh, my," Margery commented to Daniel from the sidelines. "I haven't witnessed anything that blatantly sexual since…"

"You and I were together the last time?" Daniel said hopefully, his arm going around her waist as he pulled her close to him.

Margery lay her head on his chest. "I do miss you, Daniel. But I…"

"But you're afraid I haven't changed," Daniel finished for her. "It's okay. Take your time. I'll be here."

Margery closed her eyes and relaxed in his arms. She loved Daniel. She had never stopped loving him. She was no longer that trusting young woman whom he'd taken for granted years before. But some things were still worth the risk.

"Okay, Daniel," she murmured.

His heart beating double-time with pure joy, Daniel gently kissed Margery on the lips. Tears sat in his golden-brown eyes when he looked down into her beloved face. "I'll spend the rest of my life making you happy."

"We'll spend the rest of our lives making each other happy," Margery corrected him. She smiled into his eyes.

To their left, Toni quietly observed the reunion of her best friend with the love of her life. It's about time, she thought. She looked away, only to lock eyes with an interesting-looking gentleman across the room. Wasn't that Spencer Taylor, the famed jazz pianist? He was even more devastatingly handsome in the flesh.

"Georgette," Brian Chandler said into Georgie's ear. "This is all very entertaining, but can't we circulate more? I haven't even met the mayor yet."

Looking into Brian's smooth dark brown, impatient face, Georgie stifled a groan. All Brian thought about was networking. She didn't think the brother had ever let loose in his entire Ivy League life. She was beginning to think he was only with her because she had access to certain people. People whose friendship she would never dream of using for career advancement.

She cast an envious eye at Alana and Nico. To have a man look at her like that...and have no ulterior motive.

"Georgette?" Brian said again, this time unwilling to be ignored.

Turning on her heels, Georgie walked away from him.

"Georgette, I'm talking to you," Brian said as he followed.

"Why is it you can't call me Georgie?" she said petulantly. "Would it kill you to be less formal with me, Brian? We're not in the office now, loosen up."

She kept walking. "Brian?" Turning, she realized that Brian was engrossed in conversation with the San Francisco District Attorney.

"Are you glad you came?" Bree asked Pierre as she stood locked in his two strong arms.

"Oh, yes," Pierre breathed. "It's everything you said it would be. I've met so many influential people. Thanks, babe."

"You're welcome," Bree responded. Somehow the feel of his arms was not the same for her. She had been aware from the start that Pierre wanted to act more than anything. And she also knew, from experience, that two actors trying to make a go of a relationship didn't often have positive results. But somehow she'd grown fond of Pierre, and that fondness had matured into love. She suddenly had a premonition of them going their separate ways. She shuddered.

Pierre's hold tightened. "What's wrong, sweetheart?"

"Nothing," Bree said. "Just hold me."

Studying Alana and Nico as they danced in the manner only those who had been partners for years did, Bree wished she would someday know that kind of happiness.

The Latin tune was replaced by a Gershwin song, and Genero tapped Nico on the shoulder, wanting to dance with Alana.

Alana waltzed around the room with Genero, complimenting him on his appearance and the fine job he'd done supervising the party.

Genero shrugged off her compliment. "It was nothing any culinary genius couldn't have pulled off. I wanted to talk to you about your aunts…"

"Oh, no," Alana cried. "Not again."

Genero gestured toward a lovely, petite African-

American woman in her early twenties, dancing with the commissioner.

"They set me up with her," he said. "She's a chef at The Beverly Hills Hotel."

From his expression, Alana couldn't tell whether he was pleased or not.

"Well, was it a hit or a miss?" she asked, her brows knit together in worry.

Genero grinned impishly. "She's wonderful."

"Then why aren't you dancing with her?" Alana asked, relieved. "Go ask her to be your Valentine. Must my aunts do your courting for you?"

Laughing, Genero bent his dark head to quickly kiss Alana on the cheek. "Are you sure you and Margery aren't blood relatives?"

Left without a partner, Alana made her way off the dance floor. As she wove her way through the crowd, she spotted Gina to her left dancing with her fiancé, Gary Nunn. Gina waved to her, a wide grin on her pretty face. Earlier in the evening, Alana had noticed her showing her favorite actress how to do the Electric Slide.

"Excuse me," Alana said as she bumped into a tall man.

Clovis looked down at her. "Alana, hello. You remember my wife, Alice?"

"Of course," Alana replied, smiling at the handsome, stout woman who was a foot shorter than her husband. "How are you, Alice?"

"Winded," Alice said, laughter in her deep brown eyes. She was wearing a simple white gown that fell to her ankles. It gave her a sophisticated, elegant appearance. Clovis wore a basic black tux. Alana noticed he'd trimmed his mustache.

"Well, you both look fantastic," Alana complimented them.

Alice blushed. "Thank you, Alana."

"Enjoy yourselves," Alana said as she left them.

She made it as far as the very alcove she'd been standing in before Nico had pulled her onto the dance floor where she was waylaid by Maria and her husband, Carlos.

"I think you all outdid yourselves on the food, Alana," Maria told her. "Everything was *delicioso.*"

Carlos kissed Alana on the cheek. They hadn't seen one another in some time. He was kept busy by his job as district manager for a fast-food chain.

He was around five-ten, dark-skinned and the epitome of the doting spouse. He was always affectionate with Maria. After greeting Alana, his arm was back around Maria's waist, drawing her close to him. They were both wearing black: Maria in a short, sleeveless sheath that clung to her ample curves and Carlos in a tailored tuxedo.

"Thank you," Alana said cheerfully. Reaching up, she removed a leaf from Maria's hair. "Where'd that come from?"

"Oh, my," Maria said. Tinges of red appeared on her cheeks. "We just stepped outside for some air."

She and her husband lovingly gazed into each other's eyes.

"The air must be especially good tonight," Alana joked. "See you guys later. Have a great time."

She turned around to continue walking toward the buffet tables and nearly stepped on Pierre. Bending to pick the poodle up, she tried to calm his trembling. He had been dodging dancers, more than likely attempting to locate his mistress.

Cuddling him, Alana rubbed his small head. "Poor baby. Who let you out of the bedroom?"

Undoubtedly, prying guests had been upstairs. After looking around the bedroom, they'd thoughtlessly left the door ajar.

"You could have been trampled on," Alana complained. Searching the room for Nico, she saw him dancing with Margery. She would take Pierre back upstairs, then go and convince him to take her home. She liked to party as well as the next person, but tonight on their very first Valentine's Day as a couple, she wanted him all to herself. They still had unfinished business to settle.

"All's well that ends well," Margery said happily as she and Nico did a passable two-step. "You and Alana will get married and give me plenty of grandchildren. Then this old childless soul will never be lonely again."

"As for being old," Nico began. "You will always have a timeless beauty and as for being lonely, I believe Daniel is more than willing to take care of that problem."

Margery smiled up into Nico's handsome face. "You're such a sweet boy. I'm so pleased my darling

Alana has finally awakened from her slumber and found *you*."

Toni politely smiled as Spencer Taylor told her of his recent concert dates in Boston. She felt her right foot going to sleep as he droned on about the many celebrities who had come backstage to congratulate him on his splendid performance. It was a pity that a man of such pulchritude should be a brain-numbing bore.

"You are familiar with Charles Edward Waters, the frozen-food king? He is possibly the wealthiest black man in America. He told me he thought my playing equaled the great Duke Ellington's."

Don't believe everything he tells you, Toni wanted to warn him, but didn't. She vigorously shook her leg, trying to get the blood circulating in it.

"You're right," Spencer Taylor said. "Here I am bending your ear when we should be dancing. Shall we?"

It was as good a way to awaken her sleeping member as any, so Toni accepted.

Barry White sang of love from afar on the Stingray's compact disc player as Alana and Nico cruised through San Francisco's streets. The full moon looked as though it was suspended directly above the Golden Gate Bridge.

The ball had been a resounding success. Alana expected to read about it in the society pages of tomorrow's paper. Now Margery could rest on her laurels until she started planning her wedding. Alana had a feeling she and Daniel were more in love than they were when they were first wed nearly twenty-five years ago. She was happy for them.

Nico reached over and gently massaged the back of her neck. "How do you feel? Tired?"

"A little," Alana replied softly, enjoying the feel of his strong fingers on her skin.

"Too tired to go to my place? I have a surprise waiting for you there. We haven't had the chance to celebrate our first Valentine's Day together yet."

"What kind of a surprise?" Alana asked, turning in her seat to look at him.

"It won't be a surprise if I tell you what it is," Nico countered, his deep voice husky.

He stopped the car at a red light, and Alana moved closer to him and planted a warm kiss on his cheek. Nico pulled her into his arms. "Do not do that unless you are willing to pay the price," he warned her provocatively.

"Would you shut up and kiss me?"

"And she's rude too," Nico joked as his mouth descended upon hers.

They were interrupted by the sound of blaring car horns. The light had changed to green.

Alana got back in her seat, fastening her seat belt. Nico hit the accelerator and shifted into second, then third.

"You're going to make me get a ticket yet," he grumbled, looking sideways at her with a smile on his full mouth.

Nico's house was located in the North Beach section of San Francisco in a neighborhood that had once been the home to the city's wealthiest citizens. Today the area was populated by middle-class families who wanted a nice place to rear their children.

It was a bi-level bungalow with big airy rooms that allowed the breezes from the Pacific to circulate throughout. When he'd purchased the house, three years ago, Alana had helped him decorate it. They had compromised between his love for leather and her desire to bring nature inside by going with contemporary furnishings in Italian leather for the living room with natural wood accents.

As they stepped into the foyer and Nico engaged the alarm, Alana laughed softly. "I see Mrs. Bailey was recently here."

"I'm not as bad as I used to be," Nico said, defending himself. "Mrs. Bailey comes in only once a week now and she doesn't have to berate me for leaving my shoes in the middle of the room anymore."

Nico switched on the lights, slightly dimming them. They sat together on the brown leather couch in the living room.

He grasped one of her hands in his, squeezing it gently. His dark, thickly fringed eyes looked down at their entwined hands.

"I need to know something before we go any farther, Alana." He peered into her eyes. "That day when we were swimming in the lake and you got a cramp and went under and I went in after you. Later, when we were certain you were out of danger, you looked at me in such a way…I can't begin to describe it. Did I *imagine* that look?"

Alana's heart thumped fiercely in her chest. She

never dreamed he had noticed. She had fought to subdue her emotions. For months before that fateful summer day, she had been trying to deny that she was falling in love with Nico. Then after a harrowing experience in the water, she could no longer hide from it. She loved him. She had felt so guilty.

"If I had known Michael was seeing Karen, I would have left him then," she said now. She touched his face with her free hand. "I loved you so much, Nico. But I couldn't hurt Michael. In all his life, he never had anyone who stuck by him. I couldn't abandon him."

Nico knelt before her, holding both her hands in his. His bedroom eyes bespoke his passion. "I know you must have been in torment," he said. "We were both in our own unique hell, wanting each other but remaining loyal to Michael who, unbeknownst to us, was doing as he pleased."

Rising, he pulled her up with him, and they held each other for a long while. "*Te amo,* Lana. I love you with all my heart and soul, my being." Looking into her big brown eyes, Nico took her lovely face between his hands. "I've never loved anyone else, Lana. I'm telling you this so you'll know the intensity of my feelings for you."

"I tried to bury my love for you, Nico. But, no matter how hard I tried, I couldn't do it. Sometimes it was so all-consuming, I couldn't bear to be around you."

"Those were the times you pushed me away," Nico deduced, his eyes taking in the delightful curve of her lips.

"Yes," Alana said passionately, her breasts swelling

with desire. He had to kiss her soon or she'd perish with the want of the feel of his mouth on hers.

"Un momento, mi amor," he said, as he released her. He slowly reached into his coat pocket and removed a small, red velvet-covered box. He handed the box to Alana, his hands closing around hers.

"There are some traditions my parents taught me that I cannot ignore," he said, his accent more evident due to the depth of his emotions. "Alana, you know I adore you. Will you do me the honor of becoming my wife and partner in life? Will you allow me to cherish you and protect you for always?"

Nico released his hold on her, allowing his arms to fall to his sides. Alana could not pull her gaze from his wonderful face. She knew she had heard a proposal, but the whole scene felt surreal to her.

"Alana?"

"I do," she murmured.

Nico grinned. "It's a little early for that reply."

"I will," Alana corrected herself. She screamed and jumped into his arms. "Yes, yes, yes, yes!"

Laughing, Nico set her back down. "You haven't even looked at the ring. You might not like it."

Alana opened the tiny box and smiled broadly. The ring was a two-carat diamond solitaire in a white gold setting.

"It's beautiful," she told him. "Thank you."

Nico solemnly placed the ring on her finger, and then they kissed. Coming up for air, Alana said, "When you promised to always protect me, what exactly did you mean?"

"It means I'd gladly give my life for you," Nico said, jutting out his strong square chin. "And I mean that, *querida*."

"Will you also protect my honor?"

"To my last breath."

Alana laughed softly. "Well, don't be so vigilant to-night, Nicholas Setera, because for the next few hours I just want to be your woman. Make love to me, Nico."

"As you wish," he replied, his voice husky and his eyes never leaving her dear face.

Picking her up in his muscular arms, he carried her upstairs to his bedroom, where they stood at the head of the queen-sized, hunter-green comforter covered bed.

Nico reached up and methodically removed the pins holding Alana's naturally wavy hair in its smooth chignon, dropping them onto the nearby nightstand. Her hair fell in soft waves about her face. Alana, in turn, removed his tie, placing it next to the pins, and then she began to slowly unbutton his pleated, crisp white shirt.

Her sable-colored eyes raked over him. She wanted to record every detail of this moment in her mind's eye so that she'd never forget it. Not the look of passionate longing in his dark, uniquely downward-sloping thickly-fringed brown eyes. Nor the sound of his breathing or the feel of his warm exhalation on her hot skin.

Finished undoing the shirt, she bent her head and kissed his hairy, decidedly muscular chest.

Nico grasped her by the shoulders, halting her slow progress downward. "One good turn deserves another," he said. He walked around behind her and unzipped the silvery gown, and the weight of the material caused it to slip from her silken teddy-clad figure. Alana stepped out of the dress and bent to pick it up. She tossed it onto a nearby chair.

She stood before him in a black teddy, silk stockings and her silver Italian pumps.

Boldly stepping forward, she reached for the clasp on Nico's slacks. He stayed her hand there. "As you can see, I want you very much, *querida*. But unless we want to start a family tonight, you'll have to excuse me for a minute."

Nico kissed her forehead and disappeared into the adjacent bathroom.

When he returned, Alana was lying on the bed after having removed her shoes and stockings. She looked up and was unable to suppress a gasp. Nico was completely nude except for a pair of black bikini briefs. She'd seen him in bathing trunks before, however never in an excited state.

"You should see your expression," Nico said, smiling.

He sat beside her and drew her into his arms. It was the first time their bare skin had ever touched like this, and he could not help trying to experience all the sensations of touch, feel and taste simultaneously. He breathed in her sweet essence. His hands ran over her soft, pliant body and he ran his tongue along the perimeter of her full mouth.

"Nico," Alana said breathlessly. Her eyes were closed. Her head went back as she succumbed to a euphoric feeling of pure pleasure. Nico followed the delicate curve of her throat with his tongue.

"You're exquisite," he whispered in her ear. "So lovely, you take my breath away."

"I feel like this is my first time," Alana told him, her eyes coming open. "I've dreamt of this moment so many times, and now that it's here, I'm so nervous…"

"Shhh…" Nico said.

He gently forced her back onto the bed, holding her in his strong arms all the while. They lay facing one another.

"Sweetheart, tonight is ours. From this moment, here and now, the past is dead and the future is new territory. We will explore it together."

Alana pulled him close and kissed his square chin, working her way upward to his full mouth. She couldn't believe her good fortune. Nico loved her—and she wasn't dreaming.

Epilogue

Alana rolled over in bed and slammed her hand down hard on the OFF button of the alarm. Forcing her eyelids apart, she read the lighted dial: 3:23 A.M. That hadn't been the alarm she'd heard after all.

She none too gently nudged Nico awake. "Nicholas Setera, wake up. It's your turn to go get Nicky."

Sitting straight up in bed, Nico yawned. "Didn't we just go to sleep?"

Alana laughed as she sat on the side of the bed. "It only feels like it. I'm going to the bathroom. Nicky's waiting for you."

Wiping the sleep from his eyes, Nico yawned again and finally put his feet on the floor.

"He's two months old," he grumbled. "When is he going to start sleeping through the night?"

"You're asking me?" Alana replied, smiling at the sight of her husband stumbling toward the door. "This is my first child too, you know."

"Well, what did the book say?" Nico asked, referring to the child-care manual Alana had read throughout her pregnancy.

"It said by the time he turns three months old, we will probably resemble the walking dead, and judging from your appearance, it was right," Alana said, laughing heartily.

Turning to leave, Nico said, "Well don't look into the mirror when you go into the bathroom because you might run out screaming."

Alana nearly did scream in fright when she saw her reflection in the bathroom mirror. There were dark circles beneath her eyes, and her crowning glory looked like she'd stuck a finger in an electric socket. She smiled at that haggard young woman because, even though she looked less than lovely, she'd never been happier.

She splashed cold water on her face and dried it with a clean towel. Then she cleansed her breasts in preparation for her son's three A.M. feeding, which was nearly half an hour overdue. No wonder he was screaming at the top of his lungs.

She went back into the bedroom and awaited Nico's arrival. She knew he was delayed because he was changing Nicky's diaper. From day one, Nico had been an attentive father. He never shirked his responsibilities, no matter how dirty the job.

Nico entered the room five minutes later, cuddling his son in his muscular arms. Nicky was no longer crying. He found solace in his father's nearness. For Nico's part, he was instantly transformed for the better when he held his son. He could not help marveling at the miracle that was Nicolas Shelby Setera.

He carefully placed Nicky in Alana's arms and sat on the bed next to them. He was wearing only pajama bottoms. Alana wore the top. He loved watching his wife feed their son. She held Nicky firmly against her and Nicky automatically turned his head toward her breast and suckled contentedly. Eight pounds, ten ounces at birth, Nicky had gained over two pounds in his two months on Earth. He was thriving beautifully on his mother's milk.

Alana had been observing Nicky, making certain he was positioned correctly. She could hear him swallowing, feel the slight pulling sensation. He was in his normal rhythm.

She looked up to find Nico smiling at her.

"What?" she asked, curious as to what he found amusing.

"You just took to that as if you'd been doing it all your life," Nico said, his eyes meeting hers. "He looks more like you every day," Nico said as he gently touched his son's head which was covered with an abundance of curly black hair.

"I think he looks like you," Alana disagreed. She grinned. "Of course, everyone thinks he looks like someone else. Yesterday Margery told me she thinks he has my mother's eyes."

"That's understandable," Nico said. "Connie *was* his

grandmother. But when Toni saw him, she swore he has her nose. Now *that's* scary."

They laughed.

Nicky opened his eyes. They were the same warm brown color as his father's.

"We broke his concentration," Nico joked. Then added, "Do you know what tomorrow is?" He looked up at her expectantly.

"Thursday," Alana replied deadpan.

"Does June 15th ring a bell?" Nico said, his finger trailing along her strong jawline.

"Mother's Day is in May," Alana began, seemingly unaware of where her husband's line of questioning was leading. "My birthday's in April. Your's is in July…"

"Alana Setera…" Nico said, his deep voice rising slightly.

Alana grasped one of his big hands in hers and squeezed it reassuringly. "Do you think I'd ever forget our anniversary?"

Raising her hand to his mouth, Nico kissed her fingers one at a time. His dark eyes mirrored his emotions. He'd waited a long time for this moment. Looking into Alana's eyes and seeing her love for him reflected in them, he knew it had been worth the wait. "Not for a second," he replied confidently.

* * * * *

REQUEST YOUR FREE BOOKS!

2 FREE NOVELS PLUS 2 FREE GIFTS!

KIMANI™ ROMANCE

Love's ultimate destination!